INSPIRATIONAL WINK AND THE ALTOGETHER EXTRAORDINARY NOTEBOOK

DELANEY EVERS

235
ALEXANDER
STREET

For more Delaney Evers, go to

www.delaney-evers.com

Uncontrollable urge to chat?

Reach me at delaneyeversauthor@gmail.com

Published by 235 Alexander Street LLC

CoverDesign by E. Ernst

Interior illustrations by

Andhika Sintink https://gblackid.weebly.com/

ISBN#978-0-99833464

❀ Created with Vellum

INSPIRATIONAL WINK AND THE ALTOGETHER EXTRAORDINARY NOTEBOOK

DELANEY EVERS

PART ONE

In which we meet Inspirational Wink,
learn of her life and family
and become aware of
A Great Secret, and the existence of
An Altogether Extraordinary
Notebook.

WHISPER

CHAPTER 1

They lowered Steadfast Wink into his grave on a cold and rainy spring morning. The ceremony was brief but well attended. After all, Steadfast had been born and raised in the small town of Whisper, and all his children had stayed within the community, becoming active and useful citizens.

Afterward, his only daughter, Inspirational Wink returned to the farmhouse with her mother, the same farmhouse Inspirational had been born in and had continued to live in for all of her sixty years. She stood on the front porch and looked around at the farm she had spent her whole life tending and said, very quietly,

"My heart is broken."

She had loved her father with all of her being. She and Steadfast had worked the farm together. They had been a team, from the time when, as a little girl, she would follow her father around on sturdy legs, ready to help. Whenever Steadfast said aloud he was going to go somewhere or do something, his tiny daughter would nod and say, "Good Idea" giving her the nickname that, in Steadfast's opinion, suited her much more than the unusual and—dare he say it— flamboyant name given to her by her mother.

"I've never heard of anyone else named Inspirational," he said, gazing down at the wriggling bundle in his arms.

"I know," his wife Belladona sighed happily. "She will be one of a kind."

"But what does Inspirational *mean*, exactly?" Steadfast asked.

"I'm sure we'll find out in time," she answered.

Belladona then promised him that he could name any further progeny, and she kept that promise. Which was why the three subsequent Wink sons were named in accordance with Steadfast's straightforward and logical brain: Second, Third and Fourth.

Those names, by the way, were not as unusual in Whisper as one might think.

Good Idea spent a sleepless night—or three—tossing and turning, thinking over the conversation she'd had with her brother, Second, as they walked together in the rain behind Steadfast's coffin. Fighting back tears, Good Idea explained to Second her fear, and gave him what she thought was the logical solution to her problem. He had agreed. All she had to do now was convince her mother to move past her grief and act in the best interest of the farm. For as much as Good Idea had loved her father, the farm was her priority.

The next morning the rain had stopped. Sitting in the sunny kitchen, the painted cabinets scrubbed clean, the slate floor swept, Belladona sat upright in her wheelchair. Years ago, the strength in her legs began to slowly wither away, the exact reason impossible to name by even the most learned doctor from Mirror City. Clear gray eyes staring straight ahead, thin-lipped and silent, she listened as Good Idea explained what she and her brother had decided.

"Second's two youngest sons, Before and After, will move into the extra bedrooms and continue to work the farm," Good

Idea explained. "I'll supervise. After all, I'm not as young as I used to be." Good Idea managed a wry chuckle. "And things can continue, just as before." Her voice gave away her relief. Things *would* continue as before. That was what had become the focus of Good Idea's thoughts since her father fell dead while milking his favorite cow. "I can't take any more changes, and I don't think you can either."

Belladona took a deep breath and clasped her hands together, close to her heart. "You have been the most loving of daughters," Belladona said. "You have devoted your life to your father and me. And I am grateful. I really am. Having Before and After here will certainly keep the farm going. But you cannot just continue your life here. It is time for you to go out into the world."

Good Idea shook her head. "First of all," she said, "it was a joy to care for you and help father. I could not have asked for anything more from my life." And she meant it. Working the farm, the gardens, and tending the animal had brought her a simple happiness every day of her life.

Belladona rolled her eyes. "Honestly, Good Idea, if I hadn't been awake for your entire birth, and hadn't held you in my arms and looked into your eyes the second you drew breath, I would wonder if you were, indeed, a child of my womb. If spending your whole life on this farm and doing nothing but chores is your idea of joy, it's only because you are, without a doubt, the least imaginative person I have ever encountered. You are truly your father's daughter."

Good Idea stared. "Mother?"

Belladona flapped a hand, as though waving away a bothersome gnat. "Don't 'Mother' me. You have spent your entire life in Whisper. You never ventured farther than the Three Creek Market. You never went to a dance, or even a school potluck. It's my fault, I suppose, for not pushing you earlier, because I must admit having you around has made my life much easier.

But now Steadfast is gone." Her voice choked and tears clouded her eyes. "I have a job that must be done, and it will be all the more difficult because you are, well, you."

Good Idea drew back, shocked at the words. "Mother, everything I ever needed was right here! What else could I ask for? Why would I go anywhere else?"

"Because there's more to life than what you need, that's why. What about what you want?"

"I want to be here," Good Idea insisted. "I want to live out the rest of my life here in Whisper, on this farm. It's all I've ever wanted."

Which was almost true. She had, in all her years, often wondered what lay beyond the curve of road that led away from Whisper. But every time she had thought about maybe doing something about it, a cow needed to be milked, a sheep shorn, a garden planted, or a crop harvested, and she never got beyond the thinking.

Belladona gripped the arms of her wheelchair. "Then I'm very sorry, Good Idea, because that is not what your future holds. Not your immediate future, anyway."

Good Idea reached for her mother's hand. "I know how upset you are, so I understand. I'm sure that after a month or two has passed, you'll—"

Belladona shook her head. "A month or two won't change a thing, Good Idea. I loved your father with all of my heart and soul, but he was a man with little imagination. That was the hardest thing for me to get used to. And to watch you, my oldest child, the one I had pinned all my hopes on, to turn out just like him? Well, that almost broke my heart. But it doesn't matter." Belladona gripped Good Idea's hand in both of hers and squeezed tightly. "You must leave Whisper."

Good Idea stared at her mother. "Leave Whisper?"

Belladona nodded. "Yes. You must go to Mirror City for me and retrieve something of great value. I left it there for safekeeping, but now that Steadfast is gone, I need it back, and, obviously, I can't get it myself. You have to go."

"To Mirror City?" Good Idea repeated slowly. "The capital of all the Western Realms?"

Belladona nodded.

"I've never been there before," Good Idea said.

"You've never been anywhere before."

"But that's...far."

"Yes," Belladona agreed. "It certainly is."

"How would I get there?"

"You must ride there on a strawberry roan horse. That is how I left Mirror City, and, well, it's all rather complicated." She reached into the front of her dress and drew out a small pouch, a bit bigger than a perrin fruit, on a long, silk cord. Good Idea had never seen her mother without it.

Belladona untied the pouch and turned it over. Several gold coins spilled out onto Belladona's lap, a small ring, a large, rusted key, a yellowed piece of paper folded over three or four times, and a mouse.

Good Idea stared and wondered, first, that the pouch must have been quite heavy with all those things in it, and, secondly, how long had the mouse been living there?

The mouse ran up Belladona's arm, circled her neck a few times, squeaking happily, then settled on her shoulder, bright eyes fixed on Good Idea.

"Why is there a mouse on your shoulder?" was Good Idea's first question. "Has he been in there the whole time?" was her second. And finally, "What has he been eating?"

Belladona waved all three questions away. "The first thing you must do," she said, handing Good Idea the ring, "is take this to the blacksmith. He will fit it to your thumb. Not your finger, your thumb. That will allow you to pass through the Veil."

"What Veil?" asked Good Idea, looking at the ring. It was thin and the metal dull and plain. As she slipped it onto her thumb, it felt loose. Belladona then dropped the coins into Good Idea's palm. Twelve gold pieces. She had never seen so much gold at one time in her life.

"Now, as I said, you will need a strawberry roan horse. Go to the livery and ask one of the Barnstable sisters. Give her two gold coins and she will find one that will be suitable. Make sure she also gives you a saddle. Then, go to Tuesday Fix and ask him to repair the saddle."

"Why would she give me a broken saddle?" This was getting more and more confusing.

Belladona shook her head impatiently. "It won't be broken, but it will need to be fixed. Now, once you get to Mirror City, you must find my old mistress, Weathervane Wynd. She has a shop on Seller's Street, by the River Brown. The roan will know the way. Tell her who you are, and she will take you to the cellar. Fleet will find the crack. Follow the map. Then, use the key."

"Who is Fleet? What crack? What should I use the key *for?*" Good Idea was now thoroughly perplexed.

"For unlocking, of course."

Belladona pushed the key into Good Idea's hands, but she pulled away from her mother and glared. "I'm not going to Mirror City."

Belladona's mouth formed a thin line. "But you must. This is something that only you can do, daughter."

Good Idea was torn. She had never disappointed her mother before. In fact, she had never disappointed *anyone* before. But going to Mirror City? "And what exactly is it that only *I* can do?"

Belladona sighed. "You must retrieve my magic notebook."

Good Idea sat back. "Your magic what?"

"Notebook."

Good Idea gathered her thoughts, which were many. "Mother, first of all, there's no such thing as magic."

Belladona threw up her hands. "Of course, there is. Zeppins!

Good Idea, you're not ignorant. Look around Whisper, it's everywhere. Just because you've chosen to ignore it doesn't mean it doesn't exist. You've never seen or touched an elephant, but elephants are real. So is magic."

"There's a difference," Good Idea said slowly, "between an elephant and magic."

"You're right," Belladona agreed. "Magic doesn't flap its ears and leave great piles of shit behind."

Good Idea stood. "I think that you need more rest, Mother." She stared at the ring on her thumb and the coins in her hand, then at the rusty key and, finally, the mouse on Belladona's shoulder, who now appeared to be frowning. "And I have more important things to do than go to Mirror City." She dropped the coins and the key back into her mother's lap and practically ran from the room.

She slipped the ring into her pocket, poured herself a glass of berry tea and sat out on the porch, rocking quietly in the noonday heat. Gray, her mother's cat, sat perched on the railing, watching her. Good Idea closed her eyes and tried to sort out all the thoughts running around in her head. Her mother actually expected her, Inspirational Wink, to buy a strawberry roan horse and ride to Mirror City, which was arguably hundreds of miles away, to retrieve a magic notebook? Her mother expected this? The same mother who had never, in Good Idea's sixty years, done anything out of the ordinary?

But then Good Idea stopped rocking. Actually, her mother had once been *very* out of the ordinary. In fact, when Good Idea was very young, her mother had been a storyteller, a fantastical storyteller, bringing to life wondrous tales of magic. Good Idea remembered listening, wide-eyed. Her mother was beautiful then, vibrant and practically glowing with energy.

Good Idea opened her eyes and looked at Gray, who stared steadily back at her. Her mother told stories of witches. Not just

7

witches, but witches she had *known*. And adventures. With elves. And how she had helped dreams come true.

Had they been just stories?

Perhaps not.

Good Idea had stopped listening to her mothers' tales when she began to follow Steadfast around the farm, doing little chores, even as her younger brothers continued to sit on the porch and listen. But she remembered those stories and had sometimes wondered if *that* was what lay beyond Whisper.

But to go to Mirror City? On a strawberry roan horse? To get a magic notebook?

Really?

Gray meowed loudly.

"Are you magic?" Good Idea asked. The cat rose onto all four feet and arched its back. Good Idea held her breath, waiting for it to turn into something...else. Gray meowed again and slipped off the railing and down the front steps.

"Aunt Good Idea," a voice called.

She stood and spotted Before and After coming down the drive, each with backpack and carrying a battered trunk between them.

"Just in time," she called. "I was getting your rooms ready. Come on in and help with the beds."

And then, with a new task before her, she quite forgot all about Mirror City.

HER MOTHER HAD nothing more to say on the subject of Mirror City for the rest of the day. Belladona prepared a welcome dinner for Before and After while Good Idea showed them the barns and pasture, the henhouse and the pigpen, and, finally, the carefully tended garden.

Both young men were obviously Winks. They had the same tall, strong bodies, reddish brown hair, and deep brown eyes. They looked like their father, Second, who looked like all of the other brothers, and who looked exactly like Steadfast. As did Good Idea, who had long, strong limbs and broad shoulders. Her hair, now streaked with gray, was pulled straight off her heart-shaped face and braided in a single plait that reached almost to her waist. Seeing the three of them together, the family connection was obvious.

Nothing of the petite, beautiful, gray eyed Belladona had found its way into the sturdy line of Winks.

Nothing anyone could see, anyway.

They all sat down to a table groaning under the weight of baked ham (from Wink pigs) corn and butter beans (from the Wink garden) and chocolate cake (flour milled from Wink wheat.) There was even dandelion wine from the casks Steadfast had stored in the cool of the barn.

They talked about the crops to be planted, the repair to the well, and the upcoming market at Three Creek Bridge.

"I want Good Idea to go," Belladona said. "When is it, day after tomorrow?"

Before and After exchanged looks. They had wanted to go to the market themselves, but were not about to argue with Belladona, who owned the farm where they were now living, and who had cooked them a meal better than anything they had eaten in their lives.

"Let the boys go," Good Idea argued. She loved the Market, but the ewes were due to lamb at any time. "They would enjoy the trip more than I."

Before and After exchanged another look and leaned forward hopefully.

"No," said Belladona. "I want you to go, Good Idea. There is something I need from a man called Mionarach Jones."

Before and After sat back, sighing.

"Who is this Mionarach Jones?" Good Idea asked. She knew

most of the sellers that set up their tents monthly just across Three Creek bridge. "I've never heard of him."

Belladona nodded. "Probably not. He doesn't come often, but he will be there tomorrow."

Good Idea wanted to ask how her mother could possibly know that. But while she questioned many things in her mind, she didn't often voice those questions aloud. "Can't the boys find him and get what you need?"

The boys leaned forward again.

"No. I don't think so," Belladona said. "What I need is of a rather, well," she dropped her voice. "It's of a delicate, feminine nature."

The boys stood hastily and quickly cleared off the table.

Belladona looked at Good Idea and smiled brightly. "You don't mind, do you, dear?"

Good Idea, grateful that Mirror City was apparently no longer an issue, was happy to oblige. "Of course, Mother." She lowered her voice. "Where is the mouse?"

Belladona raised an eyebrow. "What mouse?"

And that, thought Good Idea thankfully, was the end of that.

CHAPTER 2

𝒯he morning of Market Day, Good Idea washed her long hair and coiled it at the base of her neck instead of plaiting it into its usual braid. She slipped on a simple but beautifully made — Belladona made — dress, laced her best boots, and presented herself to her mother. Belladona nodded in approval. Going to Market was never just a commercial exercise. It was a place to see and be seen, and it was always good to be seen dressed in your best.

A familiar tingle of excitement ran through her. Market Day always held the promise of something unexpected happening, and although she was a woman who held to her habits, the thought of the unexpected had always intrigued her. And now, this additional errand with Mionarach Jones...why, *anything* could happen.

Belladona handed Good Idea a few coins and a slip of paper, folded many times and sealed with a blue dab of wax. "I need beeswax for my wheelchair," she said. "There's a bit of a creak in the back wheel that needs to be soothed. We need more nutmeg from Mr. Trade, and laces for my boots. Bright green, I think. Then take that bit of paper to Mr. Jones. His tent is at the very end of the row on the creek side, not the meadow side. It's purple. Give him that and he'll know what I need."

Good Idea nodded, saddled up Front, one of the two mules in the barn, and set off to the Market past Three Creek Bridge.

Three Creek Bridge was the only way in — or out — of Whisper. The town lay in the center of a large valley, surrounded on all sides by high and impenetrable mountains, with only one narrow road leading in or out of town. That road led over Three Creek Bridge. The three creeks came tumbling down the various crevices of the mountainside and came together to form the Three Creek River, a narrow slip of fast-moving water that flowed through more mountain and, eventually, to the sea. The Market lay on the other side of the bridge, but still within the border of Whisper.

The day was bright and not too warm, and Good Idea felt a rising excitement. She had been to market many times before, and always enjoyed the brightly colored tents, the low hum of conversation, the occasional song from the Player's tent. Wink's Wold lay almost exactly between Three Creek Bridge and the town of Whisper proper, so it was a short and uneventful trip. She stopped on the top of the bridge to watch the family of otters that lived in the rocks below. She laughed at their antics and waved at them and at least one seemed to wave back. She went farther along until she found the line of tethered mules and horses, tied up her mule, Front, and began winding her way through the market.

Bright green shoelaces were easy, as was the nutmeg. Buying beeswax required a bit of bargaining, but Good Idea had been haggling with these vendors since she was ten years old, when she would come with Steadfast. She bought some sweet rolls for a treat, a ripe round of cheese that smelled of grass and honey, and finally found herself in front of a purple tent, creek side.

A man stepped out of the tent, an extremely old, stooped man with very pale skin and a halo of white hair and a bright smile. His left pant leg was pinned up at the knee, and he moved slowly, with obvious difficulty, a simply fashioned crutch under his arm.

"Hello, young miss," he called.

Good Idea rolled her eyes, but then sighed. To someone as old as he looked to be, perhaps she *was* a young miss. Wordlessly, she handed him the folded bit of paper from her mother.

He held it, looking at the dab of blue wax. He broke the seal, unfolded the paper, and read it carefully. He looked up at her and smiled again. He held open the tent flap with one hand and gestured her in with a nod of his head.

Once inside, she gasped in delight.

There were shelves on three sides of the tent, shelves filled with bottles of various shapes and colors, small ornamental boxes, some closed but some open, with bits of colorful stones and dried flowers inside. There were bones of animals, large and small, hanging from the ceiling. In the middle was a small colorful rug, and a round table and two chairs of worn, silvered wood. It was the most interesting place Good Idea had ever been in, and she wanted to touch every single item and ask what it was and where it came from.

"Please, sit," Mr. Jones said. His voice was low and had a tremble in it, as though he was already exhausted from speaking. Good Idea sat, set her burlap bags of purchases at her feet, and, with eyes still wandering over the shelves, waited for Mr. Jones to find whatever her mother needed.

Instead, he sat down across from her. "You are Belladona's oldest child." he said, not a question, but a statement of fact, in a frail whisper.

She nodded. "Yes. I'm Inspirational Wink. But I am called Good Idea."

"Hmm." His eyes narrowed. "And you're going to Mirror City to retrieve the notebook?"

Her mouth opened in surprise, and she stared. "No. I'm not, but how did you know —"

"I know quite a lot about you," Mr. Jones said, his voice a bit stronger. "You are, after all, Belladona's firstborn, and that means quite a lot where I'm from. And now Steadfast is gone." Here he tilted his head. "And for that, I am truly sorry. I know you loved him very much."

Grief came back in a rush, but curiosity nudged it aside. "How do you know *anything?*" Good Idea asked.

"You are Belladona's first born. I've been watching you very carefully ever since you first drew breath."

Good Idea sat up. Someone had been watching *her?* That was kind of exciting. A bit creepy, perhaps, but exciting. Her heartbeat quickened as she leaned forward in her chair. "Really?"

He sighed. "I can't say it's been the most thrilling sixty years I've spent, but yes, I've been watching you."

Good Idea bristled. "Farm life," she explained, "has its patterns."

"Hmm. Yes. And most of your patterns are simple straight lines."

Good Idea had to admit that was true. She reflected for a moment on her life and realized that there hadn't been too many...events.

Although...

"It's not like I've done *nothing*," she argued, on the defensive now. "I devised a system to feed the chickens that did not take all morning. I trained the cows to come in from the pasture with just a shrill whistle. I've spent years negotiating with various tradespeople and neighbors for good prices and fair exchanges."

He did not look impressed. "Indeed." he said.

"So, *why* have you been watching me? Exactly?" she asked.

"Because Belladona found something quite extraordinary when she was a much younger witch," Mr. Jones began, "and —"

"Wait," Good Idea interrupted. "My mother was a witch?"

He rolled his eyes. "Of course, she was a witch. She still is. But once she married, her powers were vanquished. Now, the notebook —"

"What notebook?" Good Idea interrupted again.

"The notebook she acquired. It was quite unusual. And powerful. In fact, it was altogether extraordinary. From her description, I guessed that it was the Notebook Of Whim, an incredible object that was believed to have been lost forever in the Friends and Enemies Wars."

Good Idea frowned. "That was hundreds of years ago."

"Yes. And to think that it had been found again, well, I was very eager to see it. To verify that it was, in fact, the Notebook Of Whim."

He sighed heavily. "Then she met Steadfast, fell in love and married him. If a witch is bound to a mortal, she cannot bring anything from her former life into her new one. That includes her magical powers. It also includes any objects, especially if the object contains any type of enchantment. She had her Pouch Of Remembrance, of course, but that was not big enough for the notebook, so she was forced to leave it behind. It was a great sacrifice, as the notebook was altogether extraordinary. And powerful. Did I mention powerful? But now that Steadfast is gone, she can get it back. But she cannot get it back herself. Therefore, you, as her firstborn, must do it for her. You must go to Mirror City, retrieve the notebook, and return it to Belladona."

There were so many questions going through Good Idea's mind that she didn't know what to ask him first, so she began with the simplest.

"Who are you?"

"Mionarach Jones of the Fifth Circle Of Zellon, Master Of The First Order, Keeper Of The Staff Of Resistance," he answered proudly, a bit of spirit in the weak voice.

"Say again?"

"Mionarach Jones," he repeated slowly. "You may call me Arch."

She frowned. "Around here, names usually mean something," she said.

He smiled. "Well, I'm not from around here. And where I *am* from, my name does mean...something. Your name is also unusual."

She sighed. "Yes. My mother always told me I'd grow into it, but she may have gotten that wrong."

"Or not," he said, then coughed. "You still have something of a future in which to be inspirational."

"I suppose." Good Idea thought again. "Am I a witch too?"

He exhaled slowly. "Well, you *could* be. You come from a long line of very powerful witches. However, you are rather ordinary. You have shown a, well, marked lack of imagination. So, the chance of you being receptive to any magical influences is not strong. At all. In fact, it's practically nil."

It was surprising how disappointing his words were. All her life she *had* felt very ordinary. Yes, she was clever, but that certainly didn't count for all that much in Whisper. She wasn't pretty. She couldn't dance or sing. She didn't have a specific skill or trade. She was a farmer, which was nothing special at all. Had she been a witch, well, that certainly would have been *something*.

"Nonetheless," Mionarach went on, "you are..." He waved his hands in the air.

"Yes," Good Idea acknowledged. "Her firstborn."

"So, it is your duty to go to Mirror City and retrieve the notebook. I will assist you. The very idea of you out there in the real word alone is, well..." he visibly shuddered. "Originally, I was chosen to be the one to accompany you on this journey."

She opened her mouth to speak, shut it again, thought, then tried again. "Chosen by who?"

"When I received a letter from your mother describing what she thought she had found, I hurried to Mirror City to see for myself. Unfortunately, she had already left with your father, and the notebook was hidden. Others had heard of the letter, so a Council Of Important People was called together to devise a way to protect it. And I was chosen to help retrieve it when the time came."

"Excuse me," she said cautiously, "but it seems to me you'd have a bit of difficulty retrieving anything."

He laughed weakly and then coughed again. "I would have *extreme* difficulty," he finally said. "I was chosen, but any fool can see I'm not up to anything more arduous than sitting in a tent in the middle of nowhere." He turned his head. "Bunny," he called in a thin, querulous voice.

Good Idea looked expectantly at the open tent flap, expecting a magical rabbit to come hopping through the door. Instead, a short, thin, and nervous-looking young man stumbled in.

"This," Mr. Jones said, "is my nephew. Buadhachan Jones. You may call him Bunny. He will go on this journey with you. And Fleet, of course."

"Fleet?"

Once again, he looked as though his patience was being sorely tried. "The mouse."

"The mouse?" Good Idea asked.

"He is Belladona's familiar. He is capable of, well, any number of things."

"Like what?" Good Idea's interest perked.

"Well, the most important thing he can do is show you cracks in the Veil."

"Veil? What is this Veil? And what cracks?"

His brow wrinkled. "Do I really have to explain all of this now?"

She shrugged. "Only if you want me to go to Mirror City."

. . .

HE STARED at Good Idea for a moment, stared at Bunny, then broke into a grin. "Fair enough. Bunny," he motioned with his hand, "this may take a while. You might want to sit down."

Bunny immediately dropped to the grassy floor of the tent, bobbing his head. "Yes, sir," he mumbled.

Mionarach settled himself, his shoulders squared off, his chin lifted. "Magic is everywhere. It is part of the natural world, just like time, space, science, well, everything. But Magic is protected by something we call the Veil. It's not so much a physical barrier as a psychic one. Those who practice can travel through to both realms, but no one else can. Occasionally, people, or things, can pass through the cracks. Cracks are weaknesses in the Veil. You yourself are not magical. At all. But you will pass through a crack in the Veil with the help of a magical talisman, the ring. That will be necessary to retrieve the notebook."

"Why does it have to be retrieved at all?" Good Idea asked. "Why is it so important?"

"If it is the Notebook Of Whim, it is the only one of its kind in existence. In the wrong hands, it could be used, well, in a very negative way. Belladona needs to get it back so she can give it to me, and I can cast the necessary spells to safeguard it forever."

"Why can't you get it?"

"Because it is protected by enchantments." He took a deep breath, which brought on a fresh round of coughing. "Only her firstborn, entering Mirror City on a strawberry roan horse, will find Weathervane Wynd. Only Weathervane can take you to the cellar. Only Fleet can find the crack in the Veil. Only the map can show where the notebook is hidden. Only the rusty key can release it. Only the firstborn can remove the notebook, take it from Mirror City, again on a strawberry roan horse. Once it is returned to Belladona, only Belladona can undo the enchantments and hand it over to me so that I can finally do something with it to keep it from getting into the wrong hands."

Good Idea exhaled loudly. "That seems overly complicated." He looked annoyed. "Tell me about it," he groused.

Good Idea thought. "If all those enchantments exist, then why are you worried about the wrong hands?"

"Because if your mother should die," he said, "all the protective enchantments would die with her. Of course, finding it in the first place is the biggest challenge, even if the enchantments didn't exist anymore. Without knowing where to look for it, finding the thing is a near impossible task. Still, when Belladona passes through the final Veil, there will be a great struggle between several factions for possession of that notebook. They will tear up Mirror City looking for it. Who knows what kind of destruction will rain down." He looked uncomfortable. "There has not been a war between witches and demons for centuries, and we certainly wouldn't want to start one in this day and age."

Good Idea felt a shiver. "Demons? There are Demons?"

He nodded matter-of-factly. "Oh yes. And Goblins. And rumor has it that there is an entire syndicate of trolls trying to get their hands on it. So, you need to get it, return it to your mother, who will then give it to me to be taken care of, it once and for all."

"Oh, my." Good Idea took a long breath. "What does this notebook do, anyway?"

Arch sat back and closed his eyes. After a few moments, she shifted uneasily. Maybe he had fallen asleep. Or died. Finally, he nodded to himself, opened his eyes, and leaned forward. "It grants wishes. That's simplifying things, of course. It..." He wrinkled his forehead. "Whatever you write in the notebook will come true. Do you want a new pair of shoes? Write it in the notebook and you will get a new pair of shoes. Do you want someone to fall in love with you? Write their name and what you want from them in the notebook, and it will happen. Do you want to control the weather? Write down that you want sunshine tomorrow and sunshine you'll have." He took a long breath. "Do you want complete control of every person on the entire planet, and have them obey your every whim? Just write it down in the notebook." He stopped and watched as Good Idea's eyes grew big. "You can see, can't you, how someone may, well, abuse such a notebook?" he asked.

Good Idea nodded wordlessly. This was becoming almost too much. First, that her mother was a witch. And that, as a witch, she'd given up everything to marry Steadfast. And that one of the things she'd given up was an object that could send the entire world spiraling into chaos if it fell into the wrong hands. And only *she*, Good Idea, could retrieve this...thing?

"And that is why you must go to Mirror City, find the notebook where Belladona hid it, and return it to her," Arch said. "Bunny will assist you in this. Once you cross into the Veil, things will become very dangerous. After all, everyone else who wants the notebook will do everything in their power to prevent you from getting it back to Belladona. Or once you *do* get it to her, they will force her give it to them. Or they will just kill her. Believe me, you'll need some help."

"Wait." She pushed aside all her other thoughts to focus on what he had just said. "Why will there be people who will try to prevent me from getting the notebook?"

Arch pursed his lips. "As I mentioned, I was not the only one to know of your mother's letter. By the time your mother left Mirror City, rumors were already starting about its existence, and about the witch who had found it, and where she had gone. Over the years, the interest has not waned, and there are many different parties still interested in acquiring the notebook."

He made a face. "Nothing will be done to prevent you from getting to and retrieving the notebook, because you are the only one with the map and items needed to do that. The tricky part will be returning it to Belladona. That's where the enchantment is the weakest. Once the notebook leaves Mirror City, getting it to Belladona is kind of an open-ended situation."

"So, at that point, anyone can take the notebook?"

"Yes."

"And what would happen to it? "

He shrugged. "Nothing. But again, if Belladona dies, well, whoever has it can keep it. See, the finding it is really the hardest part. Once it is found, and if the wrong parties get their hands on it, no protection around your mother will be enough to keep her safe for long."

He held a fist to his mouth, stifling another cough. "You will leave in three days for Mirror City. It is three- or four-days travel at the most. That will be the easy part. Bunny has business for me in Mirror City that he must attend to sooner rather than later, but he will meet you in one week's time to guide you through the Veil and accompany you on your return to Whisper. He will assist in whatever way he can."

The young man, still sitting on the grass and who had not spoken a word, met her look with a smile.

Arch, upon seeing her expression, began, "He looks young —"

"He looks twelve," Good Idea interrupted.

"I'm twenty-four," Bunny said, rising. "I have spent the past five years at the elbow of my uncle, arguably the most renown wizard in the Realm. Before that, I attended the great School Of Magical Stuff in Quenruth, far to the East. I am only Master Of The Third Order, but I know all of the details of your situation and am more than capable of protecting you. The Veil can be treacherous, and it is during the trip back that the enemies will show themselves."

"And these enemies will want to what? Kill me?"

"Yes," Bunny said. "And I will protect you from that fate."

"Rather than just, say, take the notebook from me?" Good

Idea asked.

Bunny looked at Arch, who stroked his chin. "The whole idea here is for you — and whoever is with you — to do everything in their power to *keep* it from being taken."

GOOD IDEA SQUIRMED in her chair. She was not comfortable with any of this. In her sixty years, she had only been threatened by weather, bad crops and, just once, a huge black bear that wandered into her hen house. The very idea of *people* coming after her, trying to hurt her, well, it was quite beyond her level of comfort. "You will protect me?" she asked Bunny.

"That is my job," Bunny said stoutly. "Myself and all your other allies."

Allies? Good Idea relaxed a little. That sounded a little bit better. "And who are they?"

Bunny frowned. "Who are whom?"

"My other allies?"

He looked a bit flustered. "Well, I don't know. We don't actually have them yet, do we?"

"We're going to, what? Collect them on the way?" she asked, skeptical. "That doesn't sound all that promising, if you don't mind my saying so. I mean, if you're going off on a quest, and there's obviously danger lurking, wouldn't you want all those important details lined up before setting out?"

Arch interrupted, his brows coming together in what could only be described as an expression of annoyance. Or, possibly, anger. "Now, see here, young lady, I —"

"Please stop calling me that," Good Idea said crossly. "I'm sixty years old. I am an old woman and I've never been farther away from Whisper than I am right now. This entire plan is a logistical disaster. I'm supposed to ride a strawberry roan horse to Mirror City. Do you know how rare a thing that is? A strawberry roan horse? And then there's the trip itself. That will take me at least four days. That also means three nights. Where am I supposed to sleep for those three nights? How do I feed myself and this horse? When I get there, I have to find a person who was alive over sixty years ago, and living there at that time, but who knows where she is now. I'm supposed to depend on a mouse to lead me through to somewhere to find something that requires a very disreputable-looking key to unlock, and then I have to travel another three or four days back here pursued by unnamed things that want to kill me? And I will be protected by a Master Of The Third Order and some imaginary allies? Hmm?" She sat back, shaking her head. "I do not think so."

Arch seemed, for the moment, speechless. His rheumy eyes widened.

Good Idea bent to gather the bags at her feet. "I have never failed to do anything my mother asked of me," she said, "But this is a big no. You'll have to find someone else to get this notebook of yours."

"But" Mionarach sputtered, "there is no one else."

"There has to be," she argued. "There are so many inconsistencies in this whole scenario. You must have a contingency plan of some sort." She settled back in the chair. "For instance, what if my mother had died before my father?"

"That would not have happened," Arch said.

"And how do you know that? No one can predict death."

He nodded. "True. But she has been protected by a wellness spell ever since she left Mirror City."

"A what?"

"A spell to keep illness at bay. She has never been sick a day in her life, has she?"

"No. But she cannot walk."

It was Bunny who explained. "The energy needed to keep the spell active has to be drawn from somewhere. Sometimes the legs fail, sometimes the eyes." He shook his head. "That sort of magic comes at a cost."

"But what about these enemies you mentioned? Why hasn't anyone tried to kill her? To end the enchantments?"

"Well," Arch told her, "finding the notebook is a near impossible task. Killing her would not help anyone *find* the thing. And even if someone were that shortsighted, between the elves and the gnomes and the witches and the dwarves, she has been very well protected."

Good Idea's eyes narrowed. She knew who the elves were: the Fixes, who had their shop in Whisper. And the Whisper Weekly newspaper was run by two gnomes. Her mind raced. Who *else* was he talking about? "Witches? And Dwarves?"

"The Barnstable sisters are witches, of course. And Montgomery Gold? The blacksmith? He is a dwarf," Arch said.

Good Idea considered the wide and varied population of Whisper. The Barnstable sisters looked like anyone else. But she had to admit, Montgomery Gold, with his short stature and broad shoulders, not to mention the beard...

"They are here to protect my mother?"

Arch nodded. "Yes. There was no magic at all in Whisper before your mother came to live here. Why would there be? It was not the sort of place that allowed magic to flourish. And this valley is in the middle of literally nowhere. But it is a place that is, by its nature, easy to protect. Good heavens, even an army of goats couldn't get over these mountains! But all of us at the Council Of Important People knew how vital it would be to keep Belladona safe. When she moved here with Steadfast, the rest of us came."

"Rest of who?"

He shrugged. "Lots were drawn among the free people, and guardians were chosen to live in Whisper until the day came that the notebook was retrieved."

Good Idea was, she knew, very good at problem solving. Hadn't she devised a way to divert the water from a nearby stream directly to Wink's Wold, ensuring an easy and efficient way to water the cornfield? Hadn't she thought to pack old copies of the Whisper Weekly in the cracks around the windows in the upstairs rooms of the farmhouse, effectively blocking the seeping cold winds of winter? Surely there was another way to retrieve this notebook that did not involve her leaving Whisper herself. "Okay, how about this? I'll bring mother to Mirror City and let *her* get this notebook?"

"That is not possible," Arch explained in a patient tone, "The wellness spell will not work if she leaves Whisper. Once she sets foot over the border of the town, any illness or injury that was held at bay over the years will come upon her. She could very well die on the spot." He sighed. "If she thought she could get it herself, by any means, do you really think she'd ask *you* to do it?"

"That's rude," she said coldly.

"Yes. Also true," he said.

That stung, but she recognized the sting of truth. Good Idea sighed. "Mr. Jones. Arch. And Bunny. I am an old woman."

Arch nodded briefly. "Well, you certainly aren't young."

"Riding on a horse for more than half a day will hurt my back so badly I'll need another whole day in bed to recover. My eyesight is failing, and certain foods have a very negative effect on my, ahem, digestive tract. You mention enemies? The only weapon I can wield with any accuracy is a pitchfork. How could I possibly defend myself in any sort of fight? Especially against beings that are...supernatural? You speak of allies and protection, but what about me, facing these obstacles when I have never faced hardship or danger in my life? You need a hero for this sort of thing. As you have noted, Mr. Jones, I am rather ordinary."

Mionarach Jones gazed at her for a long moment. "Everything you say is true, Inspirational Wink. But, unfortunately for all of us, there is no hero to be found. You are all that we have."

CHAPTER 3

o get to Wink's Wold, one turned off the main road to Whisper and went down a long drive, lined with Vellian trees, past the cornfield on one side and the cow pasture on the other. The wood-frame house appeared first, under the shade of an elm, and the drive wound its way back to the barnyard behind. Good Idea returned to the farm just as the sun was setting behind the house, and she paused to take it all in. She never failed to stop and look over the home that she loved. She put Front in the barn, next to his brother, Back, and walked slowly into the house.

Belladona had saved supper for her, a dish covered in a plain cloth: a chicken leg, cheese, good bread and small, sweet berries.

Good Idea ate slowly. She had given her mother the bags of purchases, and Belladona had taken them into her room to sort through. As Good Idea finished her meal, Belladona slid back into the kitchen, the wheels of her chair soundless.

"Thank you for the beeswax and laces," she said. "And the sweet rolls. Before and After will eat them for breakfast in the morning, but would you like to share one with me now?"

Good Idea nodded, and her mother placed the roll on the table with two small plates and carefully sliced it exactly in half.

"You never told me you were a witch," Good Idea said after a few bites, during which she had tried to organize her many, many thoughts.

Belladona sighed. "I am Belladona Green, Of The Fifth Circle Of Zellon, Healer Of The Seventh Order. I told you stories of my past as soon as you came into the world, daughter. I spun yarns of spells and potions and curses. I told you of elves and princes in dungeons. I told you tales of curses and dreams-come-true. You just didn't believe me."

Good Idea now had even *more* thoughts to organize but had to admit her mother had a point. "So, all of those stories were true? You weren't telling us tales?"

"Well, some of them were tales. I never lost a glass slipper in my life. But yes, most of those stories were my own. I had quite an exciting life as a young woman."

Good Idea watched her mother bite into the sweet roll. "Did you ever tell us stories about the notebook?" she asked.

Belladona shook her head. "No. You see that notebook should never have been given to me. It's too long a story for now, but once I had it, and realized what it might be, I immediately wrote to Mionarach, who was a very important wizard within my circle. But before he could get back to me, I met your father." Her face softened. "Steadfast had walked all the way from Whisper to repair his father's watch. And honestly, one look at your fathers' face, and I forgot all about the notebook. He asked me to marry him that first night, and I said yes. It was going to take three days for the watch to be fixed, which gave me three days to hide the notebook. At the end of those three days, I still hadn't heard from Mionarach, so I got on the back of my pink horse and rode out of Mirror City with your father."

"And now I have to get it and bring it back so you can do

what you should have done all those years ago?" Good Idea asked.

Belladona nodded. "Yes. And while I am very sorry to put this burden on you, I'm not at all sorry that you now have to leave Whisper and finally go out into the world. Better late than never, as they say."

Good Idea swallowed the last of the roll, licking crumbs from her lips. "How do you know I can even do this thing?"

"Because you have to." Belladona patted her daughter's hand. "First, see Mr. Gold." She drew out the pouch again and Good Idea stared at it.

"Is that the Pouch Of Remembrance?" she asked.

Belladona nodded. "When a witch chooses a life with a human, they are permitted to bring with them only what can fit inside this small bag. The notebook was too large. I was lucky I could fit everything else that I needed." She poured the gold coins into Good Idea's hand. "As I said, first see Mr. Gold. Then get a strawberry roan horse. Have the saddle fixed and come back to me. I will give you the map, and Fleet, of course."

At the sound of his name, the small mouse ran up the table leg, onto Belladona's hand, up her arm and perched again on her shoulder.

"I'm afraid," Good Idea said in a small voice, and she was. As much as she had often thought about venturing beyond Whisper, now that it was a distinct possibility, she didn't find the idea nearly as exciting.

"Of course, you are. And truthfully, I am afraid for you. Don't worry though. Arch will guide you."

"No, he won't," Good Idea said. "He is too old. His nephew, who looks younger than any of my nephews, will be the one to guide me. His name is Bunny."

Belladona frowned, then brightened. "I'm sure he's very capable. And you will have other help along the way," she said assuredly.

"That's what Bunny said, but where is he going to find all these so-called allies?" Good Idea asked.

Belladona looked steadily into her daughter's eyes. "He will not find them. After all, he doesn't need them. You do. Would you really trust someone who is in his corner and not yours?"

Good Idea shifted her gaze to the mouse, still perched on Belladona's shoulder. "What can he do, exactly?"

"Well, he can find cracks in the Veil. That will be his biggest contribution. But he's very good at finding stray bits of things that are much more valuable than they seem."

"What is it like? The Veil?"

Belladona pursed her lips. "The Veil is something you pass through. It's not an actual destination. The Veil hides things, changes the shape of things, illuminates the details of a person or thing. So, if you step into a room, and then go through the Veil, you will be in the same room, but you will see it very differently."

"And that's how I'll be able to see the notebook?"

"Eventually, yes."

"Eventually?"

"Well," Belladona said, sounding a little cross, "it's not like I just stuck it in the back of a drawer somewhere. I mean, that's where I hid it originally, but since I was riding away for who-knew-how long, I knew I had to do a better job. That's why you'll need the map. To find the notebook and unlock it from its years of hiding."

Good Idea eyed her mother critically. "You had to make this as difficult as possible, didn't you?"

Belladona shrugged. "At the time, all I could think of was that it had to be carefully hidden, and I only had three days and three nights to do it in because I wanted to leave with your father." She sighed. "Besides, I was young and a bit dramatic. That's why it's all so complicated. I left on a strawberry roan horse, so only if you enter Mirror City on a strawberry roan horse will you be able to find Weathervane, etc., etc. It was all, now that I think about it, just silly. Overblown. I think if I could have figured out a way to slip a gargoyle in there, I probably would have."

"Arch seems to think that getting this notebook back here might be hazardous to my health," Good Idea said, her eyes on the now-empty plate.

"Yes, he's probably right. After all, every emperor wanna-be and has-been despot in the kingdom would want a notebook that makes wishes come true. Not to mention every hedge witch or demon around. When I first realized what the notebook could do, I almost took it directly to the Prince of Mirror City. The Prince was quite handsome and was said to be looking for a wife." Belladona smiled wistfully at the memory. "I had aspirations. But then I remembered that he didn't like dogs, and I had visions of him wiping all the dogs off the face of the earth with a few pen strokes and decided against it."

"Really?"

Belladona nodded. "Good thing too, because he turned out to be quite an ass, and a very bad prince. And I hear the new one is not much nicer."

"Getting back to my, ah, safety?" Good Idea nudged. As her mind shifted through all the various parts of this scheme, danger kept popping up on top.

"Right. Well, Arch is a wise man who knows how important this is. If he says this Bunny person will be of help, I'm sure he's right. And you can ask Weathervane Wynd for help. She raised me after my mothers' death, and I would trust her with my life. She made a Witches' Vow when I left that if help was ever needed to get the notebook, she would provide it."

"A Witches' Vow?" Good Idea asked.

"Yes. A promise made between two witches. It can never be broken."

"But won't Weathervane Wynd also be rather, ah..." Good

Idea struggled to find the right phrase. "Fragile? Will she even remember having made this Vow?"

Belladona laughed. "She will remember. And she will keep it. And I'm sure she won't be fragile at all. And like I said, you'll gather allies. If you can, find a giant. Maybe you can convince a demon. Usually, they're not on the side trying to *prevent* evil, but you could get lucky. Yes, a demon would be very handy. What, Fleet?" Belladona cocked her head toward the mouse still on her shoulder, and Good Idea could have sworn Fleet whispered in her mother's ear. "Fleet says to find an elf with a big sword. Fleet is a little old-fashioned, but he has a point. Elves are very handy in the killing-of-enemies game."

Find a giant or a demon? How was such a thing even *possible*? "I'm still not one hundred percent convinced I should even do this thing."

Belladona stared at her, then snorted with laughter. "Of course you're going to do this thing. You have to. Because if you don't, you're going to have to live with me nagging and making your life a living hell."

Good Idea stared at her mother and another uncomfortable truth sank in. All of her concerns about finding and returning the Notebook Of Whim were nothing compared to what she knew her life would be like on the farm with a disappointed and disapproving Belladona.

"You're right, Mother. I'll go."

THE BLACKSMITH HAD a sprawling establishment just at the edge of the town of Whisper, where the road met the mountain and went no farther. Good Idea found him behind the second barn, his forge glowing with heat, making horseshoes. She watched him for some minutes, intrigued. She'd never paid much attention to him or his work until now, but as she watched him, it occurred to her that he probably made swords and axes. Maybe he knew a lot about swords and axes. Maybe he was exactly the type of ally she needed on a journey that would require at least one person who knew their way around swords and axes.

He finally noticed her and paused his work, frowning. "Can I help you?" he called over the roar of the fire.

She reached into her pocket and withdrew the ring. He put down his hammer and took a step closer. He leaned forward, squinted at the ring, and nodded, as though to himself.

"About time," he yelled. "Where's your thumb?"

She stuck out her right hand. He grabbed her thumb, stepped closer, and squeezed it. Then he took the ring from her other hand and slipped it on her thumb, eyeing it with interest. He took the ring with a tiny set of tongs and held it in the flame.

Good Idea held her breath. Would there be sparks? Pink flame? Maybe a puff of magical smoke?

Mr. Gold, noticing her rapt attention, snorted. "It's just a ring," he yelled. "Nothing special here. Step back."

She did, disappointed.

He removed the ring from the fire. Would he need a special hammer? Dust it with enchanted powder?

He grabbed a pair of pliers, placed the ring in the center, and tightened gently. Then he tossed the ring into a pail of water where it hissed, then floated to the surface.

He watched, grabbed it from the water, dried it with the tail of his apron, and handed it back to her.

"There you go. Good luck."

She slipped the ring on her thumb. A perfect fit. She stepped back, looked again at the broad, powerful shoulders and obvious strength, and cleared her throat loudly.

The dwarf turned. "Anything else?" he asked, barely polite.

"Do you know why I need this ring?" she asked. She had to speak loudly over the noise of the forge.

"Course. Been waiting nigh on sixty years for that ring to show up here," he said.

"Then you know how important it is that I get to and from Mirror City in safety?"

"Of course, I know. Do you think I would have sat out the best part of my life in this ridiculous town, watching for goblins and hobs and any number of enemies that might come looking for your mother, if I didn't know?" He leaned toward her. "I used to craft the finest swords in the kingdom for the wealthiest and strongest knights. I gave that up to be here and protect her and do nothing but make horseshoes and mend broken plows while I waited for you to show up with that ring."

This was not exactly the reaction she was expecting, but she plowed on. "Then would you come with me? To Mirror City?"

His eyes grew wide, and his jaw went slack. He stared, then threw his head back and laughed. He continued to laugh for such a long time that Good Idea began to feel uncomfortable. He finally gasped, and sputtered, "Why in yaksun would I want to do that?"

"Well, it's a dangerous journey and I could use the help."

He wiped the tears of laughter from his eyes. "Dangerous doesn't even begin to describe your journey. Zeppins! Woman, you're going to have every demon and goblin and hedge witch in this Kingdom — and the next — on your tail. Not to mention the henchmen of every has-been or wanna-be, all looking for the ultimate power. I, for one, want none of that."

"But what if I fail, and the notebook falls into the wrong hands?" she pleaded.

"Then the world, as we know it, may be over. Or not. Tricky things, these magical objects. Who knows, maybe a sweet, benevolent dragon will get hold of it and give everyone in the world a boatload of gold." He settled his hands on his hips. "Now, I swore to protect Belladona, and I swore to fit the ring, and I'm bound here until the notebook is returned to Belladona. Or not. But traipsing all over the countryside with you?" He shook his head. "I'm sorry, Inspirational Wink, I really am. And I sincerely hope no one kills you in some terrible fashion before you get back here. But I'm going to stay right here by my forge."

Good Idea twisted the ring around her thumb. "All right then. Thank you, Mr. Gold. I hope to see you again."

As she turned away, he called her name. She turned. He grimaced beneath his beard.

"Here," he said, and reached under his apron and drew out a knife, small but with a beautifully wrought handle and an obviously sharp blade. He reached over and gave it to her, handle first.

She took it, looked down at it, then up at him. "Is it magic?"

He shook his head. "No. Just a very well-balanced weapon that will always find its target."

She shook her head. "I don't know how to use this," she said.

He snorted. "Nonsense. You've gutted chickens and castrated sheep. You've skinned rabbits and butchered pigs. You've been using a knife your whole life. Just because it's a pretty thing doesn't change its function. You know how to use it."

She nodded, slipped it into her belt and left the yard, head held high.

ONCE BACK INTO THE STREET, she continued on to the livery.

The Barnstable sisters were undistinguishable from one another until they took off their hats: Tress had a long tumble of white curls, and Cropped had a short, very messy bob. They were both in the stable yard, examining a rather disreputable-looking bull when Good Idea creaked open their gate. Eyes narrowed, and the bull was pushed to the side.

"Can we help you, Miss Wink?" Tress asked.

"Trouble again with that milk cow?" asked Cropped.

"Or perhaps another goat? We have a new batch of kids, healthy and strong," said Tress.

Good Idea held out two gold pieces. "My mother wants me to buy a horse," she said.

The two sisters nodded.

"A strawberry roan horse, I'll wager," said Tress.

"With a saddle and bridle," said Crop. "We have just the horse you need."

They led her into the large, quite pleasant barn and stopped in front of a stall.

"Now, this is Pink," Tress said. "Quite strong, lovely temperament. And fast. Yes, she's fast."

"We think that she is exactly what you need," Cropped said, opening the wooden door and leading out the horse by a leather halter.

Good Idea, raised around animals her entire life, looked the small mare over. She had clear, intelligent eyes and a pretty arch to her neck. She was all mottled red and white, an almost perfect strawberry pink.

"I'll take her," Good Idea said, handing over the coins. She eyed the two women as they all went back out to the yard. "Do you know why I need her?" she asked.

"Certainly," Tress said.

"She'll get you to Mirror City and back again," said Cropped.

"It's the back again I'm concerned about," Good Idea began. "You know, because of the notebook."

"Well, Pink here won't mind what you're carrying," said Tress.

"I'm sure she won't, but she might not be of much help to me if, say, I met a demon on the road home," Good Idea said.

"Now, I wouldn't be too sure of that," Tress said.

"She's not just fast, she's something of an escape artist," said Cropped.

"That's a fact," Tress said. "I've seen her twist and jump her way out of many situations."

"Why, her very first day in this stable yard," Cropped said, "she saw a snake and practically flew into the next paddock."

"She's very keen, our Pink," said Tress. "Notices every sound and flicker in the shadows."

"A horse like that is very handy on the road," said Cropped.

"A seasoned witch would also be handy," Good Idea managed to get in.

Tress shook her head. "No, sorry my dear, but we're staying right here in Whisper."

"Not much sense in putting ourselves in harm's way after living such a long and peaceful life now, is it?" asked Cropped. "Besides, there's your mother to protect."

"Well, thank you anyway," she said, leading the small horse out onto the road.

This was not going at all the way she envisioned.

THE FIXES HAD their shop off the main road, but as Good Idea walked through town, she came upon the storefront that housed the Whisper Weekly News. Hadn't Bunny mentioned gnomes? And weren't the two proprietors of the Whisper Weekly gnomes?

She tied Pink to a post outside the storefront and went inside.

There were two battered desks by the front doors, and behind them, through an opening, she could see the large printing press standing quiet and still.

One gnome stood up from behind his desk. Very thin, with an overlarge, balding head and thin and nimble fingers, he looked at her through orange eyes and bowed his head.

"It's Inspirational Wink, is it not?" he asked politely.

"Yes. May I sit down?" she moved to the single rickety chair in front of the desk, and as he nodded, sat.

"I am Mr. Tip. And this gentleman," he nodded to the second gnome, whose also balding head was bent over a long, faded piece of parchment, "is Mr. Tap. I see that you are wearing a thin silver ring on your thumb. You have also acquired a strawberry roan. We can only assume you are about to embark on a very important and possibly perilous adventure. Is there any way we can be of service?"

Good Idea felt a rush of relief. "Yes, Mr. Tip. And thank you so much for asking. I would very much appreciate if you and Mr. Tap would come with me to Mirror City." She smiled brightly. The scratching of the quill on the parchment stopped, and the ensuing silence seemed to last a very long time.

Finally, Mr. Tip cleared his throat. "I beg your pardon? Go with you? To Mirror City? I'm sorry, my dear, but I cannot imagine, not in one thousand lifetimes, why myself or Mr. Tap would want to do such a thing."

Had he not just acknowledged that she was about to embark on a possibly perilous adventure? Wasn't that reason enough for them to come with her? "I need allies," she said, raising her voice. "There *is* danger and if I'm to survive this, I need to *find* those allies. Mother suggested a demon, which, I'm fairly sure, is not ideal, and I wouldn't know how to find one anyway, and —"

"We could do that for you," interrupted Mr. Tip.

She sat back in surprise. "You could find me a demon?"

He shrugged, and the scratch of quill on parchment began again.

"We know things," growled Mr. Tap.

"And you know how to find a demon?"

Mr. Tip nodded.

She thought. "How about a giant? I think a giant might be better company."

"Undoubtedly," said Mr. Tip, looking relieved. "Finding a demon is always a very risky proposition for all involved. However, giants are, believe it or not, harder to come by."

Her shoulders slumped. "Oh."

Mr. Tap growled again. "Orc."

Mr. Tip brightened. "Of course, Mr. Tap. Very good. Yes, we could find you an orc. Half as large as a giant, of course, but nearly as strong, and they smell much better. And they probably wouldn't want to kill you, like a demon would, so that may be the solution you're looking for?"

"And this orc," Good Idea began. "Would he be an ally?"

Mr. Tip raised an eyebrow. "You mean follow you through danger and death just because he—or she—believed that the notebook you will be carrying needs to be protected at all costs? No."

Her shoulders slumped again.

"Gold," Mr. Tap whispered. "Gold."

"Yes, that's true," said Mr. Tip, nodding. "I imagine for as little as two gold coins, any orc would follow you to the ends of the earth. Their love of gold coin is unequaled, but you must set the terms of employment at the outset. Orcs are very particular about details."

"Oh," said Good Idea, relief flooding her. At least now she'd have someone – or something – on her side, even if she'd have to pay for loyalty. "Well, as long as this orc protects me, I don't care much about the details."

"That, my dear," said Mr. Tip with a gentle smile, "is not the attitude you need when dealing with orcs. The details are everything. If you're smart, have your mother set the terms. Now, it will take us a bit of time, but we will send one to your mother's farm the day after tomorrow. Will that suit?"

She stood up and held out her hand. "Yes, that will be fine. Thank you for all your help, Mr. Tip."

The gnome's hand was boney and rather damp, and Good Idea dropped it as soon as was polite, making a genuine effort not to wipe her palm on the hem of her shirt.

"You too, Mr. Tap," she called.

The scratch of a quill against parchment continued as she shut the door behind her.

CHAPTER 4

*T*he sign attached to the gatepost read 'We Fixes'.

The Fixes were elves who'd come to the town of Whisper years ago. They'd set up shop and begun repairing things that normally would have been tossed away. Wrench Fix and his wife, Button, had five sons, named for the days of the week when they were born. The oldest sons left Whisper to find Elven wives, but two sons remained and continued repairing everything and anything brought to them.

Did they use magic? Did anyone really care? They fixed things, and, in some cases, made things even better than new. Windmills that turned without a hint of a breeze, stoves that never had to be relit, and harnesses that never wore out. Folks paid dearly for these extras, and no one ever said the "M" word, but everyone knew.

Good Idea pushed her way in, tugging at Pink to follow her. The drive was tree-shaded and very narrow, but she could hear the clatter of some machinery and the laughter of a child in the clearing ahead, and she felt her heart lift. She had acquired an ally. It came at a cost, to be sure, but she felt so much better now that she knew someone large and strong would join the obviously inexperienced Bunny Jones and the totally helpless Fleet.

And now she would be seeing Tuesday Fix. Tuesday was tall and lean, like all elves, with a narrow but beautiful face, long and blond hair that was, as tradition dictated, curled in a tousle directly on the top of the head. His ears were pointed, his eyebrows came together in a gentle 'v' and he had a wide, bright, and beautiful smile. Also, like all elves, he appeared forever young. In fact, he looked just as he had when he and Good Idea were in school together where they had shared, among other things, an interest in growing corn.

He had been the most beautiful boy Good Idea had ever seen, and as a young girl she dreamed of spending the rest of her life gazing at that face and running her fingers through those golden curls. But one stolen kiss under a starry sky had left her feeling disappointed and somewhat troubled. Where had been the quickly beating heart? The trembling lips? The whispered words of longing? If she couldn't be enamored with this boy, would she ever find love?

But when she returned to the farm that evening, one of the cows had fallen ill, and her mind quickly shifted away from affairs of the heart, never to return. And although they didn't see each other often, she considered him to be one of the few friends she had in Whisper.

"Hello, Good Idea," he called. He was tossing a young boy into the air and laughing. "This is my neighbor, Tounce."

"Hello, Tounce," Good Idea said, smiling.

He looked past her as he set the little boy down. "You have a horse," he said.

"It's a pink horse," Tounce said loudly.

"It's actually a strawberry roan," Good Idea said.

Tuesday's eyes grew big. "Is that what that is? I always wondered what strawberry roan would look like. You're right though, Tounce. She looks pink." He grinned at Good Idea. "So, I suppose I've a saddle to repair?"

She nodded and watched as he loosened the girth and slid off the small leather saddle. "I don't think it's broken, though."

"It's not," Tuesday said. He looked down at Tounce. "Run up to the house and ask for a cookie, eh?"

Tounce ran off and Tuesday carried the saddle to a wooden sawhorse in the middle of the yard. "It's not broken," he said again, "but it needs to be fixed. It needs to hold on to its rider, no matter how fast the river is flowing around them. It needs to stay fastened even if someone has tried to cut its girth. It needs to keep the rider upright even if they are sick or asleep. It needs to know the words of encouragement when a horse is tired or injured. It needs to hold on to whatever is placed in its saddle-bags, even if the bags are torn or opened."

"You can do all that?" Good Idea asked in amazement.

He beamed. "It's what we do. We fix things. That's why we're here. That, and to protect your mother, of course."

She sighed, exasperated. "Am I the only one who didn't know that all of you, Mr. Gold and the Barnstable sisters, and Mr. Tip and Mr. Tap and your whole family, were here for one purpose only? To defend my mother?"

He pursed his lips, then shrugged. "Probably. After all, the more people who knew, the more likely that someone would say the wrong thing at the wrong time to the wrong person, and bring down a swarm of hobs or jitterflies, intent on killing Belladonna to unlock the enchantments and get the notebook."

"Hobs?" Good Idea asked. "And...jitterflies? I knew about the demons and hedge witches, despots and henchmen, not to mention goblins, but what even *are* jitterflies?"

"Oh, they're about that big," he said, holding his hands about three feet apart. "And they chew."

"Chew what?"

"Anything they can."

"Oh, my," said Good Idea. "This all sounds much more perilous than it did this morning."

"Well." He cleared his throat. "The saddle will be ready by tomorrow evening. I can bring it by the farm."

She sighed and nodded wearily. "That would be fine, thank you." She put her hand on Pink's bridle and turned to go.

"Good Idea?" Tuesday called. "It seems to me that you are a bit nervous about this journey of yours. And since I and my family pride ourselves on defending as well as fixing, would you like me to come with you?"

She froze, then turned back to Tuesday Fix. "Come with me?" She repeated hopefully.

"Yes. To Mirror City. You might need some help along the way and, well, *I* could be of help."

A thought struck her. "Do you have a really long sword?" she asked.

He frowned, puzzled. "Yes. I do."

But what good was a really big sword if ...? "Do you know how to use it?"

He grinned, his teeth white. "Naturally. My father instructed us all in the various ways of attack and defend, beginning at a very young age."

"Everyone else I've asked for help said no. Mr. Gold and the Barnstable sisters, Mr. Tip and Mr. Tap all said they were staying right here in Whisper."

He shrugged. "Well, their job is to protect Belladona, and after you retrieve the notebook, that's when her life will be in real danger. So, of course, they have to stay here. But" he waved his hand toward the low, thatched cottage set back from the work yard. "my father and mother will still be here, as well as my brother Friday. Although I have been vital to her defense until now, I feel certain that they will understand that you also need protection. If you'd like, I would be happy to go with you."

The beginning of a smile turned into the end of a smile that moved quickly to a full-fledged grin. "I would be very happy to have you come with me, Tuesday. Bunny — do you know Mr. Jones? He's coming, well, no, he's meeting us in Mirror City. But there's Fleet. Fleet is a mouse, in case you don't know. And I've hired an orc for two gold pieces."

He nodded sagely. "That's about the going rate for an orc. Couldn't find any giants?"

"No. At least Mr. Tip and Mr. Tap said they couldn't, and I don't know of anyone else who could procure a giant."

"We may come across one on our travels," Tuesday said. "And you could always ask the otters."

Why would she possibly want to do that? "Otters?"

"Oh yes. The otters living under the Three Creek Bridge. They guard the bridge."

How in the world could otters guard the bridge? "Otters?"

"They aren't just *any* otters now, are they?" he chided. "I mean, what good would otters do against demons or gryphons?"

"Then what are they?" she asked.

"They're shape-shifters," Tuesday said easily. "Don't know what their mother form is." He noticed her look of amazement. "That's the form they are when they're not, you know, shifting."

"So, they can become anything?"

"Within reason, I guess."

This was beginning to sound interesting. "Even into dragons?" she asked.

He laughed. "I don't know. You should go and ask them."

"How? I mean, do they understand common speech?"

"I imagine they understand all kinds of speech," he said reasonably.

She looked down the long drive and thought of the road ahead, through the rest of town, then into the farmland, and finally to Three Creek Bridge. "I can make it there before dark," she said. "I will ask them."

"That's the spirit," Tuesday said. "A shapeshifter or two in our company should make you feel safer. Now, I'll bring this saddle tomorrow night, and we can sit down and figure things out then. Okay?"

She nodded and smiled and felt so much better for knowing that Tuesday Fix was not only coming with her, but had said he'd help figure things out. She had not been impressed with Bunny's organizational skills, but Tuesday was always talking about some new thing he had studied and learned, some new skill he'd mastered. He'd be very helpful, besides being her friend.

"Come on, Pink," she said. "Let's find an otter."

GOOD IDEA WENT RIGHT past the turnoff for Wink's Wold and continued on to Three Creek Bridge. She was riding Pink without a saddle, of course, but that was how she often rode the mules. She stopped just before the bridge, slid off the horse and dropped the rein.

"Stay here," she said.

Pink nodded.

Climbing down the rocky bank was a bit tricky, but once on the bank of the swiftly running water, she looked around for the otters. There was just one, lying on top a rock in the dying warmth of the setting sun.

"Excuse me," she called. "Could I have a word?"

The otter looked up, then rose onto its hind legs and made a shrill chirping kind of noise. Seconds later, five other otters appeared from among the rocks, and they all made their way over to her. They sat in front of her on their hind haunches, eyes alert, noses quivering.

"I'm Inspirational Wink," she began.

"We know," said one otter in a rich, rather fruity voice.

"I'm about to go to Mirror City," she said.

"We know that too," the otter said.

She took a deep breath. "I would appreciate any help you could give me along the way. I've been told that there could be a bit of difficulty, and..."

At that, all five otters began to laugh, deep, bellowing laughs.

"Hear that, Tooth," one yelled to the first otter, still sitting on its rock. "She's been told there could be a bit of difficulty."

That otter too, began to laugh, and Good Idea was beginning to feel annoyed with the whole situation. "Stop laughing," she bellowed with such strength and command that she surprised herself. It had the effect she wanted: they stopped laughing.

"Look at me," she said, exasperated. "I'm an old woman with a pink horse and I'm supposed to go off and do something to keep the world from falling into what could be a rather tricky spot. Whenever I ask for help, I get laughed at. I'm getting a little tired of it. Tuesday Fix is the only one who's taken me seriously, and he said I should ask *you* for help. If you don't want to, fine. I just hope that you all can still have a good laugh when whoever comes looking for the notebook kills my mother and burns Whisper to the ground."

One otter stepped forward. "Our job is to protect your mother from anything crossing this bridge that might want to do her harm. And if you do succeed in finding the notebook, our job will suddenly become much more important than it has been for the past sixty-odd years. But it is also true that you will probably need more help on this journey than Tuesday Fix and a pink horse."

She cleared her throat. "I've hired an orc."

The otter nodded. "Very smart move. I hope you're not giving it more than two gold pieces?"

She shook her head. "No. And Bunny Jones, who is a wizard, is meeting me in Mirror City and will accompany me through the Veil and on the road back to Whisper."

The otters exchanged looks. The one who'd spoken last

stepped forward. "I am Left Ear. I will go with you to Mirror City, and, of course, come back with you. When do you leave?"

"Day after tomorrow," she said, "and —"

Tooth suddenly began his shrill chirping again, and all the otters froze.

On the road, Pink nickered nervously.

"Get beneath the bridge," Left Ear said urgently. Good Idea moved quickly across the rocky riverbank and slipped under the shadow of the bridge.

She could hear someone coming down the road.

A few someones.

The air grew very still and cold. Pink nickered again.

The steps, or, rather, shuffles, stopped at the exact center of the bridge. The otters were all crouched, ears quivering.

Someone spoke, but in a language that Good Idea did not understand, a hoarse kind of croaking sound.

The otters all looked at each other, and in the growing darkness, Good Idea could see a few of them start to swell. One otter snaked its way up the side of the embankment and, a few seconds later, she heard a smooth voice.

"Gentlemen, may I ask your business in Whisper?"

Pink made a nervous, snuffling kind of noise, and there was more croaking.

"Ah, but you see," the smooth voice continued, "it *is* my concern. As the Bridge Master, I must question all strangers entering town after dark."

There were some more croaking noises, and a hoarse voice said, in the common tongue, "T'ain't dark yet."

"I have," said the smooth voice, "a certain amount of discretion in the matter. So again, I ask, what is your business?"

Hoarser croaks, and the otters scattered. The ones who had begun to swell had grown larger than otters, larger than badgers, as large as wolves. Good Idea crept from under the bridge to try to see what was happening above her.

Then the yelling began.

Scrambling up the rocky slope, Good Idea ran toward the mare. The horse saw her, stopped moving, and placed herself between Good Idea and the bridge.

There was a man standing there, very calmly, arms crossed and shaking his head in faint disgust. There were also three very large creatures, man-like in shape, but with scales for skin and wearing capes of rough leather. Their heads were long, with wide eyes, pointed snouts and very, very sharp teeth. They were all armed with long spears that they were using now with rough skill, trying to kill the five sleek and very fast wolves that had swarmed them from both ends of the bridge. They lasted less than a minute. A loud, rather vicious minute, then all three lay on the bridge, obviously dead.

Good Idea had never seen anything so violent in all her days in Whisper. Things like this didn't happen here. Ever. Pink moved away, and the man turned to her.

"All right?" he asked.

She nodded. "Yes, but — who are you?"

He grinned. "Tooth" he answered. In the blink of an eye, the wolves all shrank back to otters and scurried off the bridge, and the three scaly bodies lay on the dark, empty bridge.

"Things are moving quickly," Tooth said. "We have not had to defend this bridge against something like this before. If you can leave for Mirror City tomorrow, try to do so."

"I won't be ready," Good Idea said.

"You must be," Tooth said. "Who knows what will try to cross the bridge next? Just stop on the bridge as you're leaving, and Left Ear will join you."

He shrank down, leaving a small pile of clothes, and slipped off into the darkness.

Good Idea looked at Pink. The horse snorted and shook her mane.

"I think," Good Idea said, "That we will have to move more quickly than I'd like."

Pink snorted.

"I also think that an otter will be a very useful thing to have with us."

And they headed back home.

GOOD IDEA DID NOT MENTION the incident on the bridge to Belladona when she got home. She simply said that she had the ring, horse, and saddle situation under control and went to bed without so much as a bite of cheese. Too much had happened in too short a period of time, and she needed to be by herself with just her thoughts.

Her mother had been right. There had been magic all round her the whole of her life and she'd chosen not to see it. What else was there in the world that she had missed? And was it worth leaving the home that she loved?

And then she realized that she really had no choice.

The next morning, while Before and After were just starting the morning chores, she slipped onto Pink's back and trotted quickly into town.

Her first stop was the Whisper Weekly. Mr. Tip, seated behind his desk, seemed to be waiting for her.

"Three trolls were found dead on Three Creek Bridge this morning," Mr. Tip said as she came through the door. "That can't be good news for you."

She shook her head. "It's not. How fast can the orc get here? By noon today?"

Mr. Tap, scratching on parchment as before, growled, "Cost another gold piece."

She had ten gold pieces left of her mother's stash and couldn't imagine what else she was going to do with the money, so she nodded. "Fine."

Mr. Tip stroked his chin. "Haven't seen trolls in a century at least. Things are getting interesting."

"Where are they from?" she asked.

"They live below the mines up Clerridach way. Rarely venture this far south."

"They're miners?" she asked.

"No. They just like living underground," Mr. Tip explained.

"Then, what do they do?"

Mr. Tip paused. "They kill things."

"Oh, my," Good Idea said faintly.

"I'll see about that orc," Mr. Tap said.

"Thank you," she said, then left the storefront and went on to the Fixes.

Tuesday met her in the yard. "Heard about what happened on the bridge," he said as she slid off Pink. "So, I guess you spoke to the otters?"

She nodded. "Yes. Left Ear will come with us. He said I should leave today. The orc will be here by noon."

Tuesday scratched his ear. "Certain fixes take time," he said.

"I don't think I have as much of that today as I had yesterday," she told him.

"Okay then. We'll do what we can, and I'll meet you at noon."

"Thank you," she said, and swung back onto Pink.

Back home, she sat in her simple room and looked around. What did one *wear* on an adventure? She had no armor or cloak, she didn't have a shield or helm. She barely had a weapon.

So, she did what she always did when faced with a dilemma — she thought about the easiest and simplest solution. She'd be traveling for days on horseback, so she would strive for comfort. She changed from her everyday dress into her father's work pants, his favorite white shirt, and stuck the knife that Mr. Gold gave her into the small scabbard that had held Steadfast's hunting knife. She found her best boots and a wide-brimmed hat that she usually wore in high summer to pick berries. She stuffed a few items in her pack: a heavy blanket, another shirt, and clean undergarments.

In the kitchen, she began to wrap food in stiff brown paper: cheese, smoked ham, and biscuits. Belladona watched in silence until Good Idea began stuffing dried apples into her pack.

"Aren't you rushing things?" Belladona asked.

"Change of plans," Good Idea told her. "We're leaving at noon."

"You'll only be on the road for three or four days," Belladona said. "And there will be an inn or two for you to stop and eat."

"I'm being cautious," Good Idea told her, slinging her pack over her shoulder. Good Idea believed in regular meals and, when possible, snacking in between.

Belladona nodded in understanding. "By all means, then. I know how you get when you're hungry."

Just then, Before burst into the kitchen. "They found dead things on Three Creek Bridge," he said excitedly. "Big, ugly dead things that carried spears. Some say they were trolls. It looks like they were torn apart by wolves, but the wolf prints were the biggest that Sherif Sure has ever seen. They're forming a hunting party to see if there are any more of the dead things that may be still alive." He noticed Good Idea. "Why are you dressed like that? And why was there a pink horse in the barn this morning? Are you going somewhere?"

Belladona narrowed her eyes at Good Idea. "Dead trolls on Three Creek Bridge? Is that why you're leaving early?"

Before looked between Belladona and Good Idea. "Leaving? Early? You are going somewhere? Are you leaving Whisper? Why would you ever want to leave Whisper? Where are you going?"

"Before," Belladona said patiently, "Good Idea has a small errand to run for me. So, if you could just run off to the barn, your aunt and I have a few last-minute details to go over." Before looked confused, but obediently left.

Good Idea turned to her mother. "I'll need the map. And where's Fleet?"

Belladona reached into the pouch around her neck again and withdrew the folded parchment, and the small mouse ran down her arm, across the wooden floor, and up Good Idea's pant leg, slipping into the overlarge pocket.

Good Idea took the folded paper and put it in the smaller pocket where she had the gold coins and the key.

"You're missing the saddle," Belladona pointed out.

"It's coming."

"And what about giants? Demons? An elf with a big sword?"

"I hired an orc," Good Idea explained. "I decided against demons. However, Tuesday Fix is coming with me. Oh, and an otter."

Belladona nodded her approval. "Very good. Tuesday Fix thinks quite a lot of himself, but I know he was trained well. I suppose the otters are responsible for the three dead trolls on Three Creek Bridge? I bet they weren't expecting anything like that so early in the game."

"I think they handled it very well," Good Idea said, looking out the window for something that looked like an orc.

"You were there?" Belladona asked. "How frightening."

"Yes, it was, rather. But it was over very quickly, I thought. Of course, I've never seen a pack of wolves take down three trolls before, so maybe it wasn't very quick at all."

"Trolls are nasty things. Don't see many around these parts."

"Yes. Mr. Tip says they live mostly underground."

"Yes, well, that's exactly the sort of thing Mr. Tip would know. So, we're waiting for Tuesday? And the orc?"

Good Idea nodded. Fleet shifted about in her pocket, and it tickled a bit, but when he settled down, there was a nice, comfortable warmth against her hip.

"Is that Steadfast's old knife?" Belladona asked, gesturing toward the scabbard in Good Idea's belt.

"No. Mr. Gold gave me a keepsake." She drew the knife out, once again struck by the beautifully wrought hilt and very sharp blade.

Belladona smiled approvingly. "It's a fine weapon. He's a very good blacksmith."

"No ordinary blacksmith could craft something so fine," Good Idea said.

"No," Belladona agreed. "He is exceptional."

Good Idea sat across the table from her mother. "I'm still very unsure about—" She waved her hands about her face. "I really don't want to do this, especially seeing those trolls last night. If that's going to be the sort of thing coming after me, well..."

Belladona made a kind of clucking sound. "Trolls aren't as dangerous as they look. They are fairly limited, reasoning-wise. They can only take orders. The ones you have to be careful of are the creatures that can think for themselves."

There was a thud on the back step, and what sounded like a very large fist knocking on the wall of the house. Good Idea hurried across the kitchen, opened the door, and found herself face-to-face with a very wide sort of person, a long torso on short stubby legs, with pale yellow skin. The head was round and bald, with a fringe of braids around the ears. There were two yellow eyes, a pug nose and a puckered mouth crowded under a furrowed brow. A large pack was over one shoulder, and a double-bladed axe was strapped across the yellow expanse of back.

"I'm Bruise." The orc reached back and patted his axe. "This is Axe. I want three gold coins."

"Three?" asked Belladona. "That's an outrage."

"I needed him—her—them—today rather than tomorrow," Good Idea explained.

Bruise grunted. "'Him' is good."

Good Idea nodded. "Very well. Now, Bruise, I think —"

"Good Idea, if you don't mind," Belladona interrupted. She turned her wheelchair to Bruise. "My daughter has never killed anything larger than a Freemont pig and will probably be quite unable to defend herself. You," she said succinctly, "must protect her from all enemies, human and non-human, as well as any magical interference. You must assist in finding and making camp and hunting for food when necessary and give aid to her companions if needed. Any treasure that she finds is her own, but any that *you* find when she is not with you, you may keep for yourself. She will be in possession of a valuable object once she leaves Mirror City, and you must make sure no one takes that object from her. Do you understand these terms?"

Bruise nodded formally. "I understand. And she will pay all expenses, will not leave me behind if injured, and will make sure my family is notified in the event of my death."

"Agreed." Belladona said. "One gold coin now, one when you find the notebook, and the third when you get her back to this kitchen."

Bruise nodded again. "Where's my gold?"

Good Idea dug into her pocket and brought out one coin, which Bruise took, examined carefully, then stuck deep into his left ear.

"I'll wait," Bruise said, and lumbered off to stand, perfectly still, by the back gate.

Tuesday Fix trotted into the yard on a fine black horse and had a very long sword strapped to his side. She was relieved to see her saddle behind him, and as he dismounted, he swung it down.

"I'll saddle up your roan," he called.

"Her name is Pink." Good Idea told him.

At those words, Bruise turned and grinned happily. "A pink horse?" He called.

"Yes," answered Good Idea. "I'll be right there in a minute."

She went back to stand in front of her mother, feeling

suddenly excited. After spending her entire life making carefully reasoned decisions, having to set off without having all that much say in the matter was oddly exhilarating. "I guess I'm off."

Belladona opened her arms, and Good Idea bent down, feeling all the love and hope in her mother's arms.

"I will see you soon," Belladona's voice said in her ear. "And you can tell me all about your journey out into the world. I love you. You can do this."

Good Idea stepped back and nodded. She was on her way. She was on her way to an adventure, something she had wondered about her whole life. And now it was happening. Her breath quickened and a smile played across her lips. An *adventure*.

"Good-bye, Mother," she said, and slipped out the door.

Before, who had returned from the barn, stood in the doorway and watched as Good Idea went out into the yard. "But where is she going?" He asked.

"To save the world from calamity," Belladona answered.

"On a pink horse? With an elf and an orc? Will that be enough?" Before asked.

"Oh, she also has an otter," Belladona reassured him. "And a mouse."

"Ah, well," Before said. "That's better. Is there more sweet roll left?"

Belladona gestured with one hand, then turned and watched as Good Idea swung up on her pink horse and disappeared down the long drive with the orc and Tuesday Fix.

Part Two

In which Inspirational Wink sets out
on her journey with a pink horse, an elf,
an orc, a mouse, and an otter, and
encounters the first of many
adventures.
Also, a paladin.

Three Creek Bridge

CHAPTER 5

They went on together to Three Creek Bridge, Tuesday and Good Idea riding, the orc walking between them, his yellow head just coming up to Pink's shoulder. They stopped at the foot of the bridge, and Good Idea called out. An otter scurried up from the river, jumping neatly onto Pink's neck. The otter turned to Good Idea.

"I am Good Idea," she said formally.

"And I'm Left Ear of the Wolf Clan," the otter responded, waggling one ear, which was slightly larger than the other.

"Wolf Clan?" Good Idea asked.

"Yes. That is my mother form, what I would be if not shifted into something else."

"Why aren't you a wolf all the time?" she asked.

The small, round head tilted. "And how do you think that would be received by the good folk of Whisper? Having a pack of wolves milling around the only way in and out of town? Not to mention visitors?"

Good Idea nodded. "Of course." She looked closer. "But that's your right ear…" she said slowly.

"No." The tone suggested this was an old argument. "That's

because you're looking at it. It's *my* Left Ear. These are *my* ears. And this is *my* name. Please don't try to convince me otherwise."

Good Idea fought back a smile. "I won't."

Left Ear nodded, then shifted into a crow. Good Idea broke into a smile of delight. She had seen the otters shift the night before, but that was in darkness and from a distance. Here, right in front of her, Left Ear swirled into a jumble of color and emerged all gleaming feathers and long, pointed beak, settling comfortably between Pink's ears.

They walked on, past the end of Three Creek Bridge, down the road to the grassy verge where the Market monthly set up its stalls, and around a curve in the road.

"Oh, my," she said quietly, looking at a stretch of road that she had never seen before. Her heart was beating faster than it had even been the night before, watching the trolls being ripped apart by wolves.

"What?" asked Tuesday.

"I've never been down this road before," she explained. "I've never left Whisper. Have you?"

Tuesday nodded. He was dressed in a fine linen shirt and soft leather trousers, his boots gleaming and the topknot of his hair softly curling. "I've even been to Mirror City before. It's a quiet road, smooth and easy even in bad weather. We should get as far as the Stop Here Inn by dark. We can stable the horses and have a good meal and a soft bed. The next night we may have to camp out of doors, but the weather should hold. Then, there's the Edge Of The Marsh Inn. Going through the Marsh is a shorter route to Mirror City, but the road is not well marked, and the quicksand can suck down a horse in minutes. And there are things in the Marsh that no one likes to talk about. We'll take the high road, and, again, if the weather is good, we'll reach Mirror City by nightfall of the fourth day."

"What if there are more trolls about?" Left Ear asked. "Or hobs? What about the sand demons said to live in the marsh?

Not to mention gryphons. They drop from the sky without a sound, you know. And there are probably dozens of witches who think they can find a better use for that notebook, not to mention —"

"Please stop," Good Idea said loudly. "I am going to try to enjoy this adventure for as long as I can. I'd rather not think about all the terrible things that might happen, if you don't mind."

Tuesday laughed. "Do you think that whatever we come across will be too great a challenge? My father trained for years as a guardian of the royal palace in Mirror City, and he taught me and all of my brothers well. Good Idea has nothing to fear."

Good Idea had never seen a crow roll its eyes before, but she thought that was what she was seeing, and choked back a giggle.

"Have you fought trolls, then?" Left Ear asked.

"No. But I've studied them. My father had us all study the various fighting techniques of all sorts of creatures, and we often had lengthy discussions about the best ways to defeat those creatures."

Left Ear ruffled his feathers. "I've studied the stars. It doesn't mean I can *be* one. Did you ever *fight* any of them? Trolls, I mean?"

"I have," Bruise said. "They're stubborn, I'll give them that. Hobs are sneaky. Not a fan. They're always climbing up on top of you or nipping at the ankles. They're so short they can't bite much higher than that, but they are nasty. Don't like the demons much either. They don't fight fair. Always going up in a puff of smoke when you're about to deliver a death blow and popping back on your head or some such nonsense."

"Hedge witches are the worst," Left Ear offered. "Never admit when they're losing."

"That's true," Bruise agreed. "You can literally be stabbing them through the heart, and they'll be trying to put together one last spell."

"You can stop now," Good Idea said loudly.

"So, elf, you've never, in your real life, encountered any of these, ah, creatures that you've studied?" Left Ear asked.

"The truth is," Tuesday said, "that there has never been so much as a midgewack in Whisper the entire time my family has been there."

Curiosity got the best of her. "Midgewack? What's that?" Good Idea asked.

"Annoying little beetle," Bruise said. "Easily squashed, but dangerous in large numbers."

Bruise and Left Ear discussed various creatures for the next several hours. The day was coming to a close, and Good Idea was beginning to wonder about the Stop Here Inn. She had made them stop for a lunch of smoked ham and biscuits, despite the fact that they seemed quite content to travel through without stopping to eat at all, something she had a hard time imagining. Her back hurt, and she was tired of hearing the non-stop conversation about all the dire beings in the world, and how they could kill you. Finally, there was a blaze of light at the crest of the next hill.

"There it is," Tuesday said. "The mead is excellent."

The horses were led into the stable, and Left Ear flew atop the slate roof of the Inn to keep watch. Good Idea, Tuesday and Bruise entered the main room of the Inn, low-ceilinged and crowded with farmers and travelers dressed in long, colorful cloaks and a fascinating variety of hats. They sat at a corner table, tucked away from the rest of the room. The innkeeper, named Full, served them ale and lamb stew, then showed them to three small but comfortable rooms under the eaves.

In the hallway, Tuesday leaned forward. "Lock your door. Stay there until morning. The common room will be much less crowded tomorrow, so don't mention Mirror City. Or the notebook, of course. Or Bunny. In fact, don't talk about anything to anyone until I get down there. We need to be careful. We don't want any information reaching the wrong ears."

She stared at him. "We just spent our entire dinner listening to you talk about all the various demons and hobs, goblin and jitterflies, and how you were going to protect me against all manner of enemies. And now you think maybe we should start being careful?"

He bristled. "In all that crowd, I'm sure no one heard us. But tomorrow morning may be different. That's all I was saying." He managed to look offended as he went into his room and shut the door.

Bruise snorted. "Bit of an asshole, that one," he said, then shut his own door.

Good Idea stood alone in the empty hallway, thinking that perhaps Tuesday Fix was not going to be exactly the kind of help she had expected.

THE FOLLOWING MORNING, the common room was quiet and empty. Good Idea spoke to the innkeeper, Full, and he promised to send out hot tea and breakfast. She sat at the same corner table as the night before, running over the last day's events in her mind. She could hear noises coming from the other side of the swinging doors where the innkeeper had vanished, and as she sat, a man came through the wide front doors, banging them open, and calling loudly.

The visitor was very tall and very thin, a gray cloak covering him from neck to boot. His hat was drawn down over his face, and his voice was low. The innkeeper hurried out, wiping his hands.

"Yes?" he asked the newcomer.

"I'm looking for someone," the man said. "A woman. Taller than most, with a long braid. She's riding a pink horse."

Good Idea shrank down, slid off the chair and crouched under the table.

Full continued to wipe his hands, and as he did, he looked past the stranger to where Good Idea huddled under the table. Their eyes met, and he arched an eyebrow.

"Well," he drawled, "why exactly would you be looking for her? Is she lost?" Full leaned forward. "Has she done something wrong?"

The man in black shuffled his booted feet impatiently. "The Prince of Mirror City wishes to speak to her, as if it's any of your business."

Full glanced at Good Idea again, who frantically shook her head.

"And would there be a reward for some such information?" Full asked slowly.

The man in gray stood very still. "Possibly."

Reaching deep into her pocket, Good Idea withdrew one of her gold coins. Holding it carefully between two fingers, she lifted it just above the top of the table, where a single beam of sunlight caught it and it shone brightly.

Full shook his head. "Haven't seen anyone like that. Sorry."

"Are you sure she didn't pass through?" The man in black asked. "She may have been traveling with an elf. Or an orc. Or both."

Full said again, "Sorry. No."

"Can I look in your barn? To see if there's a pink horse stabled?" The man asked.

The innkeeper became indignant. "No, you may not. Can't have strangers messing about with my guests' beasts." He snorted. "Don't you think I'd remember a pink horse?"

From beneath the table, Good Idea saw the black boots turn quickly, and the cloak swirling around his ankles as he left. She was afraid to move and squeezed her eyes shut. If he did come back, she'd rather not know.

"Miss?"

She opened her eyes, and the innkeeper was bent down, looking at her. "He's gone."

She backed out from under the table. "Thank you," she said.

He held out his hand and she dropped the gold coin in his palm. He bit down on it carefully, nodded, then smiled. "I guess you'll be leaving without breakfast then?"

Was he serious? No breakfast? Although, she had to admit that sitting down to a leisurely meal did not seem prudent. "Wrapped and to go, please." She stood and felt Fleet moving restlessly in her pocket. He crawled out, ran down her leg and scurried toward the cold hearth where Good Idea could see crumbs and bits of bone from last night's revelers.

Tuesday came bounding down the stairs, Bruise coming more slowly behind him.

"Morning," he called out. "I'm starving. What are we having to break our fast?"

"Bread and cheese to go," Good Idea said shortly, and told them about the stranger.

"Where is this interloper?" Tuesday said, his hand on the hilt of his sword.

"Hopefully far down the road," Bruise said. "And going in the opposite direction of Mirror City."

Fleet raced back to Good Idea, a small coil of thread in his mouth. He held it in front of her, obviously very proud of his find.

"Thank you, Fleet," she said, and he slipped back into her pocket.

Full appeared, holding a large sack. "And with your rooms, that'll be three silvers, two copper and twelve pence," he said, holding out his hand.

Good Idea glared. "I already gave you a whole gold coin this morning. You want more?"

Full shrugged. "That was for my silence. This is for your

room and this wonderful breakfast." He leaned in. "That feller could always come back," he said softly.

Good Idea gritted her teeth and gave him another gold coin. "Where I come from, men would not try to take advantage of a traveler."

"Maybe where you come from, nobody's looking for you." The innkeeper took her coin, flipped it in the air, then reached into his own pocket for change, his mood becoming more friendly. "There's no inn between here and the Edge Of The Marsh," he told her, handing Bruise the paper sack of food. "But there's a by-road, just past the waterfall, where you can camp. It's protected." He dropped silver and iron coins back into her hand. "You'll see." He peered at her sharply. "Why someone would be looking for you is the real question. And why you'd be so willing to part with gold to keep them from finding you. You don't seem to be all that interesting."

She sighed. "I'm not. At all. Thank you again."

They went out into the yard and pushed open the doors to the stable. A woman was there, clad in a long, shabby tunic, saddling Pink.

Tuesday's hand flew to his sword. "Stand back, you villain!" he cried, springing forward.

Bruise grabbed him by the back of his fine linen shirt and pulled him back so sharply that Tuesday ended up sitting in the dust and sand of the stable floor.

"Are you blind?" Bruise growled. "It's Left Ear."

Good Idea looked and, sure enough, one of the woman's ears was bigger than the other.

"You're a...female?" Good Idea asked.

Left Ear turned. "And why not?"

Good Idea shrugged. "My mistake. I just didn't realize."

"Well, it's hard to tell," Left Ear said with a bit of a grin, "unless you get a good look at the important bits. My being female really doesn't change things much."

"No," Good Idea said. "It doesn't. Did you see the man who just left?"

"He came with three others," Left Ear said. "And they rode off toward Whisper. They could have surprised us in our sleep and killed us all. They could have poisoned the horses, made us walk, then ambushed us on the road. They could have—"

"But they didn't," Bruise said.

Left Ear shrugged. "True, but I didn't think anyone would be after us going *to* Mirror City. We'll have to be careful."

Tuesday stood, brushed the dirt off the back of his trousers, and looked sheepishly at Left Ear. "Sorry, my good woman. Didn't recognize you without your feathers. I'll just saddle up my horse."

Bruise reached into the sack the innkeeper had given them, took out a loaf of bread, and bit off a large chunk. "Bit of an ignoramus, that one," he said, handing the sack to Good Idea.

She pulled out an apple and held it out, palm flat, in front of Pink. The horse nickered softly, took the apple in a delicate bite, and crunched it between her teeth.

Good Idea looked around uneasily. Yesterday, she had enjoyed the ride along the winding road to the Stop Here Inn. She had been relaxed and excited to be setting out on her adventure. But the adventuring part wasn't supposed to have actually started until she reached Mirror City. No one was supposed to be looking for her *now*. Why, she'd barely left Whisper behind. She had envisioned a few days of easy and safe travel, getting to know her companions, getting used to the idea that danger was somewhere ahead.

But it looked like danger was already here, and she didn't like that at all. While she was certain that Bruise and Left Ear could protect her, her faith in Tuesday had slipped a bit. Thankfully, she would have the young wizard, Bunny, to guide her once they reached the city.

Good Idea walked Pink out into the yard as Left Ear swirled

back into a crow and once again settled to perch between Pink's ears. In a few minutes, Tuesday trotted out, smiling his broad, beautiful smile.

"Are we ready, then? Let's be off," and he cantered ahead and out of the yard. Good Idea swung herself on top of Pink and followed. There was a small stone of worry in the pit of her stomach.

"Don't fret," Bruise said, walking beside her. His legs were not very long but moved with a smooth speed and he never seemed to lag behind the horses. "Taking out four of them would not have been too bad."

"No," Left Ear agreed. "Unless, of course, they were from, what is that forest to the west? With the trees that pluck folk off of their horses?"

"That would be Treachery Wood," Bruise said. "You're thinking of Wind Walkers. But they travel alone, mostly."

"True," Left Ear said. "Maybe they were Shade Men? Very tall and dark they were."

And they were off again, listing the many, many, *many* things that could possibly kill them on the road. Good Idea sighed and wished for, among other things, a violent thunderstorm to settle on them, to drown out the sound of their voices.

IT WAS JUST GROWING DARK, and they were approaching the waterfall. Good Idea could hear the faint sound of splashing. She was tired and there was a small blister on her left hip where the scabbard attached to her belt had rubbed through the cloth of her pants. There was an ache in her thighs from riding so long for the second day in a row, and something in the innkeepers' breakfast had not quite agreed with her, and she had pulled Pink off the side of the road several times to race into the woods, searching for a suitable tree. That had caused her to skip a lunch of cold bacon and apples, which *certainly* did not agree with her.

"Left Ear, could you fly ahead and see if you can find the byroad the innkeeper mentioned? I'm ready to stop for the night."

Left Ear stretched out her wings and flew off, heading down the road.

"A bit unnerving, that," Tuesday said. "Just, you know, changing."

Good Idea eyed him curiously. "It was you who sent me to the otters. It was you who told me what they were. I thought you knew them."

"Well, I knew *of* them, of course," Tuesday said heartily. "I'm a big shape-shifter fan. But I never actually saw them change. It's a different thing altogether, you know, to watch it happen." He shivered, his curls dancing around his face.

"I think it's quite beautiful," Good Idea said. And she did. She loved the way Left Ear dissolved into color and shape, only to emerge whole and completely different. She was looking up, following the flight of the black bird as it got smaller, when Pink suddenly stopped short.

Bruise grabbed the reins and pulled Pink and Good Idea off the road.

"Something's coming," he said.

"Really?" Tuesday leaped off his horse and unsheathed his sword so quickly that the horse startled and galloped off down the road. "Drat," he muttered. "Bad luck there."

"What is it?" Good Idea whispered. She slid off her horse and stood behind Bruise, wisely deciding it was a safer place to stand than anywhere near Tuesday Fix.

Pink shook her head and looked skyward. Good Idea followed her gaze, as did Bruise.

"Gryphons," Bruise muttered.

"Where?" Tuesday asked, straining his neck to see farther down the road.

"Only six of them," Bruise said. "Not too bad."

"Six?" Tuesday said. "Six? Gryphons? They will probably attack us from the sky," he said, looking up at last.

"Think so?" Bruise muttered. He pushed Good Idea and Pink under a huge elm tree on the side of the road. "You should be safe enough here. If any of them land and try to grab you, get on that little horse of yours and run like speercat, okay?"

She nodded, and Bruise took Axe in one hand and stood in the middle of the road, waiting.

Tuesday stood a few feet away, dancing from one foot to the other, waving his sword in the air.

"Just come and try," he yelled. A gryphon, accepting the invitation, folded its wings and dove straight at Tuesday, flexing its huge talons. The elf fell to his knees and covered his head. The gryphon, still intent on the bright blond curls, got close enough to the ground for Bruise to strike it dead with one brutal swing of Axe.

Good Idea's mouth dropped open. This was her well-trained ally? Yelling in the middle of the road, swinging his sword wildly without hitting a thing?

"Oh, dear," she muttered to herself. This was quite disappointing.

"Good move," Bruise yelled. "Try to get another one down here."

Tuesday staggered to his feet, threw Bruise an incredulous look, then turned his face skyward again, waving the sword. "Who's next?" he cried.

Two gryphons took him up on the challenge, crisscrossing each other as they gathered speed, coming at him from two directions. A third had circled behind Bruise, and the orc now had his attention divided. He shifted the Axe from one hand to the other and drew a short, ugly sword from beneath his tunic. Good Idea watched in growing fear and amazement as one of his small eyes moved across his yellow face, past his ear, until it was on the back of Bruises' head.

"Whoa," she said softly. She tugged on Pink's reins. "Did you know they could do that?"

Obviously, the gryphon didn't, because it fluttered slowly behind the orc, thinking it was unseen and safe, only to have the short, ugly sword thrust backward, directly into its breast. It fell to the ground, screaming.

The two that had been aiming for Tuesday dropped down quickly. Tuesday reached up and swung wildly, and, through sheer luck, managed to strike one gryphon on the tip of its scaly wing, just enough for it to wobble directly into Bruise's more accurately swinging Axe.

The second gryphon, seeing firsthand the consequences of a failed plan, soared upward and out of danger.

"Three down," Tuesday cheered. He was panting wildly, and his topknot of curls had come loose, releasing long blond ringlets down the front of his face.

Bruise's eye had returned to its former position on the front of his face, and both now focused on Good Idea. "Doing all right so far?" He asked.

She nodded. Apart from watching the bodies fall around her, it wasn't nearly as frightening as she would have thought. In fact, she was quite enjoying Bruise and Tuesday as they brought the gryphons down. She looked up and caught sight of something else in the clouds above them. "Look," she shouted. "Look at that!"

Bruise glanced up with a grin. "That'll be Left Ear coming back. Now, this should be fun."

What, exactly, Left Ear had shifted into wasn't clear at first, but it was much larger than a crow. It dove at one of the remaining gryphons and, with a swift snap of large jaws, bit it into two flailing parts that plummeted to the ground. Then Left

Ear took out the other two gryphons with one short burst of flame from its nostrils, lighting up the darkening sky.

"Oh, my," whispered Good Idea. "A dragon." Now, *this* was an adventure.

Tuesday, watching, waved his sword in the air again, whooping with delight as the two charred figures tumbled back behind the steep cliff.

Left Ear became smaller, and by the time she landed in front of Good Idea, was a simple crow again.

"Gryphons?" Left Ear asked Bruise. "From Girnel, do you think?"

Bruise shook his head. "No. Girneleese have green scales. I was thinking maybe Landern."

"Sounds right," Left Ear said. "Everyone okay down here? Good. I found that by-road. It's just ahead. There's a nice level patch against the cliff-side, shaded by some sizable trees, out of the wind and easy to keep watch. Just a few minutes further, Good Idea, because I know you're probably thinking about our evening meal."

Good Idea chuckled. "Yes, I am," she said, and mounted Pink.

Left Ear lifted into the air and flew lazily around Bruise's head as Good Idea turned back on the road. "Your horse is up ahead," Left Ear called down to Tuesday. "Didn't go too far. Now, those Landern Gryphons, they seemed faster than I've seen before."

Bruise nodded. "Yes. Very fast. Luckily, you came back when you did. They were pretty clever. They could have gotten in a few licks."

Left Ear backstroked through the air. "Did you do the eye thing?"

Bruise chuckled and sounded like an empty barrel being thumped loudly by a metal bar. "Yes. Had to."

"Wish I had seen that," Left Ear lamented.

Bruise chuckled again. "Next time."

· · ·

THEY MADE CAMP QUICKLY, and Left Ear once again flew off, returning with two small rabbits in her talons which Good Idea cleaned and skinned, and soon had them roasting by the fire with small potatoes from her pack.

"I will admit," she said slowly, "that watching you all at work this afternoon was unlike anything I'd even seen before, and it was, honestly, a thrill. But I think I've had all the thrills I can take for one day, so please, no talk tonight of trolls, goblins, demons..." She gave Bruise a hard look. "Or anything at all about who or what we might encounter on the road, how they can be killed, or how they can kill us. Understood?"

Bruise looked hurt but nodded.

Tuesday loosened his sword and spent most of the evening polishing it with a worn piece of leather, which was a fairly useless exercise if he was only going to be hitting things with it accidentally. Left Ear disappeared into the darkness, and Good Idea heard the branches above them rustle gently as he settled in to keep watch. Bruise took a brief nap after finishing his meal, awoke with a snort, then drew out a small volume from his pack and began to read by the firelight. The book was bound in rich tan leather with intricate gold embossing on the cover. Good Idea thought that such a beautifully crafted book was of some great social importance. She leaned over and squinted in the firelight. There was no title on the spine of the book.

"What is that?" she asked. Fleet climbed out of her pocket and slipped off.

Bruise looked up and grinned. "A Short and Woefully Incomplete History Of Goblins And Their Brethren."

"Oh," said Good Idea. "Is that why you know so much about all these things that might be after us?"

Bruise shrugged. "I like to know about what I've killed. Or will be killing." He waggled a finger at her. "Knowledge is power."

"It is indeed," Tuesday said. "I believe that book was in my family's library. Fascinating stuff. Why…"

Pink nickered, and Left Ear let out a quiet croak. Bruise stayed where he was, back against the stone cliff-face, but his hand moved to Axe.

A lone figure walked down the by-road, cloaked and hooded, leading a hulking black horse that appeared to be covered in leather armor. The figure stopped just outside the ring of fire-light and held out a hand.

"May I join you?"

"No," Good Idea said.

"Of course," Tuesday called.

"Are you friggin' kidding me?" Bruise muttered.

The figure, understandably confused, stayed where it was.

"Tell me, good sir," Good Idea asked politely. "What are you doing on this road so late at night?"

The figure took another step forward, and Good Idea saw the figure was actually a woman, tall and broad, with bright red hair peeking out from under her hood. "I am looking for some-one," she said. "Inspirational Wink."

Good Idea reached out with her foot to kick Tuesday before he could jump to his feet and introduce them all.

Bruise lifted his eyes from the book. "You a paladin?" he asked.

The woman looked surprised. "Yes. How did you know?"

Bruise shrugged before going back to reading, although his hand was still on Axe. "Recognized the sword."

Good Idea could barely see the sword, but now realized the blade flashing between the folds of the cloak bore very intricate markings. The paladin also had a bow strung across her back and a quiver of arrows.

"What is a paladin?" she asked.

"A knight," Tuesday said, finally getting in a word. "Very

highly trained. Usually attached to a person of high rank. Usually *not* roaming around the roads in the dark."

"I am Avanoline, Third Paladin of the House Of Nemroth Falls, Captain to the Honorable Duke Haggerty and Protector of his Lands," the paladin said. "But you can call me Regret. Montgomery Gold, who fashioned this sword for me many years ago, told me that this person, Inspirational Wink, might be in need of assistance on the road to Mirror City. I came looking to offer that assistance."

"Why?" asked Good Idea. She noticed Left Ear had dropped from his high perch and was now sitting on a low-hanging branch, listening.

Regret sighed. "I was once, as this good elf said, attached to a duke in the North. My job was to protect his lady from harm, and I failed." She was silent, and Good Idea could see the anguish on her face. "I have been on the road to redemption ever since, offering help wherever I could."

"Oh," Good Idea said. "And how long have you been on this road to redemption?"

"Forty-six years," came the answer.

"You don't look so very old," Good Idea said.

"I am of the Jaspeion," Regret said. "We are long-lived and therefore usually chosen for a life of service."

Left Ear ruffled her feathers. "How many others have you offered assistance to? If you don't mind my asking."

"One hundred and twenty-three."

"And how many other failures have there been?" Left Ear asked. "If you don't mind telling."

"None."

Bruise let out a snort and took his hand from Axe.

"But you are still seeking redemption?" Good Idea asked. "Surely by now you can consider the score settled."

Regret sighed again. "It will never be settled."

Good Idea considered. A stranger walking up to them in

the night seemed suspicious, but if Mr. Gold had sent her...but had he? "And how was Mr. Gold when you found him?" she asked.

Regret almost smiled. "Complaining about making horse-shoes instead of weaponry."

Yes, Good Idea thought, that sounded like the blacksmith. She decided to trust this paladin, who obviously *did* know Montgomery Gold. Besides, after seeing Tuesday in action, a trained knight would probably come in handy. "Well, if you are still looking to offer aid," she said, "I am Inspirational Wink. Call me Good Idea. And we would be pleased to have you join us." She held out a bit of rabbit still left on the spit. Having eaten her fill, she was feeling generous. "Dinner? We also have potatoes and some rather stale biscuits."

The paladin nodded and pushed back the hood. She was, Good Idea saw, quite beautiful, with an oval-shaped face, and red hair that glinted from deep copper to rose gold. The only sign of age were the fine wrinkles around her eyes of deep blue, and at the corners of her perfect bow mouth. She nodded, took the spit and delicately picked off the remaining rabbit meat before she handed it back, arranged her cloak, and knelt down by the fire.

Tuesday cleared his throat. "I am Tuesday Fix, of Whisper. This is Bruise," he nodded to the orc, "and the crow is Left Ear. Welcome."

"Can you tell me," Regret asked, "the purpose of your journey?"

"No," said Bruise.

"Of course," said Tuesday, and Good Idea kicked him again.

"I am on an errand for my mother," Good Idea said.

"And there is a certain element of danger involved?" Regret asked.

"Yes," Good Idea said. "So far, we have encountered a small

group of the Prince's men seeking us, but we managed to avoid them. We did not manage to avoid six gryphons."

Regret nodded. "But you managed to defeat them?"

"Yes, we did." Good Idea smiled. "And it was quite splendid."

Regret looked thoughtful. "Perhaps you don't need my help?"

"Oh, no," Bruise said. "We do. Good Idea has never had to kill anything larger than Freemont pig, and Tuesday is almost as inept. Left Ear here," he nodded to the crow, "is a shapeshifter. Very handy. But an extra sword would be a great help."

The paladin looked at the crow. "What clan?"

"Wolf," she answered.

Regret nodded, then turned to Good Idea. "This errand for your mother takes you to Mirror City?"

Good Idea nodded. "Yes. Once there, I am to complete my errand and then I am to return to Whisper." Fleet had once again made his way to her shoulder. She could feel his whiskers twitch against her neck. "We all thought that the trouble would begin on the return trip, but it seems that we've come to the attention of our, ah, detractors sooner than expected."

Regret nodded. "Montgomery Gold hinted at something to that effect. That help might be needed sooner rather than later."

"And what led you to Mr. Gold in the first place?"

She shrugged. "Word had gotten out that someone was looking to hire an orc." She looked at Bruise. "Usually if someone wants to hire an orc, they are in desperate need. When I came to Whisper, and realized that my old friend Montgomery lived there, I went to him first. He told me to seek you out. So, here I am."

"Your horse," Good Idea observed, "seems to be ready for battle."

"We are always ready for battle." She opened the front of her cloak, revealing a cuirass of dull silver. "His name is Vigilant, and now I must bed him down for the night. I will be glad to take the first watch."

Left Ear croaked. "No, night watch is my job. I can usually sleep during the day. Unless I'm killing gryphons, that is." She flapped her wings and flew upwards, settling again in the tree.

"All right then. I'll just bid you all good night," Regret said, stood, and shook out her cloak. "You seem worthy. I give you my pledge of protection. And I bid you good night." She bowed her head briefly and led the massive horse away from the firelight and into the darkness.

"Wow," Tuesday said. "She's beautiful."

"Got a bit of a guilt complex, that one," Bruise said before closing his book and stretching out to sleep. Good Idea felt Fleet tap her gently and she looked at him. He was holding a something that looked like a small nut, bright red with tiny black specks. He waved it at her.

"Why, thank you, Fleet," she said.

He went back down into her pocket. Her eyelids grew heavy as she watched the fire a bit longer, until the tuneless whistling of Tuesday Fix lulled her to sleep.

CHAPTER 6

*T*he next morning there was cheese and the rest of the cold potatoes for breakfast, and they were back on the road early. Regret took the lead, her massive horse moving with surprising grace. Left Ear slept for a bit between Pink's ears, then woke and she and Bruise began a lively discussion about the differences between land and water Kelpie. Tuesday had ridden ahead and kept trying to engage Regret in conversation. He was doing most of the talking, with little or no response from the paladin.

The sun rose higher and Good Idea stopped to remove her cloak, put on her hat, and moved the knife scabbard to the other side of her belt. By noon she was already tired, her back ached, her neck was sore, and her shoulder chafed from her pack. The joy of the first day's ride had faded, as had the thrills of yesterday's encounter with the gryphons. Today she was hot, tired, aching, and once again hungry, and beginning to think that maybe adventuring wasn't going to be much to her liking after all. Tuesday, discouraged in his attempt to impress Regret, dropped back to ride beside her, and he noticed her discomfort.

"You can sleep," he told her, "and never fall from that saddle."

"I'd forgotten," she said. "Perhaps after lunch."

Regret had gone off the road and returned with three guinea hens, all neatly shot through the head with an arrow. Good Idea cleaned and roasted the birds while Bruise foraged the nearby woods, returning with berries, tender greens, and small, succulent mushrooms.

"A midday feast," Tuesday declared.

"Yes," Left Ear said. "One I'd like to partake of." She then shifted into a woman again, this time entirely naked.

Good Idea blinked. "Where are your clothes?" she asked.

"Why would I have clothes?" Left Ear asked, squatting by the fire.

"Tooth had clothes on Three Creek Bridge," Good Idea said.

"He always keeps clothes by the bridge in case he needs to shift. A naked man is never taken seriously," Left Ear said.

"You had clothes in the stable last night," Good Idea pointed out.

"I found a tunic in the barn, and as there were strangers about, I thought it prudent to not be naked, as it would raise questions." She looked at her, eyes glinting with humor. "But here, among you all, there would be no questions. Or so I thought. Do you want me to be a crow again?"

Good Idea glanced around. Regret seemed not to have noticed the shifters state at all, and Tuesday, after one appraising look, ignored Left Ear entirely. Bruise seemed oblivious to everything except the food before him.

"No," Good Idea said. "You deserve to enjoy this food as much as the rest of us." As a woman, Left Ear was not young, as there was gray in her light brown hair, which fluttered above her shoulders. Her features were quite pleasant, with eyes a beautiful shade of green. Her body was small and rounded, which Good Idea found quite nice, as her own body was tall, broad and quite angular.

"Have you been at the Three Creek Bridge for sixty years as well?" Good Idea asked.

Left Ear shook her head. "No. Our clan is quite well-known in the protection game. I've only been in Whisper for about five years. Before that I was in Pressory."

Bruise and Regret both looked up.

"Lots of action in Pressory," Bruise said, admiration in his voice.

Left Ear shrugged. "My clan has been an ally of the elves there for generations. We always meet our obligations."

"So, you've seen quite a bit?" Regret asked.

Left Ear shrugged again. "When needed," she said. Good Idea was beginning to think that there was more to LeftEar than just changing skin.

They washed in the bubbling spring that had been running alongside the road and were soon moving again. Feeling full and sleepy, Good Idea dropped the reins from her hands, slumped forward, and napped.

When she awoke, the sun was low in the sky, and she was very thirsty. "What did I miss?" she croaked.

Left Ear answered. "Bruise and I had quite a discussion on all the ways to kill and skin a manticore," she said.

Good Idea blinked. "Sorry to have slept through that," she mumbled.

Tuesday who had once again been riding alongside Regret, dropped back by her side. "She doesn't say much," he said, nodding toward the figure of the paladin riding ahead. "Tried for hours. Wouldn't even tell me about that Duke and his Lady."

"I imagine," Good Idea said, "that she was responsible for the lady's protection, and she somehow failed."

Tuesday frowned. "Think so?"

Good Idea reached for her water skin and took a long drink. "And possibly she feels guilty or ashamed and doesn't *want* to talk about it."

Tuesday continued frowning, then shook his head. "But here we are, companions on the road, practically brothers-in-arms. Surely that sort of bond ferments an exchange of confidences?"

Good Idea sighed. "Tuesday, she only came to us last night."

"But still…"

"Have you told her any of *your* secrets?" Good Idea asked. She was usually not one to tease, but something about Tuesday Fix brought out the bit of mischief in her.

"Indeed," Tuesday said. "Why I told her all about my fencing lessons, dueling lessons, bareback riding lessons, and all about how we use just a bit of magic in our fixes."

"And was she impressed?"

He frowned again. "I couldn't really tell, but I don't think so."

He looked so dejected she quickly changed the subject

"Are we there yet?" she asked.

"Another hour, I imagine," he said, his confidence back. "Probably less. Left Ear took off a few minutes ago to fly ahead, but I think we're close to the Edge Of The Marsh Inn."

The landscape had changed. Gone were the tall cliffs and verdant woods. Around them the land was flat and mossy green, no trees but waving grasses. The sky was more gray than blue, and the breeze was hot.

"What's that smell?" she asked.

"The marsh," Tuesday answered.

"The dead things in the marsh," Bruise corrected him. "That's how you can tell when you're getting close."

"That's also why we go around rather than through," Tuesday said.

A lone, familiar shape high in the sky came to them, and Left Ear settled between Pink's ears. "The inn is just ahead," she said, "but it is deserted."

Regret pulled her horse around and drew up next to Good Idea. "Deserted?" she asked Left Ear.

The shifter ruffled her feathers. "Stable empty. Outbuildings empty. The inn itself is empty as well. Deserted. Looks like folks left in a hurry. There are half-eaten plates of food on the table, chairs overturned, all the fires out and cloaks still hung on hooks. I tried to find any other living thing to tell me what had happened, but there was nothing." Her head bobbed. "Maybe there was a raid, and they were all taken. Or a spell was cast, and they walked into the marsh and drowned. Not so much as a cockroach to be seen, so perhaps a deadly gas settled upon them, dissolving them and leaving not even ash behind."

Regret blew out slowly. "I will ride ahead. Left Ear, show me, please." She looked between Bruise and Tuesday, then blew out again. "Tuesday, you come with us. Bruise, you stay here and keep Good Idea safe."

Tuesday looked annoyed. "And who are you to be giving orders? After all, I am a friend of Good Ideas. We've known each other most of our lives, and I offered to come with her before you. I should be in charge."

Regret looked at Good Idea, her face blank, but Good Idea didn't hesitate. "Tuesday, she may be a stranger, but you your-self said she is a well-trained knight. And she has, shall we say, *practical* experience. Regret is in charge."

He opened his mouth to argue, but Regret wheeled her horse and galloped down the road, Left Ear flying ahead. Tuesday set his jaw, glared at Good Idea, and kicked his horse to a gallop after them.

Bruise watched, sighed, and motioned to the side of the road. "Let's wait," the orc said. "In this marsh, I can see trouble coming a long way aways. We should be safe until they get back."

"Left Ear certainly had a few interesting theories," Good Idea said.

Bruise snorted. "Bit of a worse-case scenario type, that one."

"What do *you* think happened?" Good Idea asked.

He shrugged. "Fey. Fairies can do that. Clear out a place of all living things, even the roaches. They aren't like you and me, and no live beings can stand to be with them for long."

"So, they're still there?"

"Possibly."

"Will they want to kill us?"

"Don't know. Because I don't know if they want you to succeed or fail at whatever you're doing." He looked at her. "Are you ever going to tell me what you're doing?"

She sighed. "I suppose so." She dismounted and dropped into the soft grass at the edge of the road. Fleet ran up to perch on her shoulder, and she could feel his little body tremble.

"Is that mouse part of it?" Bruise asked. "Or just a very devoted pet?"

"He's part of it. This is Fleet." She looked sideways at the mouse. "I think Bruise should know."

Fleet's whiskers twitched, and he settled more comfortably on her shoulder. So Good Idea told Bruise everything; her mother first telling her to go to Mirror City, Bunny Jones, the blacksmith, the witches, Tuesday fixing the saddle, the trolls at Three Creek Bridge, and the final moments with Belladona, taking the map and hearing her mother's words in her ear.

"That," Bruise said at last, "is a pretty impressive tale."

"But it's not a tale," Good Idea said. "It's all true, and I really am not comfortable with any of it. I have never wanted anything more than to spend my life on the farm, tending to the animals and watching the garden grow. I admit that I some-times wondered what it would be like to leave Whisper, and perhaps see a bit more of the world. But this," she waved both hands in the air, "is preposterous."

"I suppose it is, but it doesn't look like you have any choice. In fact, it looks like the fate of all of us lies with you, and that this is the most significant thing that any single person will ever do. I guess I'm quite honored to be a part of it all."

She glanced at him. "Does that mean you'll help me for free?"

Bruise shook his head. "Not a chance. I don't do anything for free. In fact, if I had known this was so important, I would have asked for much more."

She sighed. Fleet slipped from her shoulder and disappeared, returning a bit later with a very small but very heavy stone, the color of a new leaf.

"Thank you, Fleet," Good Idea said.

Bruise pulled another book out of this pack and read in the light of the setting sun until they heard the sound of hooves.

"Follow me," Regret called. She was alone. "It's safe now."

Bruise grunted. "I doubt that, but let's go anyway."

.

The Edge Of The Marsh Inn was a large, multi-storied building, quiet and dark. There was a flicker of firelight from inside the inn itself, lighting the courtyard. As they dismounted, Tuesday hurried out, holding a lantern.

"I'll take care of the horses," he said. "Go on inside."

Inside, the inn was large and high-ceilinged. Left Ear was behind a long bar, dressed again, this time in a plain dress slightly too big for her, with a glass of ale in one hand. The smell of cooking meat filled the air. She looked up when Good Idea came in.

Regret, leaning against the bar, was not wearing her cloak, nor was she wearing the armor Good Idea had seen the night before. The paladin was dressed in plain black leather trousers and a loose-fitting leather tunic, her sword strapped to a wide belt low on her hips, a small dagger strapped to her calf, and a fairly substantial-looking axe across her back instead of the bow and arrows. Good Idea wondered how she could move so easily carrying all that weight. She felt a movement against her leg. Fleet crawled out of her pocket, down her leg, and went off into the darkness.

"There was plenty of food left behind," Left Ear called. "We'll eat well tonight."

Good Idea breathed a sigh of relief, then looked around. "Where did everyone go?"

Left Ear and Regret exchanged glances. Bruise, coming in behind, looked around and grunted.

"Fey?" he asked.

Left Ear nodded. "Looks like. Probably just came through a day or two ago. Most of the food was unspoiled."

Bruise grunted again. "So, about the time we set out?"

Regret took a mug of ale that Left Ear had poured for her. She took a long sip, then looked at Good Idea and Bruise. "It's good ale."

Bruise set down his pack and went up to the bar where Left Ear was busy pouring.

Good Idea eased the pack from her back and stood before Regret. "Just because I said you were in charge, Regret, doesn't mean I don't need to know every single thing that is going on at all times," Good Idea said, surprised at the strength in her voice. "Tell me." She was used to ordering around cows and sheep, and even the goats had learned to heed her every word. Telling people what to do was not something she was used to, but it felt rather good.

Left Ear ducked through the open door behind the bar, and Good Idea heard the clatter of crockery.

Regret shrugged. "The fey are, well, there's magic about them, of course. A very particular kind of magic that they can turn on or off as they please. So, one of them could walk in here and we'd never know. Or they could leave fairy dust and in minutes we'd leave. We'd be compelled to leave. We wouldn't think about our families, or responsibilities, nothing. All we'd have on our minds is getting as far away as possible as quickly as possible. It's quite amazing, actually." She took a long drink of her ale.

Good Idea pondered this. "What do they look like? I mean, if they were here and not, you know," she waved her hands around, "driving everyone away, would we know them?"

Regret shrugged. "There is something called glamour. They can change the way they look. Not like Left Ear in there," she said, nodding toward the noise in the kitchen. "It's different. They can look like themselves, small, with long, pointy fingers and toes, bright colored skin. They have wings. Or they can alter their appearance to look more human."

"So," Good Idea mused, "the day we left for Mirror City, a bunch of fairies walked in here and made everybody leave."

Regret nodded.

Tuesday came in, slapping his hands and smiling brightly. "The horses are in for the night, and wait...ale? It smells excellent"

"You're an ale expert as well?" Regret asked.

"As a matter of fact," the elf began.

Regret waved a hand. "Pour yourself a mug. We're discussing the fey."

"A subject," Bruise said, deadpan, "of which I'm sure you know a lot about."

Tuesday chuckled, nodded his head, and put on his, 'If You Don't Mind My Saying So' look. "Actually, my father and I spent plenty of time discussing the fey," he said. He sidled next to Regret. He leaned toward her and dropped this voice. "They are a very interesting species."

Fleet jumped up on the bar, carrying a small, shiny object in the shape of a star. He held it in both tiny paws.

Good Idea looked and smiled. "Thank you, Fleet."

He carried it down to the pocket, then came back up to the bar and sat in front of Regret, whiskers twitching.

"This is Fleet," Good Idea told the paladin. "He's with me, so please don't try to kill him or eat him."

Regret reached out a tentative finger, and Fleet allowed her to stroke his nose. "What does he do?" she asked.

"So far, he only brings me fairly useless objects," Good Idea said. "But we'll see when we get to Mirror City."

Fleet scurried off the bar, and Left Ear came back in with a tray laden with plates of roasted potatoes and pork.

"Very good," Tuesday said, a bit of gravy on his chin. "You did an exceptional job in the kitchen, Left Ear."

"Especially since most of the meals I've eaten in the past eight years have been of the raw or partially rancid variety." Left Ear grinned. "Don't get to cook much as an otter. Lucky for us, most of the meal was prepared and just waiting to go into the oven."

Good Idea laughed. "Very lucky. Going forward, I'll stick to the cooking."

They ate in silence, huddled around the bar rather than clearing off any of the hastily abandoned tables. Finally, Good Idea pushed her plate away and sighed. "So, the fairies cleared out this place pretty much at the same time we left Whisper, so they must have guessed we were coming here. This is the only way to get to Mirror City, right?"

Left Ear nodded. "Unless you're flying, yes. The question is, of course, how did they know you were *going* to Mirror City?"

Tuesday shook his head. "The question is, why did they clear out the place? Because they wanted it empty for us, with no one to ask questions or cause trouble?"

"Or," suggested Left Ear, "because they had something planned for us and didn't want anyone to interfere."

Regret looked at them. "I know nothing of the purpose of your journey, but I don't need to know. I have found that too many details can lead to a more personal connection, and I avoid that at all costs." She looked pointedly at Tuesday, who raised his perfect eyebrows in a picture of innocence.

She continued. "I don't need to know why you want my help, only that you do. Obviously, there are things you all need to discuss, so I'll find a room upstairs. Goodnight."

She turned and went swiftly up the staircase, leaving the four of them in the flickering candlelight.

Tuesday sighed. "I think she's starting to like me," he said in a soft voice.

Bruise snorted and Left Ear ducked her head.

Good Idea had been very happy living with her parents for the whole of her life. Her brothers were all married and had families, so she had plenty of nieces and nephews to keep her company when she wanted the company of children. She had never had any real interest in a romantic relationship of her own, and never cared to marry. She knew she was rather naïve on the subject, but even she could see that whatever was happening between Tuesday and the paladin had nothing to do with 'like.'

"I told Bruise everything," she said.

Left Ear nodded her approval. "Good. What do we think? The fey know of our purpose and want to help, or they know and want the notebook for themselves and are laying a trap to stop us?"

"Can we get them here?" Good Idea asked. She looked around at their blank faces. "You know. *Ask* them. Wouldn't that be the easiest thing to do?"

"I suppose, although most folks I know try to avoid them at all cost." Left Ear said slowly. "But how?" She looked at Bruise. "I haven't had much to do with them, have you?"

Bruise shook his head. "No. But Tuesday here had lots of discussions, right?" He looked at the elf, straight-faced. "Were any of those discussions about how to find them?"

Tuesday's face lit up. "Yes. Rather, no. It's almost impossible to *find* them, but I've read extensively on how to summon them."

He stopped and took a drink of ale.

Good Idea recognized a dramatic pause when she saw one

and waited a beat. "Well, tell us," Good Idea said finally. "How do we summon a fairy?"

"We need a circle of stones and Mellonwood moss," the elf said.

"We could find that easily enough," Bruise said, looking impressed.

"We also need a gift of wine or ale," Tuesday continued.

"Also easy," said Left Ear.

Tuesday looked very pleased with himself. "And lastly, a linnet."

Bruise narrowed his eyes. "A what?"

"Linnet," Tuesday explained. "You create a circle of stones, put the moss in the center with the linnet, pour over the wine or ale, and then burn the lot."

"Oh," Bruise said.

"What's a linnet?" Good Idea asked.

"No idea," Tuesday said.

They stared at him. He glanced around at them, an exasperated look on his face. "You asked me if I could tell you how to summon a fairy, and I did. Finding a linnet is something else altogether."

Good Idea sighed. "Let's get some sleep. Maybe in the morning, Regret will have another idea. But now, I'm bone tired."

Left Ear shifted and flew out the half-open window and the rest went upstairs. At the top of the stairs was a room where Regret had left the door ajar, and they could see her inside the room, a single candle burning as she sat, motionless, in the one straight-backed chair.

"Goodnight," Regret said again, softly.

They found rooms and were soon asleep.

A VOICE WAS SINGING, a voice immediately recognizable as Bruise, so Good Idea awoke in a state of mild confusion.

Singing? She dressed and followed the sound to a room at the end of the hall, where Bruise sat in a huge copper tub, scrubbing his body with what smelled like lavender-scented soap, and singing slightly off-key.

The orc caught sight of her and waved. "I'll save the water when I'm done," he said happily. "The copper holds the heat, and there's nothing like a good, hot bath after a few days on the road."

Having ignored the grit between her toes for three days, a bath seemed just the thing. "Let me know when you're done," she called. Fleet popped out of her pocket and skittered across the stone floor, scrambled up the side of the tub, and launched himself into the water. Bruise laughed delightedly and splashed the mouse gently, and Good Idea heard him squeak with pleasure.

Downstairs was full of the smell of bacon. Left Ear was again at the bar, eating a plate of bacon and eggs, and thick toast spread with honey.

"I said I'd cook," Good Idea protested.

Left Ear shook her head. "I'm just serving. You can thank Regret for the actual cooking." She cracked a smile. "She found me in the kitchen wrapping the eggs in strips of raw bacon, trying to stuff them into stale rolls."

Good Idea laughed. "That's really not bad logic. At least you're trying. I feel badly for taking this food. We will pay them back when we return."

Regret and Tuesday were sitting by the newly lit fire, also eating.

"I don't know when you think *you'll* be back this way," Regret said, "but chances are the people who left here won't return for at least a week."

"We're almost to Mirror City," Tuesday said. "We should be there by nightfall. Our, ah, errand," he leaned toward Regret and dropped his voice, "which is highly confidential," he said, then leaned back again, "should only take a few days, wouldn't you say, Good Idea?"

Good Idea shrugged. "I certainly hope so. I need to be back at the farm by the new moon. The ewes are lambing, and I should be there."

Regret nodded sagely. "You seem confident in your ability to complete your mission," she said to Tuesday.

"He's got a bit of that all right. Confidence, I mean," Bruise muttered.

"Of course, I have," Tuesday said heartily. "Our success was assured the day we set out from Whisper. Things are going exactly to plan. And now, with you in our party," he leaned toward Regret again, flashing his perfect smile, "why, we'll have this whole situation taken care of in no time."

"And yet here we are," Regret said, staring back at him, "in a deserted inn with no explanation as to where everyone went or why. Was that part of your plan?" she asked, her voice deadly serious.

Tuesday's jaw dropped, he frowned, shut his mouth and went back to his breakfast.

The food was heaped on a platter in the center of the bar, and Good Idea helped herself. "We were wondering how to get in touch with the fairies who did this," she said around mouthfuls of scrambled eggs. "I'd like to ask them why. Do you have any suggestions?"

Regret shook her head. "I don't know anything about that," she said.

"I do," Tuesday said to the paladin, looking quite pleased with himself.

Regret looked up, surprised. "You do?"

"I told you," he said in a patient voice, "that I am something of a scholar when it comes to magic and things in its orbit."

"You may have," Regret said, "but I don't think I was really paying attention. So, you know how to summon a fairy?"

"Indeed," the elf said.

"Then why haven't you?" Regret asked.

"I don't know what a linnet is."

Regret thought. "A linnet is a seed, usually found in deep woods. They're scarce. And beautiful, I'm told. Bright red with speckles."

Good Idea put down her fork and reached into her pocket, around the string and star-shaped object, and pulled out the red nut Fleet had given her. "Is this a linnet?" she asked.

The paladin nodded. "Yes, it is. Where did you get it?"

"Fleet," Good Idea answered. "One of the things he found and brought to me that I thought was useless."

Tuesday seized the linnet. "I'll find some stones and gather some moss," he said.

Good Idea sighed. "I guess this means no bath," she said. "But I must finish my breakfast."

When she went outside, she found them all standing around a small circle of stones, gray-green moss heaped in the middle, and the small red nut atop the moss. Fleet ran from her pocket up to her shoulder, chirping happily, as Tuesday poured ale over the lot and lit the fire.

There was a whoosh of green smoke, and the air vibrated. Left Ear shifted into a crow, leaving the dress in a pile on the ground. Tuesday pulled out his sword, and Bruise unsheathed Axe. Regret was in her armor, one hand on her sword hilt.

The fairy appeared in another whoosh of green smoke, long, slender fingers waving as he stepped from the smoldering moss. He looked around at them, his wings folded against his body, his skin a rippling bright pink.

"I am Thistle," the fairy said in a high, thin voice. "Who has called me?"

Skin tightened and the hair on Good Idea's arms stood on end.

"We just have a few questions," Regret said. "We mean you no harm."

Good Idea's discomfort eased, but she still felt the faint urge to get on Pink and ride away as quickly as possible. She glanced around and saw Tuesday backing away slowly toward the barn, and Bruise's face pucker in distaste. Left Ear, as a crow, ruffled her feathers.

"We were wondering," Good Idea began, and then she cleared her throat. "We were wondering why this place is empty. Was it because you knew we were coming?"

The fairy came to the edge of the stone circle but did not step out of it. "You are Inspirational Wink?"

Good Idea nodded.

"We are aware of your quest." The voice was neither male nor female, but something of both. "It is important to us that the notebook is found."

"Did you empty the inn?" Good Idea asked.

"Yes," Thistle said. "The Prince's men were here, waiting for you. We thought it best that they be elsewhere when you arrived."

Good Idea opened her mouth to speak, but Regret shook her head sharply, leaned toward her ear and whispered, "Never say 'thank you' to the fey."

"That was…kind," Good Idea said.

"We have saved you and your party from possible harm," the fairy went on.

Good Idea wanted to say, 'thank you' again, but since she trusted that Regret knew more about the subject, simply nodded and said, "I understand."

"We ask for something in return," Thistle said.

"Of course," Good Idea said, with a sinking feeling in her stomach. She didn't have much to offer a magical creature.

"Once you recover the notebook, you must take it immediately back to the person it belongs to. It has been hidden for years, but there have always been those who would try to find it. You must promise not to give or sell the notebook to anyone else. You may be tempted, or threatened, but you must swear to protect it." Thistle looked very serious.

"I swear," she said. "I will return it to my mother."

The fairy looked curiously up at her. "And what will she do with it? Will she use it?" the fairy asked. "She can protect the notebook?"

"She knows who can," Good Idea said.

The fairy considered, then stepped back and bent to put a small leather pouch on the ground. "Very well. You can summon us. These only need to be burned in a silver chalice and we will come to you. We will help if we can." And with a final puff of green, the fairy was gone.

"Well," Regret said. She turned to Good Idea. "I don't know what your quest is, but if the fey are going to help you, it must be very important. They are singularly self-involved." She stepped into the circle and picked up the pouch, opened it, and spilled its contents into her hand. There were three linnets, but smaller and flecked with gold. She dropped them back into the pouch and handed it to Good Idea.

"A rare gift," she said. "We should be on our way."

She walked toward the stable and left Good Idea staring at the pouch in her hand. She looked around at the remaining faces watching her. "The trolls. The gryphons. The Prince's men at the Stop Here Inn. And here." She tightened her grip on the pouch of linnets. "Someone else was watching my mother all these years, waiting for my father to die, and for me to leave to fetch the notebook."

"Someone who was not interested in protecting her," Tuesday said.

"Yes." Good Idea agreed. "Gather our things. Make sure to pack the food. And let's go."

CHAPTER 7

*I*t was hot on the road. Good Idea settled her hat firmly on her head. Pink plodded, head down. Left Ear slept between Pink's ears, occasionally stretching her wings. Tuesday and Regret rode together ahead, Tuesday's voice floating back to her as he spoke, Regret nodding occasionally. Bruise walked next to Good Idea, humming to himself.

The sky was pale yellow, and the gray-green grass stretched out in three directions. To the south, the land was dark brown, and a haze hung in the air.

"Is that the Marsh Road?" Good Idea asked Bruise.

Left Ear lifted her head. "Yes. Quicksand everywhere. It's absolute death to leave the road. You get sucked down in minutes. But the road itself isn't all that safe either. There's Marsh Rats big as oxen that hunt in packs. Also, harpies. Flocks of them. Or you could get taken by a Choke Snake—"

"Enough, Left Ear. Please," grumbled Good Idea.

The shifter ducked her head under her wing and was silent.

Once again, it was Good Idea's insistence they stop for a noonday meal, biscuits and cold ham, eaten sitting at the side of the road. Left Ear pecked at dry bread and cheese. There was no shade, not even a rock to lean against, and the dust rose around them.

"I don't mind if you're naked," Good Idea told Left Ear." if you want to eat with us."

The crow cocked her head. "No worries. But I should have packed that dress from the inn, just in case." She tilted her head. "I wonder how they feel in Mirror City about folks walking around naked?"

Good Idea laughed. "I'm sure it won't come to that. Surely there must be at least one dry goods shop somewhere."

Bruise grunted. "No worries about that. I packed something for you. Forgot shoes, though."

Left Ear looked pleased. "Why, thank you. But I'll wait until Mirror City. We should be halfway there, no?"

Tuesday stretched his legs in front of him. "I would think so," He looked around the circle of faces and shook his head. "Sadly, there are no signposts, or even landmarks, to help us measure our journey."

Regret coughed gently. "See there," she said, pointing. They all looked, and far beyond the sea of grass was the faint outline of a mountain range. "The Rocky Tops. They came into sight about an hour ago. When we can make out the divide between the two ranges, we're halfway there."

Tuesday, eyes following her finger, whistled softly. 'Why, that's brilliant."

Regret scowled. "That's geography. We have a way to go." She pointed again, this time up the road ahead. "That troubles me."

Far down the road, the sky was dark, and there were faint flashes of light.

"A storm," Good Idea said. She glanced around. "If it's bad, there's nowhere to take shelter."

Regret nodded. "Exactly. And since storms are unlikely this

time of year, it could be an unnatural event. More magic." She blew out. "I hate magic."

"Tuesday is an elf. Bruise is an orc. And Left Ear is a shifter," Good Idea pointed out. "They *are* magic."

Regret nodded. "Yes. They are born with it and live simply with it. That I can understand. But some who are born with magic try to manipulate it, try to use it for some purpose to further their own gain, and that's what I can't abide."

Good Idea took a breath. "My mother was a witch," she said. "And when we get to Mirror City, we will be joined by Buadhachan Jones."

Regret narrowed her eyes. "I've heard of him. He is a wizard."

"Yes," Good Idea said, surprised. She would have thought Bunny too young to have made a name for himself. She felt Fleet slip from her pocket.

"He has, I have heard, manipulated magic in very unnatural ways," Regret said.

Good Idea went on the defensive. "I don't know about that. I just know I will meet him in Mirror City."

"Are *you* a witch?" the paladin asked.

Good Idea shook her head. "No."

"I wouldn't think so," Regret said.

"Would it change your opinion of me if I were?"

Regret tilted her head. "I have found, in doing what I do, that personal feelings of any kind are not very useful. My only opinion of you is that you seem very ordinary, and that would not really change if you were a witch."

"I am ordinary. Unfortunately, I must do an extraordinary thing, which is why I need the help of these fine folk, and I also need the help of Bunny Jones. You say you hate magic, but I feel that I may be in need of it in the coming days. Will that bother you?"

"Yes," came an instant reply.

"Do you wish to leave our party?" Good Idea asked, feeling her heart sink at the prospect.

Regret shook her head. "I gave you my pledge of protection. I will stay with you until you release me."

Good Idea breathed a sigh of relief. She'd felt much safer once the paladin had joined them and considered telling her the entire story of where she was going and why but thought she would wait until asked.

Left Ear was looking down the road. "That could be witch fire," she said. "Or maybe dragon fire. Nothing worse than witch fire. Even in a rainstorm, it can't be put out. Or maybe those heat balls that demons sometimes play with. What are they called?"

"Heat balls," Bruise grunted.

"Exactly, but —"

"Let's go," Regret said, standing.

Good Idea stood and searched the grass. "I need to wait for Fleet."

Tuesday shook down his pants leg. The linen shirt looked rather scruffy, and his bright curls were limp in the heat. "What could that mouse be looking for here?"

Good Idea shrugged. "I don't know, but he's the reason we had a linnet. Oh, here he comes."

The mouse ran up her leg and sat on her shoulder. He was holding a feather, pale gold striped with blue.

"Thank you, Fleet," Good Idea said, and the mouse disappeared into her pocket. "Okay then, let's see what lies ahead."

THEY HAD PASSED the divide that Regret had told them was the halfway point a few hours before. The storm before them was just at the edge of Mirror City. The clouds were so low as to cast the entire landscape in darkness, and the rain, as they looked ahead, blotted everything from view. The thunder was deafening, and the air was suddenly cold.

Left Ear had flown ahead, and now she returned, looking exhausted and windswept.

"I couldn't make it to the other side of the storm," she said. "Not even as an eagle. I couldn't fly above the clouds, and the winds kept pushing me back. I guess I could have shifted to a dragon and made it through, but that takes so much energy. If we encounter anyone in the middle of this, I want to be of some use."

She shifted into an otter and Bruise opened his pack, offering her a ride and protection from the storm.

Dismounting, they donned cloaks and blankets. Tuesday had on a cloak of blue silk, edged in what looked like white fur, very regal but fairly useless against the rain. Regret threw a cloak over her armor, and Bruise pulled a tattered blanket from a baggy pocket to wrap around his shoulders. With her hat tied firmly to her head with a thick, woolen scarf, Good Idea pulled on her cloak, worn but weatherproof.

As they got closer to Mirror City, the pounding of the rain was split only by booms of thunder, and the darkness broken by the brilliant bursts of light that seemed to come from every- where all at once. They huddled in a tight formation, Bruise and Regret leading, Tuesday and Good Idea close behind. Vigilant blocked some of the wind, and Tuesday's horse was large enough to offer a bit of protection, but Good Idea felt that she was going to be swept away at any moment.

"Remember," Tuesday shouted, "You can't fall from the saddle, not in the fiercest weather."

She wasn't so much worried about falling, as being swept out and away by the wind, Pink and all.

They traveled, it seemed, to Good Idea, an inch at a time. After what seemed like hours, the lightning began to strike the ground around them, causing the pools of water to sizzle and spark.

Tuesday, drenched and shivering, fought to control his horse. Vigilant seemed unfazed by the tumult, as was the horse's rider. Pink had shied at the first bolt that struck the ground beside her, then plodded on through the rest. Bruise, head down, reached back to grab the bridle of Tuesday's horse, pulling the skittish animal forward.

There was no stopping. Good Idea was already exhausted from the pounding of rain on her shoulders, and the incessant roar of the thunder. Her bones ached, and her vision, which tended to blur when she was tired, could not focus on anything other than the back of Regret's head. Which is why she never saw the Bug Bears as they burst from the darkness.

Pink reacted first, stopping suddenly and spinning away, improbably galloping back down the flooded road. Good Idea clung to her and finally pulled her to a stop, turned her, and watched as a Bug Bear took down Tuesday's horse with one giant claw.

She knew what they were, as Bruise and Left Ear had discussed them in length the first day on the road, but she'd never imagined them to be so terrifying. They were much bigger than the bears that lived in the mountains around Whisper, and fiercer looking. They had huge heads and teeth that gleamed in the dim light, claws that looked as long as daggers, and stood as tall as Regret sitting upon Vigilant. Regret used this to her advantage and sliced off the head of the nearest one with one clean sweep of her sword.

Bruise had Axe out and was swinging madly, trying to keep two of the creatures away from Tuesday, who was on the ground, trapped by the body of his dying horse. There was a roar, and Left Ear sprang from Bruise's pack, which had been thrown to the side when the attack came. She shifted from otter to wolf to something much bigger than a wolf and leaped on the back of one of the attacking creatures, dragging it to the ground and tearing at its throat until it was still.

Bruise succeeded in killing one of the Bug Bears attacking Tuesday, and the elf had rolled away and drew his sword, slashing wildly. Good Idea, trying to control her rising fear, watched as Regret calmly turned her horse and rode down another, cleaving it neatly in half. There were three of the creatures left, and Good Idea was so caught up in watching the battle that she never registered that one of the Bug Bears was galloping toward her, fangs bared, and roaring.

Pink shot off the road, churning through the wet grass, circling back to where Regret and Bruise were fighting the remaining two Bug Bears. Tuesday was there in the mix, but Good Idea could barely see him. Her eyes blurred from fatigue and rain. Pink seemed intent on rejoining the group, which seemed very sensible to Good Idea, as she felt completely incapable of defending herself against the attack of a creature so impossibly wild and dangerous. All she had was the small knife that Mr. Gold had given her, and she would have had to take off half her clothes to reach it. She could hear the Bug Bear behind her and felt its hot breath on her back.

This was danger, real danger, and her heart pounded to the beat of Pink's hooves. Only the small horse could save her now. Pink kept a steady gallop, and suddenly Good Idea saw Left Ear running toward her. Pink lowered her head and kept on running. Good Idea flattened herself against the horse's neck and Left Ear soared over her. She risked a quick look behind her and saw the Bug Bear on the ground and Left Ear atop the creature, snarling and tearing.

Pink slowed and when Good Idea looked ahead, she saw the remaining Bug Bears lying on the ground. She also saw Bruise and Regret huddled together over Tuesday, who lay on the ground, covered in blood.

Good Idea felt her heart give a lurch as fear for own safety became fear for Tuesday's. As Pink skidded to a halt in the mud, she slid off and hurried to them.

"Is he hurt?" she panted.

Regret was on her knees beside Tuesday, who was still and very white. She was binding a wound in his leg from strips of cloth Good Idea recognized as ripped from Tuesday's own fine linen shirt.

"He needs attention, and the kind of care I can't give him," Regret said, her voice tight. "Luckily, this is not a magical wound, but he is losing blood. We must get him to Mirror City." She looked up. "The storm is stopping. We might be able to travel at some speed."

"Put him on Pink," Good Idea said at once. Although Tuesday was not the hero she had been hoping for on this journey, he was still her friend, and she couldn't bear the thought of something dire happening to him. "She will carry him safely and he will not fall from the saddle. But I must enter the city on her. I must."

Regret nodded. "There will be plenty of places for you to find shelter before you reach the city proper. I will meet you just outside the walls in the morning."

Regret stood, and Bruise easily lifted the limp form of the elf onto the small pink horse.

Good Idea patted Pink's nose. "Take care of him," she whispered.

Regret swung back onto Vigilant and reached for Pink's rein, but the smaller horse shook her head and started down the road. The rain lessened, and as Good Idea watched them ride off, the horses broke into a gallop.

Left Ear came up behind Good Idea, her long wolf's snout at her shoulder. "I can shift into a horse," she offered.

Good Idea shook her head and stroked the rough fur of the shifter's back. "No. I can easily walk."

Left Ear bared her teeth in a wolfish grin. "Hardy country

stock," she said, then shifted quickly back into an otter and crawled back into Bruises' pack. The orc shouldered the pack, put Axe on his back, and looked down the road after Regret and Tuesday.

"The storm has lessened. Perhaps it knows it's been defeated. I bet we have no more trouble on this road," Bruise said.

Her legs felt like lead, her shoulders ached from the pack she'd slung over her shoulder, and she was chilled to the bone. But as they walked, the rain became a fine mist; the thunder faded away, the lightening stopped, and just as Good Idea thought she could not take another step, she heard Bruise give a snort.

She lifted her bowed head. There were lights, peeking through the heavy fog and the darkness, and beyond that, a massive wall towering in the dim light.

"Mirror City," Bruise said. "We're here."

BUILDINGS EMERGED from the fog as they approached Mirror City. They stopped at the first inn they saw, a small, rather shabby-looking place called the Not Too Bad Inn. There was a warm light shining through the downstairs windows, and the smell of baking bread wafted through the air.

The buzz of conversation barely rippled when they went in, and Good Idea sank into the first empty chair she saw. Luckily, the table it was next to it was also empty, but she didn't think it would have made a difference. Bruise went to the bar, spoke briefly to the innkeeper, then joined her.

"We have two rooms," he said.

She lifted her head. "And?"

"And I've asked for stew, bread and ale," he told her. "It wouldn't do to skip a meal now, would it?"

Good Idea nodded, too tired to speak. She closed her eyes and listened to the conversations floating around her, mostly about the storm, flooding on the riverfront, and something about how several wizards in the city had been attacked and were now cursed with no memory.

There was a clatter as plates and mugs were set down before her. She opened her eyes and began to eat. She'd been so shaken by what had happened during the storm she hadn't realized how hungry she'd been.

"We're close to the walls of the city," Bruise said, slipping a chunk of cooked carrot into the small opening at the top of his pack. An otter's paw snaked out to grab it.

"Good. As soon as we meet Regret and find out about Tuesday, we must enter the city. I need Pink to find this Weathervane person." The stew was delicious, or maybe she was just very hungry. Either way, it was hot and filling.

"He may be in a Care Home," Bruise said cautiously. "He was bleeding an awful lot."

"How many of those are there in Mirror City? One or two, I should think." Good Idea said, considering.

Bruise looked at her and shook his head. "Never been to a big city, have you?" he asked, slipping a small bit of meat into the outstretched paw.

"No. I've never left Whisper. Why?"

He chuckled. "I think you'll be in for a bit of a shock."

She waved the words away. How big could a city possibly be? The valley surrounding Whisper was home to hundreds of acres of farmland, streams and a dozen small lakes. Whisper itself had several shops on the main street, its own mill, a lumberyard and a school, everything needed to keep the community thriving. What else could a city offer? She finished her meal and drank down the rest of her ale. She and Bruise followed the innkeeper up three flights of stairs to large, comfortable rooms. She peeled off her clothes and turned down the covers, but a spark in the window caught her eye. She looked out.

To the East, where they had come from, there were a few residual bolts of lightning. That was what had caught her attention. Then she turned and looked West.

There was the solid black of the wall that surrounded the city, but her room was high enough to see beyond that. And what she saw must have been a thousand twinkling lights. Maybe more than a thousand. They stretched out as far as she could see. She opened the window and leaned out to get a better look.

Maybe *ten* thousand lights.

She closed the window and crept into bed, thinking that shock did not even come close to describing what she felt. But she was too exhausted to think about it much and was soon asleep.

GOOD IDEA AWOKE to find that Fleet had been busy through the night. On the bedside table was a cork from a bottle of wine, three kernels of corn, and seven wooden matches. She thanked him, slipped all his gifts into her pocket, and took another look out of her window.

On the other side of the wall around the city there was nothing but buildings as far as she could see: brick, limestone, wood, two-and-three-storied, with balconies and multi-paned windows that glittered in the sun. Many of the rooftops were of a pale material that gleamed in the light, reflecting the sun into her eyes so brightly that she had to blink.

Like mirrors.

She went downstairs to find Bruise and Left Ear, human and clothed, waiting for her.

"Did you peek outside of your window this morning?" Bruise asked.

Good Idea nodded. "Yes. I can't believe there are so many

people living in one place. And all those buildings...some looked taller than Grangers Mill."

Bruise grinned.

"Taller than Granger's Mill?" Left Ear said. "Oh, country girl. Just wait."

Good Idea waved away the words. "We'll find Regret and enter the city. Then we'll have a proper breakfast and decide how to proceed."

Stomach grumbling, Good Idea frowned. "We *will* be able to find a proper breakfast, won't we?"

"You'll be able to find ten proper breakfasts," Left Ear told her.

Good Idea's eyes widened. "Ten? There are that many places to eat in Mirror City?"

"There are that many places to eat on just one *block* in Mirror City," Left Ear teased.

Good Idea felt her cheeks redden but laughed quietly. "I think I have a bit to learn."

"You have a plan?" Left Ear asked, her green eyes bright with interest.

Good Idea felt Fleet move around in her pocket. "I try to always have a plan," she said. "Even if I don't exactly know what I'm doing." They walked out into the cobbled street and toward the massive wall.

Regret was mounted on Vigilant with Pink by her side, was just outside the open gate that led into Mirror City. She nodded to them and motioned them to follow. Good Idea swung up on Pink and looked through the stone archway that marked the entrance to Mirror City. She rode cautiously through and waited for a ringing of bells, a clap of thunder, anything to signify she had fulfilled the first part of her quest.

Pink snorted.

As they made their way through the cobbled streets, Good Idea had to make a conscious effort not keep her mouth from hanging open. There were shops selling everything from pre-made clothing to weapons, shoes, furniture, books, elixirs, and dry goods. There were inns and taverns, food stalls and vendors pushing carts full of wares through the crowded streets. Good Idea would have wanted to stop and enter each and every doorway, just to see what was inside, but resolutely stayed atop Pink, hands clutching the pommel of her saddle.

They followed Regret through the winding streets and eventually reached a tall gray building with a sign that read 'Care Home For The Severely Dehydrated And Profusely Bleeding.' They dismounted and Regret led them up the steps and through the tall double doors.

"About Tuesday," Regret said. "He needs at least three days here before he can even think about getting on a horse again. He's very lucky. Apparently, Elves take longer to die from these sorts of injuries than regular folk. But here's the thing."

The paladin rubbed her eyes. "While I was waiting for the healers to make their assessment, I kind of just wandered around the various floors." She chose her words carefully. "In the last few days, several wizards were attacked. No one knows why, or by whom. They weren't hurt, just cursed. Their memories were erased." She cleared her throat. "They're here. In a special ward. And one of them is named Buadhachan Jones."

Good Idea's heart sank. "He's *here*? And has no memory?"

Regret shrugged. "If I were to guess, someone realized you were going to get help from a wizard, and simply targeted every one of them they could find."

The journey here not been what Good Idea had expected, and the encounter with the storm and the Bug Bears made her realize there was actual peril, not just adventure, in this journey. Although she didn't have much faith in Bunny — he was very *young* — knowing he would be with her had given her an additional ounce of confidence. But if he had lost all memory, what use could he be to her?

"Can you show me?" Good Idea asked.

Regret nodded and led them through a warren of hallways and up several flights of stairs.

"You must have spent a long time waiting," Left Ear remarked to Regret.

The paladin nodded. "Hours. Right through here."

Through an open doorway was a large cheerful room with a high ceiling, lots of windows, and clean, white-sheeted beds lining the walls. A female elf in a white uniform hurried over to them.

"Can I help you?"

Good Idea nodded, scanning the faces in the beds. "Yes." She found who she was searching for. "May I speak with Mr. Jones?"

The elf nodded, and Good Idea approached carefully.

Bunny Jones was sitting at the edge of his bed dressed in white pajamas. His legs didn't quite reach the floor, so he swung them back and forth, humming tunelessly. His face, looking even younger than she remembered, lit up when he saw her.

"Hello there!" he said happily. "It's good to see you."

Good Idea felt a surge of relief. "It's good to see you, too. How are you feeling?"

He waggled his head from side to side. "Oh, you know. A bit groggy. But otherwise, I feel right as blizzard."

She frowned. "Isn't the saying...right as rain?"

"Is it? Well, if you say so. May I ask you something?"

Wonderful, Good Idea thought. He wants to get filled in on our journey so far. He probably wants to know about the allies I have collected. She couldn't wait to tell him about the gryphons. And the fairy. "Anything."

He smiled broadly. "Who are you?"

The relief she'd felt trickled away like the last drops of a spring in high summer. "You don't know who I am?" she asked.

He shrugged. "I don't know who *I* am," he admitted.

"You're Buadhachan Jones," she said.

"So they keep saying," he said. "But I think that's a fairly ridiculous name for a person, don't you think? What's *your* name?"

"Inspirational Wink."

He snorted. "Another ridiculous name."

She sighed and sat down in the chair across from him. "You don't remember me? Or your uncle, Mionarach Jones? Or the altogether exceptional notebook?"

He frowned, looked very thoughtful for a full minute, then shrugged. "No. Sorry."

The elf Care Person came up to his bed. "The kind of magic needed to erase memory permanently is very dark indeed, and usually does physical damage as well. This is obviously a Short-Term Memory Curse. We have no idea when *his* will return," she said. "But he's young and in pretty good shape otherwise. He can go home with you as soon as we get him dressed."

Good Idea looked up, alarmed. "Go home? Where?"

The elf looked confused. "Don't you know?"

Good Idea shook her head. "I was supposed to meet him here. I know nothing else about him except his name and that he was supposed to help me."

"Well, I'm sure that once his memory returned, he'll be of great help." The elf leaned down and shook Bunny's shoulder gently. "Let's get dressed, Mr. Jones. You'll be going with your lovely friend here."

"No, he won't," Good Idea objected.

The Care Person straightened. "He can't stay here indefinitely, and you're the only person to come forward to claim to know him."

"But what am I supposed to do with him?" Good Idea asked. Her mind started churning. He was the one who was supposed to be taking charge and guiding her through the most dangerous part of the journey, and after what she had just gone through, she was very apprehensive about what, exactly was

going to happen next. Looking down at his open — and empty
— smile, she did not think he'd be of much help.

The elf shrugged. "Just feed him, I suppose, and try to keep
him out of trouble. He has a tendency to wander. I'll get him
ready and bring him downstairs in a few minutes."

Good Idea stood and sighed. Once again, things were not as
she expected. She had spent her whole life carefully planning
events, and those events had always happened exactly as she
anticipated. This need to pivot was unsettling. She smiled
brightly at Bunny. "I'll be waiting," she said, and went back out
into the hallway.

Expectant faces waited for her.

"Is it really him?" Bruise asked.

"Did he know you?" Left Ear asked.

"Yes, and no," Good Idea said as they followed Regret back
through the stairways and hallways. "He doesn't know me. He
doesn't know anything, apparently. But the Care Person said it
was temporary, so I guess the best we can do is hope his
recovery happens sooner rather than later."

Regret then showed them to Tuesday's room, a much
different ward, shuttered and dark, the air moving slowly
through half-opened windows, and the beds filled with
moaning bodies. Tuesday was at the very end, his face paler
than usual, his blond hair a tangled mess on the pillow, his chest
rising faintly.

"He's still unconscious," Regret explained. "He's been given
poppy and willow bark, so he'll sleep through the next day or
two. He lost a lot of blood, but they say he'll make a full recovery." She looked at Good Idea. "Riding that horse saved his life.
She ran the whole way, jumped over ruts in the road, dodged
lightning, and he never slipped from the saddle."

Good Idea reached out and stroked Tuesday's cheek. "He
fixed the saddle. He's a very good fixer."

Left Ear made a noise. "Good thing, too. Cause he's not

much of a fighter." Good Idea stifled a laugh but heard Bruise and Regret chuckle behind her.

"We need to collect Bunny," Good Idea told them, and they left the ward and made their way back down to the small lobby.

Bunny Jones was waiting for them, sitting expectantly on a straight-backed chair, the Care Person standing beside him. He was dressed in what Good Idea assumed was his official wizard outfit: a long, purple robe, adorned with gold stars and pale blue crescent moons. A large leather pack was at his feet, and he was holding a tall, beautifully carved walking stick.

The Care Person handed Good Idea a roll of parchment. "These are his release papers. He is now officially in your care. He needs no special attention, but his memory will come back faster if you can talk to him about things in his past."

Good Idea took the parchment and stared at it. "I don't know anything about his past."

The elf shrugged. "Well, I don't know what else to tell you. Things will come back to him at random. It's started to happen already. Memory is a funny thing, so if he starts to babble, pay attention. He may be remembering something important. That's all, except to keep an eye on him. Like I said, he likes to wander. Good luck."

Bunny stood and waved as the elf disappeared down the hall, then he turned to Good Idea. "I'm going with you?"

Good Idea nodded.

Bunny looked around at the assembled group. "Are they coming too?"

She nodded again.

"Wonderful! This looks like it's going to be so much fun."

Left Ear rolled her eyes, and Bruise looked at the ground, shaking his head.

"And tell me again?" Bunny asked Good Idea. "Who are you?"

She sighed. "You can call me Good Idea."

Bunny grinned. "Excellent. And who am *I* again?"

"*Bunny,*" Good Idea, Left Ear and Regret shouted, all at the same time.

Bruise grunted. "Bit of a useless idiot, this one," he muttered.

Leaving the Care Home For The Severely Dehydrated And Profusely Bleeding, Good Idea was inclined to agree.

CHAPTER 8

*B*reakfasting at the Fine Food Eatery, Bunny seemed delighted with everything he saw. Regret kept as far away from him as possible at the end of the long table where they sat. Good Idea was still waiting for Regret to ask for the details of what they were looking for, and why, but the paladin never once asked a question.

"So, we need to get to Weathervane Wynd," Good Idea said, digging into a heaping plate of crispy bacon and toast and trying to ignore the problem of what to do with Bunny. She had always found it easier to deal with one problem at a time. "I have no idea where her shop is, what it's called, or even if it still exists. Apparently, Pink will find it. From there, we follow Fleet, who will show us through the Veil. Once through, we have a map, and then we use the key."

"Straightforward," Left Ear said.

Good Idea shook her head. "Not at all." She pulled out the map and spread it on the table. "Look at this map. Does it make sense to anyone?"

They all leaned in. The map was obviously old, faded, and the parchment cracked. As Good Idea stared down at it, all she saw was a series of lines, intersecting larger lines, blotches in square and rectangular shapes, and a fat, squiggly line running across the edge.

Regret frowned. "What's the problem?"

The problem was obvious. There were lines and squares and markings that seemed to spread out over an inordinately large area. And, even moving it around on the table, there was no clear way of determining where the top or the bottom even *was*.

"Everything is the problem," Good Idea said. "What is this even a map *of*?"

Regret glanced at Bruise, who shrugged.

"She's never been in a city before," Bruise explained. "She never left Whisper."

Regret exhaled loudly. "This is just a street map, Good Idea." She pointed with a finger. "This is the shop, Weathervane's shop." She moved her finger to several of the various blotches. "These are buildings." She squinted. "I know this city pretty well, and there are a few streets here that I don't think exist in the real world. But if you're going through The Veil, you'll be able to see things and go places that others can't."

Good Idea stared at the map in wonder. "This is *all* Mirror City?"

Bruise nodded. "Pretty big, isn't it?"

"It's huge," Good Idea said, her voice hushed in awe. "So, it looks like we leave the shop after we go through The Veil." She put her finger on the small star. "Here? Then just follow the map through town."

Bruise, leaning forward, nodded. "Looks like. But can we all go through?"

Good Idea sat back. "What do you mean?"

Fleet ran from her pocket to her shoulder and sat, quivering.

Left Ear glanced around, then shifted, leaving her clothes in a pile on her seat. She appeared a few seconds later on Good

Idea's shoulder, and she and Fleet engaged in a lengthy and, from what they could all tell, animated conversation.

Bunny gasped. "Your friend disappeared," he whispered.

Good Idea patted his hand. "I know. But it's okay."

He leaned toward her. "And there are two mice on your shoulder. I think they're talking to each other."

"That's okay too," she assured him.

"Is that normal?" Bunny asked.

"It is for us," Good Idea answered.

Left Ear spoke up. "Fleet says he can hold the Veil open for all of us to pass through, and as long as we stay together, he can then lead us out and close the Veil behind us." He looked at Regret. "But the paladin has no talisman or magic. She may not pass through."

Regret frowned. "That's not good. I've never been behind the Veil, of course, but I've heard that there are creatures there that don't exist in the real world. You'll need protection, and that is the only reason I am here. If I cannot pass through…"

"I have Bruise and Left Ear," Good Idea said. "And Bunny is a powerful wizard."

"About that," Left Ear said, her voice dropping, "Fleet doesn't think it's a very wise to bring the wizard. He heard what the Care Person said about Bunny. Without memory, he can cast no spells to help us. And if he wanders off and gets lost behind the Veil, we may never get him back."

"Well," Bunny said, "This Veil place sounds very dangerous, and if you want my advice, this Bunny person should *not* be allowed through."

"Oh, my," Good Idea muttered. "But else can we do with him?"

"If I were you," Bunny said, speaking with authority for the first time, "I'd find a nearby inn and check him into a room, then hire someone to watch him. If, as they say, he *wanders*."

"Makes sense," Bruise said.

Good Idea had to agree, although the idea of going through the Veil without the paladin or the wizard made her feel decidedly anxious.

First things first, Good Idea thought as she turned to Regret. "Did you notice an inn close by? Within the city walls?"

Regret thought. "I passed The Rider Man inn. Seemed safe and clean enough."

Bunny nodded approvingly. "Very good. And where are we going again?"

Bruise shook his head sadly. "A bit of a useless git, that one," he muttered.

BY THE TIME they got to the Rider Man Inn, Bunny forgot that he thought he was going with them and embraced Plaid, the barkeep, as a long-lost brother. Good Idea paid with another gold coin, for a room and quite a bit extra for Plaid to watch him. Regret was waiting for her outside, Pink standing beside her, ears twitching expectantly.

Good Idea patted her nose. "You know where to go?"

Pink snorted. Good Idea swung up on her back, Fleet on one shoulder, Left Ear on the other, and they began walking through Mirror City.

Regret rode beside Pink, Bruise walked behind, and the people seem to part as they wove their way through the crowded streets. They were going toward the River Brown, and when they reached the waterfront, several canals had been made to allow smaller ships to dock closer to the shops and warehouses. They crossed over several wooden bridges that spanned the canals until Pink turned into a narrow street marked Seller's Street.

The lane was busy and wet, the muddy water having spilled up and out of the canal during the recent storm. Pink finally stopped in front of a narrow shop. Its door and window frames were painted a bright green, the small sign hanging above the door read "Ye Olde Shoppe Of Various Herbs Potions And Cures".

Good Idea slid off Pink and opened the door slowly, Regret right behind her. Fleet and Left Ear, also a mouse, were perched on her shoulders. Bruise stayed just outside the door.

Inside, the only light came from the windows, and the single aisle was narrow and well-worn. Bunches of drying herbs hung from the darkness of the ceiling, and the shelves that lined the walls were full of glass jars and bottles, unmarked, but full of both dried and liquid material.

"Hello?" Good Idea called.

There was a shuffle from a curtain hanging by a counter at the very end of the aisle, and a woman stepped out.

Good Idea had assumed that Weathervane Wynd would be an old woman. After all, she owned the shop Good Idea's mother had worked in as a girl, and her mother was over eighty years old. But this woman was young and beautiful, tall and statuesque, with jet-black hair piled high on her head and held in place with jeweled pins, deep green eyes and rich brown skin that was as smooth and gleaming as polished wood. She was dressed in black and held a long staff carved with runes.

The green eyes narrowed. "Yes?"

Good Idea stepped a little closer. "I'm looking for Weather-vane Wynd."

The woman nodded her head slowly. "That's my name. How can I help you?" Her voice was low. The eyes flickered past Good Idea to Regret, and even farther to the shadow of Bruise hulking by the doorway.

"I...I'm Belladona Green's daughter. My name is Inspirational Wink."

The green eyes widened. "Belladona's daughter? *You?*"

Good Idea squared her shoulders. "Yes."

The woman moved down the aisle until she stood directly in

front of Good Idea, the beautiful eyes searching. Red lips parted in a smile.

"Yes," Weathervane Wynd said softly. "Belladona's daughter. And how is your mother?"

Good Idea smiled back. "She is quite old and frail. The years have not been as kind to her as they have been to you."

Weathervane laughed, but it was a rather sad sort of sound. "Maybe not. But her years have been filled with the love of a husband and family, whereas mine have been rather empty. I suppose you are here to collect the Notebook Of Whim?"

Good Idea nodded.

"And I must take you down to the cellar." Weathervane looked thoughtful. "Do you know what she plans to do with it?"

"She will give it to Mionarach Jones so that he can make sure it doesn't fall into the wrong hands."

Weathervane raised an eyebrow. "Is he here with you? I don't know him myself, but I understood Mionarach Jones was now also old and frail."

Good Idea nodded again. "You are correct. His nephew, Bunny, will assist me in getting it back to Mionarach Jones."

"But Bunny Jones was one of the wizards that was recently cursed," Weathervane said.

Regret spoke up. "You seem to know an awful lot about it."

Weathervane nodded. "I do. Mirror City is vast, but the magical community is a tight-knit one. We all know each other's business. We're safer that way. Which is how I know that Bunny Jones is in a Care Home with no memory."

Good Idea nodded. "Yes, or he would have been with us going through the Veil. But that is apparently a temporary thing, and I'm sure that by the time we start back to Whisper, he will be just fine. Once we get back, my mother can give the notebook to Mionarach, and he will do what is needed."

Weathervane arched a perfect eyebrow. "And what is that, exactly?"

Good Idea frowned. Fleet made a few chirps. "What do you mean?"

"What, exactly, is Mionarach Jones going to do? Destroy it? How? It's a powerful, magical object that others have probably tried to destroy before this. Does he think he can hide it? Belladona hid it, and look how many people know and are hovering around, waiting for it to be revealed, even if they can't take it themselves. Or does he plan to use it?"

"I, well…" Good Idea faltered. "I don't know." She frowned, thinking. "He said he was going to safeguard it."

"Again," Weathervane challenged. "How?"

Good Idea looked at Regret for some sort of encouragement, realized that Regret had no idea what she and Weathervane were talking about, then looked sideways at Left Ear. "Does Fleet know?" she whispered.

Left Ear and Fleet began chattering back and forth, and at one point, Left Ear scurried across the back of her neck to perch at Fleet's side.

Finally, "Fleet has no clue," Left Ear said sadly.

Weathervane, who was completely unfazed by two mice having an obvious conversation, spread her hands wide. "I've always known the notebook's power and was gratified when Belladona told me she had protected it with a series of enchantments. Such a thing needs protection. She also told me that, someday, her firstborn would come to retrieve it if she could not come herself, and I was to take whoever came down to the cellar. Beyond that, I don't know where it is or how to find it. But I know that you'll have to go through the Veil, and that is dangerous. And I also know that my shop has been watched for decades, waiting for you to show up. Once you have this notebook, there are many who will do anything to take it from you. You will be in constant danger. And you are going to go through all of that to give it to an addled wizard, and you don't know what's going to happen to it next? Why would you do that? Why give it to him?"

Good Idea had spent her entire life looking at things in a simple, straightforward way. Because, when you lived on a farm, pretty much everything you did *was* simple and straightforward. There was not much room for nuance when castrating sheep or mucking out stalls.

But Good Idea was very good at problem solving and had always looked at any tricky situation and found the fastest and easiest solution, given enough time to reason it all out. She needed to find the next logical step. So, she stalled for time. "What would you do with it?" she asked.

Weathervane Wynd looked completely flummoxed. "Why, why..."

Regret snorted. "If I had sixty-some years to think about something like that notebook, I would have a million different scenarios in my head what *I* would have done."

Weathervane looked long at the paladin, who returned her stare. "You don't know what she's here for, do you?" the witch asked slowly.

Regret shook her head. "No, I don't. Nor do I care. I pledged to protect her. That's all that matters to me. What she does, and why, is not my concern. Keeping her safe is."

Weathervane nodded. "It must be nice to have your path so clearly set before you."

Regret smiled. "It is."

Weathervane shifted her gaze back to Good Idea. "I would have fed the hungry," she said softly. "I would have cured the dying in the Death Homes. I would have made hearths that were forever lit, so that people could always be warm. I would have stopped the Prince from thirsting for more and more power. I would have given the goblins all the riches they wanted, so they would never feel the need to ransack villages for more wealth. I would have softened the claws of gryphons and Bug Bears, so that they could never hurt another soul." She smiled sadly. "That's what I would have done for a start, anyway."

Good Idea stared. "It could do all that?" she asked in a whisper.

Weathervane nodded. "Yes. Or I could have turned all my enemies to stone, taken dominion over all the creatures of the world, and hoarded wealth unimaginable." She shrugged. "Power is a tricky thing. You never know what you will do with it until you get it."

Good Idea shifted uncomfortably, and Regret snorted.

"Having said all that," Weathervane continued, "knowing what the notebook was, I've never felt comfortable knowing that just anyone could find and use it. Something *should* be done with it, and since it's not my choice anyway, maybe it's just as well that the final decision be given to the old wizard. I certainly wouldn't want to have the responsibility of the fate of the health and safety of the entire world resting with me."

"I didn't want that responsibility either," Good Idea said. "Can I tell you?" She glanced back at Regret, then leaned closer to Weathervane Wynd. "I did not want to come to Mirror City. At all. I may have thought about a bit of an adventure beyond Whisper, but I certainly never imagined anything quite like *this*. Now, the first day was just fine, going along the road and all, but that next morning, at the Stop Here Inn, men came looking for me. The *Prince's* men. Can you believe it?" The words came pouring out of her, like water from a dam suddenly broken.

Weathervane's mouth dropped open. "Ah, no…"

"Then, there were gryphons. Now, that was rather exciting. Do you know that an orc can move its eye from one side of its head to the other?"

"Actually," Weathervane began, "I did, but —"

"After that Regret here joined us. I must say that made me feel safer, but then there was the Edge Of The Marsh Inn. Completely deserted!"

Weathervane took a small step back. "Oh?"

"And *then*," Good Idea continued, her voice rising in excitement as she gestured with her hands, "then, the *fey*. We all just stood in a circle and burned some moss and a linnet and poof!" Her hands moved more wildly. "A fairy."

"Poof," Weathervane echoed faintly.

"But what really got me scared was that storm. And the Bug Bears. Do you know how huge they are? And fast?" She was speaking so quickly now that the words ran together. "Why, poor Tuesday is in a Care Home now, and I'll have to go through the Veil without a wizard, and I've got to tell you," Good Idea dropped her hands and blew out loudly through her mouth. "I'm not looking forward to *that*. At all."

Weathervane, overwhelmed by this unsolicited flood of information, glanced over Good Idea's shoulder to Regret, her eyes wide. The paladin had nothing to offer.

"No, I don't suppose you are," Weathervane said at last.

Good Idea's shoulders slumped. "True, Bruise and Left Ear can come with me, but Bunny was supposed to act as guide. I didn't actually have much faith in him. Why, he looks like a child, although he says he's twenty-four. But what am I supposed to do *now*?"

Weathervane looked blankly at Good Idea, blinked a few times, then seemed to gather her thoughts. "Would you like some tea?" she asked.

Good Idea was suddenly desperate for something as ordinary as a cup of tea. "Oh yes. That would be lovely." A thought struck her. "And perhaps a bit more?"

Weathervane indicated a small table next to the counter and disappeared behind the curtain. Good Idea went and sat down gratefully. Left Ear and Fleet ran down her arm to perch on the edge of the lace-covered table. Regret stood, looking down at Good Idea, frowning.

"What?" Good Idea asked.

"Do you really think it's wise to tell her so much? You don't know her."

Good Idea shrugged. "No, I don't. I don't know you, either. But my mother said I could trust her, so I will. I have no choice. Especially since I want her to take us through the Veil."

Weathervane, coming back through the curtain, stopped abruptly. "Excuse me?"

Good Idea looked up in surprise. "Well, that was fast."

Weathervane set down a tray on the small table. Fragrant steam rose from a small white teapot, and beautifully frosted cakes sat on a bit of lace.

"You want me to do *what?*" Weathervane asked as she poured the tea into a delicate pink teacup.

Good Idea took the cup and drank deeply. Kiffenberry tea. A favorite. Then she took a bite of teacake. And another. "I was hoping you'd take us through the Veil."

Weathervane sank into the chair opposite. "Why would I do that?"

"Because Bunny can't," Good Idea said simply. "And as a witch, I assume you know your way through, and around, the Veil."

Weathervane nodded. "Of course, I do. I've been in Mirror City for over two hundred years. But I rarely leave my shop. I don't have to. I have quite a reputation as a healer, you know. Why, folk of all kinds come from throughout the Realm for my potions and cures. Whatever business I have with magic folk, well, they come to *me.*" She poured tea for herself and sipped delicately. "I suppose the question should have been, why would I *want* to take you through the Veil?"

Good Idea stared down into the pale blue liquid. She had one chance, she thought, to convince Weathervane, so her argument had to be a good one. She finished the teacake.

"Your reputation," Good Idea said at last.

Weathervane frowned. "What has my reputation to do with anything?"

"Well," Good Idea said, her thoughts coming together, "if the notebook should fall into the wrong hands, everything would descend into chaos. That's what I've been told. And if it were to get out that I asked you for help and you turned me down, well, it would be almost as though the health and safety of the entire world *did* rest on you and you... failed."

Weathervane put the teacup down, her eyes narrow. "That's a very interesting argument."

Good Idea drank more tea. "Yes. I think it is."

"I am a healer. I have learned many things from other witches, things beyond my natural powers, but I am not sure I could help you in any sort of altercation."

"I have Bruise and Left Ear and Regret for that. What I will need from you, more than anything else, is guidance." She drew a deep breath and played her last card. "And there's the Vow you made to my mother."

Weathervane sipped her tea and thought for a long moment. "Yes. That's right. My Vow. Your mother..." her eyes grew teary. "Belladona was very dear to me. I raised her, you know. She was such a bright, beautiful thing. Talented, too. It broke my heart when she left, although I recognized true love. And I did promise that, if she ever needed assistance, I would be there for her. I suppose, then, I must offer that assistance to *you*."

Good Idea had no idea what the Veil was like. But if it was, as Arch had said, going to be the most dangerous part of her journey, she certainly didn't want to go it without someone who knew their way around. And now, it seemed, she had the help she would need.

Weathervane put down her teacup. "I suppose you have something to help you find the crack that you need?"

"Yes. The mouse."

"You'll need a talisman to get you through the Veil."

"I have a ring."

"Does she?" Weathervane nodded toward Regret.

Good Idea shook her head, and Weathervane sighed. "Then she cannot come with you."

Good Idea frowned. "I was afraid of that. There's no way around it?"

"The Veil will tolerate anyone who is touched with magic, or anyone who has a talisman. That is why there are so many magical creatures on the other side. They can live there in relative peace. Only those with powerful magic, a witch or wizard or demon, may pass through without aid. You and those in you party cannot enter without aid. That is where your mouse comes in." She pointed to Fleet. "The other mouse is a shapeshifter, and out there," she gestured to Bruise, "is an orc. They are touched enough to be tolerated once let in. But without a talisman, even if she managed to slip through, the paladin would not be allowed to live. Beyond the Veil is a sacred place to those who travel there, and strangers will not be borne."

"I pledged to protect you," Regret said.

"I somehow think you will have plenty of opportunity to protect once we begin our journey back to Whisper." Good Idea smiled at Regret. "Get Bruise."

The paladin nodded and went back out of the narrow shop.

"Will my horse be safe until we return?" Good Idea asked.

Weathervane nodded. "I will cast a protection spell." She sipped more tea. "I see she is a strawberry roan, the same as your mother's horse was when she left."

Good Idea nodded. "Part of the enchantment,"

Weathervane rolled her eyes. "I'm sure."

"Once through the Veil," Good Idea explained, "there's a map, and a rusty key...it's quite elaborate."

Weathervane smiled. "That sounds just like Belladona."

Bruise came into the shop, his bulk crowding the narrow aisle. "Are we ready?" he asked.

Good Idea nodded. "Yes. Regret must stay behind, but we have Weathervane here. She will travel with us through the Veil."

"She a witch?" Bruise asked.

Weathervane pushed back the chair and stood, drawing herself to her full height. "I am Weathervane Wynd Of The Third Circle Of Laramee, Healer Of The First Order, and Keeper Of The Staff Of Mending."

"And she was a friend to my mother," said Good Idea. "Which means more to me than all else."

"I'm Bruise," the orc said. "One of these mice is Left Ear. And the other is Fleet."

"Follow me," Weathervane said, lifting her staff and sweeping back through the doorway behind her.

Bruise shrugged their shoulders. "A bit full of herself, that one," he said.

"Indeed." Good Idea looked sadly at the remaining teacake and followed the witch through.

THEY FIRST WENT through a series of hallways lined with bottles and jars, books and scrolls, baskets and boxes. Weathervane opened a narrow door and started down a long stairway, then through another set of hallways, these barely lit, the walls hidden behind thick, dusty curtains. Then there was another stairway, again very steep that went on for so long that Good Idea wondered if they were going to the very center of the earth.

The stairs finally ended in a vestibule with four doors, one of each of four paneled walls. Fleet chirped excitedly.

"He can sense the crack," Left Ear translated. "Through the third door."

The third door was wide with elaborate carvings in a language Good Idea had never seen before. Weathervane turned the ornate glass knob, and they faced another passage, this one completely dark. Weathervane held her staff aloft, and a pale blue light lit the space.

It was a large, stone-floored room, the ceiling so high it vanished in the darkness. There were three openings in the rough-hewn walls, leading in different directions, and Good Idea felt the stirring of a cold breeze.

"Where are we?" she asked.

"Beneath Mirror City. These are the old tunnels, made by the First Dwarves," Weathervane told her.

"Which way?" Good Idea felt Fleet on her shoulder, trembling, and he began to squeal.

"What's wrong?" Good Idea asked, but the answer presented itself in the next breath.

From each of the openings there stepped a creature, four-legged and snarling. They now shone in Weathervane's light.

Good Idea froze, and Left Ear sighed.

"Cave Cats. I hate them to my core. Nothing fights dirtier than an angry cat," the shifter said.

"I was hoping they had given up," Weathervane said. "They were here to guard the tunnels, but since no one has been down here in decades, I thought they may have just gone home."

"What do we do now?" Good Idea whispered.

"Get back," Bruise told her as he swept the Axe off his back.

Left Ear sprang from her shoulder and shifted into the brutish wolf's form that had taken down the Bug Bear. As she leaped, a Cave Cat sprang to meet her, and the two creatures hit the stone floor, growling, snarling, and tearing into each other.

Good Idea moved quickly backward until she hit the wall. Bruise stepped forward, swinging Axe. One of the Cave Cats caught a blow to its massive shoulder as the blade missed its neck. A great taloned paw swiped at Bruise, who jumped back just in time to keep from being slammed to the floor.

Weathervane held her staff in front of her. Her lips were

moving swiftly, and a wave of pale green light flowed from the tip of The Staff Of Mending and enveloped the head of the third Cave Cat. Caught in the light, the creature did not move, only snarled in frustration, its body frantically clawing the stone floor, but its head frozen in place.

Good Idea gazed at the scene before her, thrilled at her first encounter with what was real live magic in action. She also felt totally helpless. She was jolted into action as the Cave Cat that was wrestling Left Ear gained the advantage and fought its way to the top of the wolfish body. The powerful red teeth clamped around the wolf's throat and Good Idea watched as the Cave Cat settled itself in, gnawing at the neck. She reached for the knife in her scabbard, not knowing what she would do, exactly, but knowing that Left Ear only had seconds to live before the Cave Cat chewed through her throat. But then Left Ear was gone, and the Cave Cat stared at the empty space where she had lain a second before. Good Idea watched the otter slip from beneath the Cave Cat's body. Left Ear shifted again back into her wolf shape, sprang onto the back of the Cave Cat, and this time, her teeth began their own death grip at the neck.

Bruise and his opponent seemed well-matched and were circling each other at one end of the room, so Good Idea looked at the third Cave Cat, locked in Weathervane's magical beam. She worked her way around the room until she stood behind Weathervane.

"Can you do that to its whole body?" she asked.

"For just a moment, yes," came the reply.

"I can get close enough to kill it," Good Idea said, pulling out the blade Mr. Gold had given her.

"Good," the witch replied.

The head of the Cave Cat may have been immobile, but the limbs were violently flailing in all directions. Staying away from the beam, Good Idea extended her arm, knife in hand.

"Now," she called, and the beam broadened, and the entire

body of the Cave Cat froze. Good Idea stepped closer and looked at the head of the beast, trying to find a spot where the blade could do the most damage. But as she moved her hand forward, the knife made up its own mind and went directly into the side of the beast's neck, right below the ear. The knife had an exceedingly sharp blade and slid through the thickly furred skin with ease. She sprang back, and with a small 'pop' the beam was gone and the Cave Cat, with one wild look around, slumped to the stone floor.

"Well, good for you," Bruise called. His own Cave Cat lay twitching, and he took one long step to where Left Ear had her opponent pinned down.

"Move, buddy," Bruise growled. Left Ear backed away and Axe came down on the prostrate Cave Cat, severing the head.

Weathervane looked pale and rather strained, but she was smiling. "I think we will have no problem as we pass through," she said.

Good Idea pulled her knife from the Cave Cat and wiped the blade clean on the leg of her trousers.

Left Ear padded over to her. "Are you okay?" she asked.

Good Idea nodded.

Left Ear moved her ears. "Pretty good for someone who'd only killed a Freemont pig before," she teased gently.

Good Idea laughed. "I think it was more Montgomery Gold's knife than anything else."

Fleet, who had hidden himself in her braid, crawled out, down her body, and hurried to the mouth of one of the openings.

"Through there is your crack in the Veil," Weathervane said, pointing with her staff.

Good Idea gazed at the knife in wonder before she slid it back into its place on her hip. She then looked down at the Cave Cat lying lifeless at her feet. She had slaughtered sheep and pigs during her life on the farm. Killed chickens, put down an aging mule, and once beheaded a weasel that was raiding the henhouse. But this felt entirely different.

Then she took a breath and thought again. No, it was not different. Not at all. She had killed before because that was what was needed for her to do her job. She had a new job now, and a different set of needs. And the knife Mr. Gold had given her was ideally suited for those needs.

"Then let's go," she said.

Part Three

In which Inspirational Wink and her company travel through the Veil and find an Altogether Extraordinary Notebook.

Castle Splendid

CHAPTER 9

The corridor was low ceilinged with smooth stone on the walls and rough cobbles beneath. Good Idea kept looking for something to announce their arrival at the Veil and was surprised when Fleet paused before what appeared to be a sliver of light in the wall. He turned, whiskers twitching, and disappeared through it.

Good Idea stopped.

"Follow the mouse," Weathervane prodded.

Good Idea stared at the sliver. "How?"

"Just step through," Weathervane said. "The mouse will hold it open."

Good Idea took a deep breath and a long step and, much to her surprise, found herself in another corridor, the same size and shape as the one she just left. Fleet was there, sitting up. She could have sworn he was smiling.

"Harumph," said Bruise as he bumped into her from behind. She took a few steps forward and turned to see him stepping from what looked to be a perfectly solid wall. Behind the orc, she saw the sliver again.

"Well, that was odd," Bruise mumbled, moving away from the wall.

Next came Left Ear, still as a shaggy wolf.

"Easier than shifting," Left Ear exclaimed. Then she grinned. "But not nearly as much fun."

Finally, Weathervane Wynd stepped through, looking perfectly unruffled.

"The map?" she asked. She waved her staff, and the light it had been giving vanished, but the passage was brightly lit. Good Idea looked around.

"Where is the light coming from?" she asked.

"Magic," Weathervane replied. "The map?" Good Idea handed it over, and the witch unfurled the parchment, eyes narrowed. "That's too bad," she said.

"What?"

Weathervane sighed. "I was afraid of this. The map is old, and things have changed. We need to get back to my shop, follow the river, then up…" She squinted. "Right. Up Willow Way. Then into Weir Town. That's not nearly as safe as it used to be. Once we get there, things look complicated." She folded up the map back into a small square and handed it back to Good Idea. "But let's get there first. Follow me."

"Where are we?" Good Idea asked. Fleet climbed up her leg and slipped into her pocket.

"Exactly where we were before," Weathervane answered, turning down the corridor.

It looked to be the same as the corridor they'd been in just moments before, but well-lit and with a vague vibration in the air. The passage ended in a large room, and Good Idea stopped short. The bodies of the Cave Cats were there, still and bloody.

"This way," Weathervane called, and passed through a door. They were back in the same room they had been in before, with four doors. Weathervane shut the door behind them, and they began to climb the stairs, which were, Good Idea thought, more of a challenge going up than they were coming down.

"I'm too old for this," she muttered. Weathervane, several step above, turned and looked at her. "Would you like some help?" she asked.

Good Idea nodded, trying to catch her breath. Weathervane waved her hand and a shower of pale light drifted down onto Good Idea's head.

The ache in her back vanished. The throbbing in her thighs ceased. Her breathlessness was gone, and the vision in her bad eye, which had gotten blurrier with fatigue, sharpened. "Thank you," she said. "Is this, I mean, will this last?"

Weathervane shook her head. "No. But if you wish, we can work on something more permanent later." She turned back and climbed more stairs.

"I wish," Good Idea said fervently

Left Ear, who had shifted back into a crow and perched on Bruise's shoulder, looked back at her. Good Idea had never seen a crow grin before, but she was sure that's what Left Ear was doing, and she had to laugh.

They came to the long hallway, the one that had had its walls covered in curtains. Now, shelves were visible and there were so many objects, some in bottles and jars, some just sitting out in the open, that Good Idea could have stood there for hours just looking.

"Why couldn't we see these before?" she asked.

"Because we are now through the Veil. You will now be able to see the things that exist in the magical world. Any object or creature with even a hint of magic about them will be visible. You and these companions of yours will be seen by everyone on this side of the Veil, you, because you are wearing the ring, and these two because of what they are." Weathervane looked back and flashed a brief smile. "By the way, good job killing the Cave Cats."

Bruise shrugged. "It was fun."

They faced another round of stairways, then that long, very long hallway, and finally they passed through the door into Weathervane's shop.

The entire place practically twinkled with golden light. Every surface gleamed, and the hanging herbs filled the air with their scents.

"Oh, my," Good Idea whispered. This was even more amazing than the tent of Arch Jones.

They stepped out into the street, and there stood Pink, just where Good Idea had left her, head down in sleep.

"I can see her," Good Idea exclaimed.

"Did you really think she was an ordinary horse?" Bruise asked.

"No," Good Idea said slowly. "I guess not.

Beside the small roan was a tall shadow, but Good Idea could not see what was casting it. She looked around some more as Weathervane began to walk away.

"Where's Regret?" She called.

Weathervane turned. "She is there," she said, pointing. "You cannot see any being or object that has no magic. While magical beings can be easily seen in the real world, non-magical things, through the Veil, only cast a shadow."

Good Idea looked around. "So I should avoid walking into all shadows?"

Weathervane nodded. "Unless you want to stumble over every stray cat, loose barrel or sleeping vagrant, yes."

There was much more magic around her than she ever would have thought possible. The side street was not shabby at all. Instead, the shops were painted in bright colors, the glass windows gleaming.

As they turned onto the wharf, the ships were shining in the sun, their paint gleaming, the sails billowing white. About half the men working the docks were visible to her, all dressed in bright colors, their features clean and sharply defined. There were even a few dogs nosing among the barrels and crates.

Good Idea felt like a six-year-old again, going to Market for the first time with her father, excited and slightly overwhelmed. She had just passed this way, yet it seemed completely different, colors more vibrant, the air crisper, the sounds sharper. She saw fewer people and squinted to find the many vague shadows of people and the larger shadows of ships.

She hurried to walk by Weathervane's side. "Are all these people, well, not people?" she asked.

Weathervane had been dressed in a simple black dress when they first walked into the shop, but once she stepped through the Veil, the dress became a gown of dark green silk, ruffled and festooned with what looked to be real roses. She walked briskly on high-buttoned shoes that slapped against the cobblestones. "Most are witches or wizards. Many are fey who have toned down the natural inclination to drive humans away. There are shapeshifters, of course, and demons."

"So, outside of the Veil, you can't see, ah, demons?" Good Idea asked.

"Only if they want you to see them. And they usually don't. They are very frightening." She nodded to a small gathering of creatures, their bodies squat and hunched, faces scarred, skin scaled and red, each with several eyes and at least two horns.

Good Idea glanced behind at Bruise, who seemed totally unimpressed by his unnatural surroundings. Left Ear, perched on the orc's shoulder, appeared to be asleep.

Good Idea dropped back to walk with Bruise. "Are you seeing all this?" she asked.

Bruise grunted. "Yeah. A bit of a freak show, this is."

"I know. It's wonderful," she said, and Weathervane, a few steps ahead, turned with a smile.

"Yes," the witch said. "It certainly is."

· · ·

134

WILLOW WAY WAS CLEARLY MARKED with a tall sign with a bright green arrow pointing up a narrower street, and as they passed onto the way, the atmosphere suddenly changed. The buildings looked shabbier and seemed to lean over the narrow cobblestones. The shop windows were grimy with soot, and the residents were dressed in older, less fashionable clothes and walked with heads down, feet shuffling quickly.

"Weir Town," Weathervane announced. "Let me see the map again."

Good Idea handed over the map, and Weathervane examined it closely.

"Is the Weir in Weir Town a person or place?" Good Idea asked.

"Weirs stick to their own kind," Bruise said. "They aren't inherently evil, just disagreeable."

"Very disagreeable," Weathervane muttered. "And finding our way to the next waypoint on this map might get tricky. In the past several years, the Weirs have become very distrustful of everyone." She folded the map and looked around. "Luckily, many know of me. As I said, I have something of a reputation. Let's go."

Weir Town got darker and drearier as they went on, until they at last came to a dead end, a deserted warehouse in front of them, several shuttered shops along one side or the street, and a disreputable-looking tavern on the other side.

Weathervane squared her shoulders. "Let me do the talking," she said, and pushed open the large door to the tavern.

Pints And Bread Tavern was smoke-filled and smelled of stale ale. Half the tables were occupied by cloaked figures, hunched over their empty mugs. All muttered conversations stopped as they entered. The barkeep, at the far end of the smoky room, stopped mid-swipe and rested his hands on the grimy bar.

"Whatchadoinhere?" he shouted. "We don't serve the likes of

you." He pointed, but Good Idea didn't know if he meant her or Bruise.

Weathervane kept her head up and smile bright. "It's Adam Maltman, yes? I'm Weathervane Wynd. You know of me, I'm sure, and I helped your wife a number of times. Tonic for youngest? A lingering cough, I believe?"

Adam Maltman was very tall and very thin, with a bluish cast to his skin, ears large and pointed like the rabbits Good Idea had trapped back in Whisper, and broad, six-fingered hands. He narrowed his eyes. "Yes. I know you. But that don't change the question."

Weathervane went to the bar and spread the map on the scratched surface. She pointed.

"I believe this is your establishment?"

He squinted at the map for what seemed to be a very long time before nodding. "Yar, that's me."

"Well then, if you could just allow us to go upstairs and through your attic. We need access to the roof," Weathervane explained pleasantly.

"What for?" The Weir asked.

"We're looking for something," Weathervane said. "It was hidden years ago."

Adam Maltman's expression changed. "That pretty little thing with those big gray eyes? I remember her like it was yesterday. I was just a lad when she came through. Sweet-talked me da into climbing up on my roof. Said she had to hide something of great importance."

Good Idea stepped forward. "I'm her daughter," she said.

Adam frowned. "Are you sure? She was a beauty. You're very ordinary."

Good Idea signed. "Yes, I know. But I am her daughter. Her name was Belladona Green. She sent me to retrieve what she hid."

"And that would be the NoteBook Of Whim?" Adam asked.

Good Idea froze. "How do you know that?" she whispered. She had thought that the notebook was something of a secret that her mother had tried to keep. Instead, it seemed as though everyone knew about it.

The barkeep shrugged. "Every few years there be a demon come asking about it, if I know where it is, or how to find it. I never say a word. Don't trust a demon as far as I can throw him."

Weathervane looked at Good Idea. "There are watchers here in the Veil," she said softly.

Good Idea nodded. "There are watchers in the real world too. That's why Bruise and Left Ear and Regret are here. Mionarach warned me." She looked at Adam. "Will you allow us to go through?"

"And why should I?" he asked.

There were more gold coins, of course, but she was loath to use them up so early in the journey. There was no way of knowing what lay ahead, or what it would take to get through. How long would those gold coins last?

But would Belladona have had to pay her way through the Veil?

"Why did your da allow my mother through?" she asked.

Adam's face softened even more. "She was such a soft and pretty thing. Had a voice like an angel."

"She is now old and in a wheelchair," Good Idea said. "But her eyes are as clear as spring water and gray as a thundercloud."

"She held me on her lap as she talked to me da," Adam said, his voice growing wistful. "Said she had fallen in love and could not take the notebook with her."

"She had fallen in love with my father," Good Idea told him, her voice choking with grief. "He died, and now I must get the notebook back for her."

Adam's face fell. "He died? Ah, now that's a sad thing. I

remember her eyes lit up like stars when she spoke of him. I'm sorry. Were they happy together?"

"Yes," Good Idea said. "Until the very end."

Adam pulled a dark kerchief from his back pocket, wiped his eyes and blew into it rather noisily.

"It would be a real kindness for her," Weathervane said. "For Belladona, that is, if you let us through."

He chewed on his lower lip for a long time before nodding his head grudgingly. "Follow me."

Every eye seemed to watch as the barkeep led them up a narrow stair to the second floor. He drew a large ring of keys from his pocket and unlocked a door at the end of the hallway.

"Go on up, and out through the window. But there are the Pidge Folk on the roof. They make their own rules." Adam Maltman shrugged. "They may let you pass, they may not. I can't help you there."

The stairway was steep, and Weathervane picked her way carefully up the narrow treads. Good Idea followed, and they wound their way through a steep-roofed attic, crowded with old furniture, dusty crates, and broken barrels until they found their way to a grimy window.

Weathervane pushed it open. "After you," she said to Good Idea.

Good Idea climbed through and found herself on a flat rooftop, surrounded by chimneys and other rooftops, with the whole of Mirror City and the River Brown stretched out before her.

Bruise stood next to her, and Left Ear stretched her wings, flying up into the brilliant sun.

"Very good," Weathervane said, closing the window behind them.

"Not so good," a voice croaked.

· · ·

THE AIR ABOVE THEM DARKENED, and there was a flurry of wings. In seconds they were surrounded by what Good Idea could only guess were Pidge Folk. They were the size of large geese, with broad wings of soft gray and long graceful necks that ended in heads that had very large eyes and long beaks that opened to show very large and sharp teeth. Small arms protruded from a broad breast, ending in three-fingered hands. And in each hand was a short, wicked-looking knife.

"I am Grayback, leader of the Pidge Folk. We don't abide strangers in our domain," the largest said. "You can go no farther. Return the way you came, or we'll peck your eyes out and feed them to our children. We'll tear your legs off and drop them in the River Brown. We'll scatter your arms in the Marsh to the far south. Then we'll put your head on spikes to discourage others from daring to tread where they're not welcome."

Weathervane drew herself up. "I am Weathervane Wynd of The Third Circle Of Laramee. I'm sure you've heard of me?"'

Grayback tilted his head. "No."

Weathervane squared her shoulders. "I am a healer of some renown."

Grayback ruffled his feathers. "We don't get sick much."

"I have a shop on Seller Street," Weathervane said, her voice rising in frustration. "Surely you've frequented Ye Olde Shoppe Of Various Herbs Potions And Cures?"

He shook his head. "Still no. We don't have much of a reason to go down to Seller Street. We have barely a reason to leave the rooftops"

Weathervane drew a breath, obviously not used to this kind of response. "Well, it doesn't matter. As a long-time resident of Mirror City, I know of no authority that gave you power over the rooftops. We have every right to be here and travel without fear. We are on a mission of some importance and will not be stopped by the likes of you." She flourished her staff. "Move aside."

The Pidge Folk, more than a dozen, ruffled their feathers and began cooing to one another. Weathervane stood patiently. Bruise slowly drew out Axe. Overhead, Good Idea saw a shape circling, snorting smoke.

Grayback stepped closer. "Listen," it said in a low voice. "We're all rather new at this. I mean, it wasn't even my idea to claim the rooftops. But the flock, well..." It clasped its hands around the small knife. "Can't you just turn around and go away? Please? I really don't want anyone to get hurt."

"Then why the elaborate threats?" Good Idea asked.

"Well, you see, for years, all sorts of folk have been traipsing over our rooftops, disturbing our nests, and wreaking havoc up here." Grayback looked over its shoulder at the rest of the flock and stepped even closer. "We finally decided to do something. We put the word out, and it's worked so far. We've been left alone. But now you're here, and if I let you pass, I'll lose all respect. They may even banish me from the flock. So, what do you say?"

Weathervane shook her head. "We need to get from here to the Pilgrim's Tower." She pointed to a narrow spire in the middle of the field of rooftops. "And this is the only way. In case you haven't noticed, we have an orc who could easily kill half of you with one blow."

"And see that fellow up there?" Bruise asked, pointing to Left Ear circling slowly. "That would be a shapeshifter. Right now, I believe she's in the form of a dragon."

Grayback drew back his head. "You would fight us? All of us?"

"Only if you don't allow us to reach that spire," Weathervane said.

"It is that important?" Grayback asked.

Good Idea nodded. "Very. I have no desire to stand here and

argue with you. I never wanted to be here in the first place, and I want to make it back home as soon as possible. But I understand your predicament." She thought. Once again, money seemed an answer. "What if we *paid* our way across?"

Grayback stepped back and began to coo. A lengthy conversation followed, the heads bobbing up and down, teeth bared. Good Idea sighed. Finally, Grayback stepped forward again.

"The flock has consented to payment," it said.

"What do they want?" Good Idea asked, worried now.

Grayback turned its head. "We require payment in gold."

Good Idea's shoulders slumped. Weathervane looked at her. "Do you have any gold?"

Good Idea nodded glumly and fished a single gold coin out of her pocket, holding it out to Grayback.

The beady eyes widened, and the Pidge Folk began to angrily coo.

"What use is a coin for us?" Grayback snapped. "We have no use for that. What other gold to you have?"

Good Idea thought quickly. She had no jewelry. The knife she bore was wrought in silver. She looked at Weathervane questioningly, but the witch shook her head.

Fleet ran up her shoulder and chirped. Good Idea turned to see the mouse, and in his paws, he held a single feather, pale gold striped with blue.

Good Idea took it and held it to show Grayback. "How about this?"

The Pidge Folk gathered around, cooing softly. Grayback took the feather between two of its three fingers.

"What a treasure," he whispered. "A gold feather. We have never seen anything so fine as this." He stepped back. "This is a worthy payment. Thank you for not making us kill you," Grayback said formally. "You may continue."

The air was full of the sound of wings again, and in seconds, the rooftops were empty.

Bruise sniffed. "Bit of an odd bird, that one," he said.

Weathervane looked at Good Idea coolly. "I'm beginning to think there's more to you than one would guess. Well done." She tapped the rooftop with the Staff Of Healing and pointed. "That way."

Left Ear flew closer, changing from dragon to crow, and settled again on Bruise's shoulder. Fleet made his way back to Good Idea's pocket, and the company began its way carefully across the rooftops of the Veil.

CROSSING the rooftops was no easy task. First, there was the variation of materials. Some rooftops were slate, hard underfoot and thick with moss. Some were wood shingled, easy to cross, but one had to be watchful of rotten patches where a foot might break through. And then there were those that shone so brightly that Good Idea couldn't look at them without squinting. She just kept her eyes facing front and followed Weathervane's back, trusting the witch.

And the spire did not seem to be getting any closer. Good Idea saw the sun begin to dip in the west, and it still seemed that they had not gotten any closer than they had been hours before.

Then, suddenly, the spire was directly in front of them, tall and narrow, built of smooth white stone.

"How did that happen?" Good Idea asked, astonished.

"Magic," Weathervane said. She walked around the spire, feeling the surface with her hands, then stopped, nodding to herself. "Here," she said, and pushed against the marble.

A doorway opened up before them. More stairs? Good Idea's back ached again, and the vision in one eye was blurring. But there were no stairs, just a round room with high windows up against the dome of a ceiling. They gathered in the center. Weathervane looked at the map again and began feeling her way around the smooth walls.

"There must be a crack or hidden switch," the witch muttered.

"And this is exactly where we're supposed to be?" Good Idea asked.

Weathervane blew out in frustration and pointed to a spot on the map. Good Idea stared, but the map made no more sense to her now than it had that morning.

Left Ear suddenly flew up into the dome and settled on something just above one of the windows. "There is a small wooden perch here," she called down. "And it moves."

Good Idea looked up, but in the growing dark, she could barely see the crow.

"Is there another?" Weathervane asked.

Left Ear flew across the room and settled again. "Yes. Here's another one. It moves too."

Good Idea looked back at the map. "What is that writing?" she asked, pointing to tiny runes near to where she thought they might be.

Weathervane squinted. "It says 'Cannot use magic.' That's very unhelpful, because it means I can't cast a spell on either perch. We obviously need to pull on them, so we have to find another way." She looked up again. The tiny perches were so high up on the wall that no one could reach them.

"Maybe we could stand on each other's shoulders?" Bruise suggested. "Then we could pull on one and Left Ear the other?"

Weathervane looked insulted. "I don't stand on other people," she said. "Nor do I let other people stand on me."

Good Idea looked at her squarely. "Do you have another suggestion?"

Weathervane sighed and shook her head.

Good Idea scrambled on to Bruise's shoulders. Weathervane, after rearranging her skirts, carefully put her foot into Bruise's cupped hands, then climbed onto his head, and finally pulled herself onto Good Idea's shoulders. She stretched, but the small bit of wood sticking out above the window was still too high.

"How on earth," Weathervane grumbled as she unceremoniously slid down Good Idea, then Bruise, "did Belladona find a way to pull on both of them? She was a tiny thing."

Good Idea was tired and hungry. "Maybe we can reach them from the outside?" she suggested.

Weathervane brightened. "Maybe." But as they all turned to the doorway that led back out to the rooftops, the door silently slid shut.

Weathervane examined the door, or rather, where the door had been, because now the wall was smooth without a seam or crack showing.

"I believe," Weathervane said, quite unnecessarily at this point, "that we are trapped in here."

Left Ear flew down. "I can fly out and gather food," she offered.

Good Idea was about to say a few words of encouragement when Bruise grunted.

"No need," the orc said, and pulled from his pack a loaf of bread, several apples, a head of cheese and half a meat pie.

"You brought all this?" Good Idea asked, delighted

"And more. For a few days anyway," the orc answered sheepishly. "I didn't know how long we'd be through the Veil, and I wasn't sure there would be eating places, or what kind of food they'd serve. I didn't want to eat anything unnatural." The orc grinned. "Besides, I know you get a bit cranky if you don't eat."

Good Idea sank to the cold floor. She took the loaf of bread, broke off a chunk, and chewed. "I do not get cranky," she said.

"Maybe not *cranky*," said Left Ear, pecking away at the bread. "But longer time between meals does affect your mood. It's a good thing he's a bit of a planner, that one," the shifter said.

Good Idea looked up in surprise, then glanced at Bruise. He met her look, matched her grin, and they all began to laugh.

CHAPTER 10

*W*hen Good Idea awoke the next morning, her back ached from sleeping on the hard floor, her mouth was dry, and, as she slowly came to her feet, she saw that everyone else was awake, and there was still no apparent way out of their prison.

There was, however, a small fire in the middle of the floor and Bruise was cooking slices of bacon, each slice pierced through and hanging from a slender stick, dangling over the flame.

Weathervane and Left Ear were in whispered conversation, but seeing that Good Idea was awake, the witch motioned her over.

"We have been discussing possible methods of escape, and there appears to be none," Weathervane told her. "So, we must figure out how Belladona got from this particular place to the next spot on the map, which appears to be directly beneath us. Left Ear volunteered to fly back to Belladona and ask her, but considering how long it would take, and the dangers that may be on the road, that is our last resort. You, as your name suggests, seem to come up with good ideas. Any thoughts on how we can get something on both of the perches at the same time? Theory being, of course, that the floor will then move in some direction, preferably down."

"I assume," Good Idea said slowly, "that you cannot change into a bird of comparable size and fly up there too?"

Weathervane had been waving a crispy piece of bacon to cool it off. She stopped waving and glared. "No, I can't."

The bacon was hot and crispy and the bread not to stale. The room had smooth walls which led to high, narrow windows. Now that it was light, and Good Idea was more rested, she could clearly see the small perches protruding from each side of the dome.

"My mother did not use magic," she mused. "What else did she have that could have helped her, I wonder?"

Fleet popped out of her pocket and squeaked.

Left Ear flew down, quickly changed into a mouse, and had a long, animated conversation with Fleet. Good Idea smiled as she watched them, each making wide motions with their tiny front legs, and she could almost understand what they were saying to each other. Left Ear finally turned to Good Idea.

"Fleet was with her, and she had thin, strong twine. He carried the twine up to each perch and tied it. When both pieces were attached, she pulled, and the floor lowered. As the floor went down, she held on to the twine until it snapped. That was over sixty years ago, and the traces of the twine have since disappeared. It was a very clever plan."

Weathervane sniffed. "And do any of you have any twine in your packs?"

Bruise shook his head. Good Idea could only find the tiny ball of thread Fleet had given her earlier, which seemed to be very long but too thin to be of any use.

Silence fell. Good Idea watched the sun move from one of the high windows to the next. They could spend days here, she realized, and she wanted to have this entire episode done with as soon as possible so she could return home. Then she looked at the two mice on her shoulder. "Left Ear, is your weight as a mouse enough to weigh down the perch?"

Left Ear shifted back into a crow to fly and land on the perch, then became a mouse again. Good Idea could see the answer to her question. As a crow, the perch lowered. As Left Ear shifted to a mouse, the perch lifted back into its original position.

She reached into her pocket and found the small, green stone that Fleet had found. She held it out to him. "Can you carry this while you climb up to the perch?"

The mouse reached over to take it, held it for a moment, then shook his head.

"Left Ear," Good Idea called. "Come and get this. Fleet is going to climb up to the perch. When he does, please give this to him to hold, then fly back to your own perch."

Left Ear flew down as Fleet began to climb the wall. Good Idea was worried that the walls would be too slick, or perhaps the climb would be too much for the tiny creature, then remembered that Fleet had done this once before already.

She watched as Left Ear flew to the top of the dome, circling slowly. When Fleet reached the perch, Left Ear dropped the small stone from his claws. Fleet caught it, and Left Ear flew to the second perch.

There was a sudden jolt and the room shuddered. The floor began to move slowly downward. Fleet scrambled down the wall, but Left Ear flew and scooped him up gently. The floor dropped fast, then faster, and Good Idea worried they would hit bottom with a crash. She grabbed on to Bruise, who appeared to share her fears.

"I hope we don't die when we hit bottom," the orc said.

But there was a sudden whoosh, and the floor slowed and practically floated to a stop.

Good Idea looked up. The top of the dome was so far above that the light from the windows barely reached them.

There was an open archway before them, a long passageway, and, where Good Idea saw the passage curved to the right, a faint glow.

Weathervane consulted the map once again. "Thank the stars. We're almost there. What are we looking for, exactly?"

"Something that unlocks," Good Idea said. "I have a key."

"That's unhelpful," Weathervane said.

Left Ear dropped Fleet back onto Good Idea's shoulder, and the mouse chirped.

"No pocket?" Good Idea asked. "I guess you want to see this last bit through? All right then. Let's get this done." She nodded to Weathervane, and the witch cast a light ahead and led them toward the faint, quivering glow.

THE GLOW, when they rounded the corner, came from a large, open furnace. There were figures in front of it, short and muscular, with long beards: dwarves working at a forge. One was holding a long blade over an anvil, striking the red-hot metal with a heavy hammer. One was pushing on bellows as tall as it was. Two more dwarves were shoveling coal into the open door of the furnace.

None of the dwarves noticed the approach of two tall women and an orc, or a crow flying above the sparks and smoke. They were very intent on their task, which seemed to be the forging of a very long, very strong blade.

"Excuse me," Weathervane called.

One dwarf, shoveling coal, stopped, turned and, seeing the group, put down his shovel and approached them.

"How did you get down here?" he asked gruffly. His beard was bright blue and there was black coal dust on his face.

Weathervane pointed behind her.

148

The dwarf frowned. "No one has used the spire lift in decades," he said.

"Well, we did." She shook out the map and pointed. "Now, we need to get *here*."

The dwarf leaned over and squinted in the dim light. When he straightened, his face was grim. "You can't get there from here," he said shortly, and turned away.

Weathervane grabbed the long braid of his hair and stopped him. "Someone did once. And we need to get there again."

The dwarf, his back still to them, reached behind to jerk his braid out of Weathervane's grasp. "Then follow me," he said.

They passed many similar furnaces and forges and seemed to be going deeper and deeper underground. Fleet had long since made his way back into Good Idea's pocket, and she didn't blame him. She didn't like the hot, smokey air, the noise of pounding hammers, and the bursts of flame from the furnaces either. They finally came to a tall, narrow doorway, and the dwarf stopped.

"Go on through," he muttered, and headed back the way they came.

Weathervane pushed open the door.

The room was mercifully cool and quiet, and Good Idea relaxed. She blinked against the sudden brightness, and found herself in an obvious throne room, long and broad, with a raised dais at one end, complete with a very ornate throne guarded by two armed dwarves.

One stepped forward. "Who wishes to have an audience with our Queen?"

Good Idea raised a tentative hand and waved it. "I do. I am Inspirational Wink, daughter of Belladona Green, who has been this way before."

"And what is the nature of your visit here?" the dwarf asked.

Weathervane spoke. "We need to find an object of great

importance that lies here in your realm, and we've been told we can't get there. But we must."

The dwarf bowed swiftly and turned, marching through one archway to the left.

Weathervane looked around. "I've heard of the Dwarf Caves beneath the city, of course, but never had a reason to visit. Dwarves are touchy creatures, very loyal but quick to anger."

"Brutal in a fight," Bruise added. "You always want them on your side."

Left Ear scratched her side with a large paw. "Now, Morten Dwarves, they are the fiercest. Never saw a one back down. Once saw a troop of them take down a Querrian Dragon."

"I fought with them against a goblin hoard over in Lake Borne, fifteen years ago. Bragget Dwarves, but yes, they were great warriors."

"You were at Lake Borne?" Left Ear asked. "Those were goblins from the Nether Caves, no?"

"Yes. I've fought goblins before, but I thanked the gods every night for those dwarves with me."

Weathervane glanced at Good Idea. "Interesting conversation," she said quietly.

Good Idea rolled her eyes. "It's been an education I never knew I needed," she answered.

While they waited, Left Ear and Bruise discussed the various breeds of goblins and their strengths and weaknesses, best fighting techniques, and even their sleeping habits.

"Now, a Phonifur goblin can sleep standing up. They never have to leave the battlefield," Bruise said.

"I never knew that," Left Ear told him. "I thought the standing sleepers were only—"

Good Idea never found out anything else about the standing sleepers, because the dwarf returned through the same archway, followed by four other dwarves in single file, each dressed in red robes, their beards and hair braided in gold. Finally, a smaller, more slow-moving dwarf entered, in a simple red-and-gold robe, and a circlet of pale silver on her balding head, her beard almost reaching the floor.

The Queen stood before her throne, turned, and held her arms out. The two dwarves flanking the throne each took an arm and lifted her up and back until she was sitting high above them. She glowered.

"Which one of you is the child of Belladona Green?" she asked in a querulous voice.

Good Idea stepped forward. "I am. I am Inspirational Wink."

"And who are all these others?"

Weathervane Wynd stepped forward. "I am Weathervane Wynd."

The Queen nodded slowly. "The healer? I have heard of you."

Weathervane glowed. "It is gratifying to think my good reputation has spread so far throughout the Realm."

The Queen tugged at her beard. "What makes you think your 'good' reputation has spread? Maybe I've heard that you are a talentless fraud."

Weathervane blanched and stepped back.

"This is Bruise," Good Idea said quickly, not looking in Weathervane's direction. "And Left Ear of the Wolf Clan"

Left Ear, who had been sitting on Bruise's shoulder, shifted instantly into a wolf, a large, imposing wolf.

Good Idea felt a twitching as Fleet once again climbed on to her shoulder. "And Fleet," she added.

The Queen leaned forward and looked Good Idea up and down. "I am MerriDon Gold, Queen of the Mullon Dwarves of Mirror City, and Defender of The Vein Of Sorrow."

Good Idea bowed quickly, as did Weathervane and Bruise. Left Ear stretched her front legs out before her and ducked her shaggy head.

"My understanding," the Queen continued, "is that you need to find the Notebook Of Whim, which Belladona Green placed here many years ago. Unless there is another object of great importance that you seek?"

"No, that's the one," Good Idea said. "Can we retrieve it now?"

The Dwarf Queen shook her head. "No. There is no way for someone who is not Dwarf Blood to find the way."

Good Idea waited for something else, but the Queen settled back, closed her eyes, and began to snore.

"Ah, your highness?" Good Idea said.

The Queen opened her eyes.

"You know how important this is?" Good Idea asked.

The Queen nodded. "Yes, of course I do. After all, I sent my most favored nephew, Montgomery Gold, to that village. What was it called? Whisper? Yes, I sent him to help protect her."

Good Idea tilted her head. "Mr. Gold is your nephew? He gave me a very nice knife." Good Idea reached into her belt and withdrew the finely crafted knife and held it up for the Queen to see.

The Queen squinted, and her face softened. "He does such good work, my Monty."

Good Idea nodded. "I'm sure you understand that we need to get the notebook. Can you," she paused. She'd never spoken to a queen before, but sensed she had to be delicate in her request. "Can you, in your wisdom, possibly advise us on the best way to retrieve it?"

Bruise leaned over and whispered in her ear. "Good move."

The Queen considered this. Her brow puckered. Finally, she snapped her fingers and one of the red-robed dwarves hurried forward.

"This is one of my most trusted captains, Mica. He will take you." She turned to Mica and waved her hand. "Take them to the Cave Of Abandonment."

Mica bowed and mumbled. "The Cave Of Abandonment? Aren't there new reports of hobs in those tunnels?"

The Queen leaned her head in the direction of another dwarf, who scurried forward and whispered in her ear. Queen MerriDon nodded. "Yes. So be careful through there."

Mica, bowing even lower, mumbled again. "And the troll?"

Good Idea looked sideways at Bruise with growing anxiety, but the orc's tiny eyes brightened with anticipation. Then she turned to Weathervane, who sighed softly. Left Ear wagged her tail. Was she the only one even slightly troubled by this growing list of adversaries?

The Queen, listening again to her advisor, sighed. "Yes. Apparently, there's a troll. There's always been a troll." She tugged at her beard. "Your point?"

Mica cleared his throat. "Perhaps I can take a few more soldiers with me?"

Queen MerriDon drew back, looking astounded. "More soldiers? Whatever for?"

Mica glanced over at Good Idea, whose eyes had grown quite large.

"Your Highness," Good Idea said, "I was given this task, to be sure, but I am quite unequipped to deal with these kinds of enemies."

"Then why were you given it?" The Queen demanded.

"Because there was no one else. Believe me when I tell you I did not volunteer."

The Dwarf stuck out her lower lip. "Well, that seems to be rather short-sighted."

Good Idea sighed. "That was my thinking exactly. But there's just me."

"Yet you have ..." The Queen waved her hand in the direction of Weathervane and Bruise. "What are they for, then? And you've got a wolf with you. Do you really think you need more help?"

"Queen MerriDon, to be perfectly honest, I don't know if I do or not," Good Idea said. "But in the past few days I have encountered dangers I never imagined. I have all the faith in the world in my companions, and they have served me well, but if your own captain feels the need for additional help, then I am going to humbly bow to his judgment."

Queen MerriDon narrowed her eyes. "I quite clearly remember your mother coming here and asking of me a great favor. I granted that favor and prepared quite an entourage to ensure her safety. In exchange, she promised to return that favor, and she never did. You're lucky I'm allowing Mica here to go with you. After such shabby treatment, I should really just turn you away completely."

Why was everyone so difficult? Good Idea had thought that everyone who knew about the Notebook Of Whim, how important it was to be dealt with, would be eager to help her. But she'd been stymied every step of the way so far, and she was getting rather tired of it all.

She cleared her throat. "What did you ask of her?"

The Queen frowned. "What do you mean?"

"What favor did you ask of my mother that she refused?"

The Queen looked confused for a moment, then squared her shoulders. "To be honest, I never got around to asking her for anything. The whole thing just slipped my mind."

"I see," Good Idea said reasonably. "So, in truth, my mother never went back on her promise to return the favor. There *was* no shabby behavior."

Queen MerriDon leaned forward on her throne. Her advisors, who had been whispering to each other, fell silent. Mica, still bowed down almost to the floor, let out a small whimper.

The Queen stood. "Then you," she said in a cold voice, "shall owe me *two* favors."

"Yes, your Highness," Good Idea said. "That's only fair."

"But" the Queen continued, "there will be no more soldiers. You seem very able to defend yourselves. Mica, you shall act as their guide. I expect you remember the way?"

Mica, forehead to the floor, whispered, "Yes."

"Good." She stood. "Take them through. And for pity's sake, don't let the dragon eat them."

Mica seemed to blanch under his beard but straightened and walked over to Good Idea.

"Please. Follow me."

BRUISE AND LEFT Ear began an immediate discussion about the most effective ways of dealing with trolls. Good Idea wished she was not close enough to hear them, because their discussion focused primarily on how to get *away* from trolls.

Weathervane, walking next to Good Idea behind the dwarf, muttered, "I wonder if she meant it. That remark about me being a talentless fraud."

"I'm sure she didn't," Good Idea said tiredly. Her mind was thinking about hobs and trolls and dragons, not Weathervane Wynd's reputation. She sighed. She was having trouble seeing in the darkness. Her shoulders hurt, her pack chafed, and she was very hungry. "The least she could have done," she muttered, "was offer us something to eat."

Mica, holding a lantern high and proceeding with, Good Idea thought, a lot of caution, spoke over his shoulder. "The Queen never offers anyone a meal. Sometimes we don't get fed for days. Rather miserly, our MerriDon. Fresh food is very hard to come by, and she likes to keep it to herself. And why not? After all, she is the Queen." He went around a rather substantial puddle of water and lifted his robes with one hand to avoid any splash.

"And does she exaggerate?" Good Idea asked hopefully.

Mica shook his shaggy head. "No. Sadly, there's a very good chance we'll be attacked by any or all of the creatures she mentioned. Lucky for us, Scale Face has grown very lazy in his old age, and barely opens one eye at a time."

"Scale Face?" Weathervane said.

"The dragon. Been here a very long time and has pillaged just about as much as his cave can hold, so things have been quiet. If he went after any more treasure, he'd have to expand his lair. And like I said, he's very lazy." He swatted away a thick, dusty cobweb, then grumbled as he brushed the debris from his shoulders.

Good Idea, half an ear to what Bruise and Left Ear were saying, asked, "What, exactly, are hobs?"

"They're a nuisance, that's what they are," Mica explained. "Small, hairy things that just try to ruin anything and everything they come across. They used to be quite useful little buggers, a century or two back, but someone pissed them off and they turned into the most annoying creatures you can imagine. Just one of them is too little to be of any danger, but they have learned to travel in massive hives and have been known to take down a giant."

Weathervane shivered delicately. "And the hobs here are angry?"

"Oh, they've been mad as yaksun for years." Mica stopped as the passage split, peering down one dark tunnel, then the other. "This way," he said, turning left.

Bruise and Left Ear had moved on to dragons, so Good Idea tried to engage Mica in discussing anything other than something that could possibly kill her. "Mica, were you here when my mother hid the notebook?"

He nodded. "Yes. Lovely girl, your mum. She caused quite the stir down here. Dwarf women are fine, but we rarely come across a woman whose face you can actually see." He shot a grin over his shoulder. "The beard, you know."

"Did you take her to the Cave Of Abandonment?" Good Idea asked.

He nodded. "Yes. Me and about fifty other soldiers, as well as the Queen and twelve of her advisors. It was put together very quickly, or the entire kingdom would have been there. Had a regular caravan going on. Very nasty going, though. The passage hadn't been used in years, and the dirt was incredible. Ruined my best pair of high-heeled boots. Lovely they were. Had a bit of gold trim around the laces." He sighed at the memory. "And I'll wager no one has set foot down here since."

Mica slowed even more and approached the next curve of the tunnel, practically on tiptoe. He held a hand up, signaling them to wait, and peeked around the corner. He drew back with a sigh.

"Well, that's not good," he said mournfully. "They're there."

"Who?" Bruise asked.

"Hobs," Mica answered.

Bruise's face lit up. "Really? Hear that, Left Ear? Hobs." The orc looked at Good Idea. "Watch your ankles." He grinned and rounded the bend in the tunnel, Left Ear running alongside.

In a matter of seconds, there seemed to be a lot of squealing going on, so Good Idea inched up and around the bend to see what was happening. It was not pretty. There were tiny torches on the sides of a largish, high-ceiling cave sort of room, and there appeared to be a swarm of tiny hairy, lop-eared, sharp-fanged creatures attacking Bruise and Left Ear. Bruise was swinging his axe, and appeared to be killing a number of them, but at least a dozen had crawled up his back, and an equal number hung from his legs, despite his best efforts to shake them off.

Left Ear was doing no better as her jaws snapped wildly, but the hobs had swarmed up her back and were hanging onto her fur. Left Ear changed tactics and shifted into an enormous eagle, but the hobs still clung as she circled the ceiling. She dropped down and changed tactics again, this time seeming to disappear entirely. But Good Idea saw the small mouse slip away from the confused hobs and scurry to a quiet corner where she shifted again, this time into a large crocodile with incredibly large jaws and a slick, scaly hide that none of the hobs could grab hold of.

Mica came up from behind, sighed heavily, drew his stout sword, and entered the fray, swinging.

The hobs squealed even louder, and Good Idea saw another group of them emerge from a crack in the stone wall and began to climb Mica.

"Well, this doesn't look promising," Weathervane said, looking over Good Idea's shoulder.

"They're practically small enough to step on," Good Idea mused. "But they're just too quick and squirmy to catch."

"Hmm," Weathervane said. She drew herself up, held out her staff, and a wavering kind of light pulsed from it. It filled the room in front of them with a haze, then she brought the staff down upon the ground with a sharp, loud bang, and everything before Good Idea slowed down to a literal crawl.

"Oh, my," Good Idea said, delighted again by magic in action. "Now, that's clever."

She and the witch came out of the passageway and began to stomp on the hobs. It was very messy, squishy work. Bruise, Left Ear and Mica had also been affected. The expressions on their faces changed in comic slow-motion as they saw Good Idea and Weathervane stomping on the now considerably slowed hobs. Good Idea pried the clinging creatures off their bodies and stepped on them as well. In a few minutes, the stone floor was littered with twisted, hairy bodies and pale, green blood.

"Are we ready?" Weathervane asked.

Good Idea nodded, and the witch tapped the stone floor again with her staff, twice this time.

Bruise, Left Ear, and Mica startled back into normal movement.

Bruise looked around at the bodies, then at Weathervane. "SloMo Spell?" he asked. "Excellent."

Left Ear shifted back into wolf shape. Mica brushed some green blood and flecks of hair and skin off of his red robe, then tried to rub a particularly large stain off the white cuff.

"This will never come out," he whined. "Couldn't you have just set them on fire? Ash would be so much easier to clean."

"I could have," Weathervane said, "but then I would have had to burn you up as well."

Mica made a face and tried to wipe the blood and gore off his sword. Bruise grabbed it from him, and, large tongue protruding, licked it clean.

Mica took the sword back with some dignity. He said, somewhat stiffly. "The good news is, we're halfway there." He pointed with his sword, now gleaming. "That way."

Weathervane followed him, and Bruise, coming up behind Good Idea, grumbled, "Bit of a prisspot, that one," and went on through.

CHAPTER 11

*M*ica led them down a few more very tall and wide tunnels. When asked about the large size, he shrugged, "They're this big because this is how large Scale Face is. He enlarged most of the tunnels when he was much younger."

Good Idea did not find that thought comforting. She'd read about dragons, of course, but had believed in them as much as she'd believed in magic. Now that she knew that magic was real, she tried to remember everything she'd ever heard about drag-ons. Then, she stopped, because what she remembered was not making her feel any better about her situation. Left Ear had *become* a dragon, but Left Ear had been on her side, and Scale Face certainly was not.

After several sharp turns, Good Idea realized that the Queen had been right. No one would have been able to find their way through this maze of passageways. Belladona had made no attempt to map it at all. The map took them from the spire lift to the last X that marked the location of the notebook with nothing but a feeble, wavering line.

Mica, though, moved with confidence, if not speed, and he

finally turned into a much smaller, dampish kind of space.

"Here we are," he announced.

The Cave Of Abandonment was not particularly impressive. Weathervane tapped her staff and light flooded the cave. There were a few rocks on the ground, a rough-hewn niche in the far wall, and a steady drip of water coming from somewhere.

"This is it?" Good Idea asked.

Mica shrugged. "Well, the only time anyone ever comes here is to leave something behind. Doesn't need to be all spiffed up for that now, does it?"

Good Idea walked across the rocky floor, looking. "So where, exactly, do you retrieve what's been left?"

Mica stuck his lower lip out, thinking. "I don't think anyone has ever done that, to be honest."

"You mean," Good Idea asked, "that not one person has ever come back to get what they left behind?"

Mica clucked his tongue. "It is called the Cave Of Abandonment, after all. Not the Cave Of Just Leave This Here A Bit."

Good Idea fished the rusty key from her pocket. "Then what is the use of this?"

Mica shrugged. "I'm sure it fits somewhere," he said.

The key would surely open something: a chest, a drawer, a door. But there was nothing of that sort that she could see. The walls were very rough and jagged, the niche empty, the floor rough but without an obvious trapdoor, and the ceiling dissolved above them into darkness.

Weathervane looked disgusted. "Are you sure this is where we're supposed to be?"

Mica nodded. "The Cave Of Abandonment. Yes, this is it."

Good Idea sighed. "When you brought my mother here, what happened?"

"Well, there were many speeches," Mica began.

"About what?" Good Idea asked.

"About the Notebook Of Whim, of course. About how it

needed to be hidden. Protected. How dangerous it was. That sort of thing."

Good Idea frowned. "I thought it was, I don't know, a secret?"

Mica chuckled. "We're dwarves. We don't really talk to anyone else. We rarely leave our caves and tunnels. Sure, some of us go to the surface and live there for years. Montgomery Gold, for instance. But Dwarves never tell non-dwarves anything of importance. That's why your mother came to us. We know how to keep secrets."

Weathervane nodded. "That is very true."

"So, then what?" Good Idea urged.

"Then she placed the notebook in the niche there, and we left," Mica said.

Weathervane walked over to the niche. It was barely more than a narrow shelf hewn into the stone. She ran her hands over the surface of the surrounding wall, then turned to Good Idea. "Come here," she said.

Good Idea went to her, and Weathervane took her hand and pressed it against the cool stone.

"Can you feel that?" the witch asked.

The stone was cold to the touch, and rough, but beneath her palm Good Idea felt a small dimple. She took the key and placed the end against the indentation, and it slid smoothly into the stone. She turned it, felt a satisfying click, and stepped back.

The wall beside the niche slid open.

There was a much larger cave behind the gap. Weathervane held the light high and leaned in.

There were piles of things everywhere: large chests, pieces of furniture, books, pots and pans, piles of clothing and, off to one side, a cannon.

"What is all this?" Good Idea asked as she walked through. She felt as Fleet ran out of her pocket and saw him vanish beneath an overturned spindle.

Mica, clucking with delight, clapped his hands. "Look at all of this! Why, this must be hundreds of years' worth of abandoned things."

"All this stuff was left down here?" Bruise asked, opening a small chest filled with gems.

"Oh, no," Mica said. "This is from all over the city, I expect. People are always just *leaving* things everywhere. I always wondered where it all went. Now I know. It makes its way here."

"Then why did my mother *intentionally* come down here?" Good Idea asked.

"Well, she couldn't just leave the notebook lying around, could she? No, she had to make sure some idiot didn't accidentally pick it up and start ruining the world." Mica was rummaging through a stack of swords, some old and rusty, but some quite new and beautifully made.

"But where's the notebook?" Good Idea asked.

"There," Weathervane said. She had worked her way into a far corner and was standing by a heap of books. One small book in particular gave off a pale glow.

"Can you get it?" Good Idea asked, hurrying over.

Weathervane shook her head. "No. There are enchantments, remember? Only Belladona's firstborn child can retrieve the notebook. If anyone else touches it, well, who knows what would happen."

Good Idea had to reach high up and over to grab the notebook with her fingertips. She gave a gentle tug. The notebook slid into her hand as a small avalanche of books tumbled to her feet.

It fit perfectly into her palm and was bound in plain brown leather. Aside from the glow, it looked very ordinary. Good Idea opened it carefully. All the pages were pearly white and seemed to shimmer. She could feel it vibrating in her hands, a faint, steady thrum of magic.

"Oh, my," she said.

Bruise cleared his throat. "You owe me one gold coin."

Good Idea looked up. "What?"

"The terms," Bruise said. "One gold coin when you find the notebook." He held out a massive hand, palm up.

Good Idea turned to Bruise. "Can't you wait until we leave this place and get back out into the real world?"

"No," said Bruise. "Those were the terms."

A very loud, deep roaring noise came rumbling down the tunnel and into the cave.

Mica sighed. "Well, that's not good. He's awake."

"Who's awake?" Weathervane asked.

"Scale Face," Mica said. "And you'd better pay your orc. It's all in the details, you know, and I can guarantee you that this one here will stand by and let you get eaten by that dragon if you don't pay what's owed."

Good Idea frowned at Bruise. "Would you?"

Bruise shrugged. "It's what was agreed." The hand stayed out, palm up.

Good Idea tucked the notebook under her arm, dug into her pocket for a gold coin and placed it in Bruise's hand. The roar became louder.

"I thought," Weathervane said, as she glared at Mica, "that the dragon was lazy and not interested in any more treasure."

Bruise, after sticking the gold piece deep into one ear, grunted. "Dragons are tricky beasts. They not only love to hoard their own treasure, they also don't like anyone else getting their hands on anything of value. Just in case, you know, they decide they might want it somewhere down the road."

Mica cleared his throat as he wiped a feathering of dust off his shoulder. "I suggest, now that we've found what we needed to find, that we get out of here before we find our passage is blocked."

That sounded to be excellent advice, and Good Idea hurried

out of the cave. When they were all out, she turned the key again, and the wall slid back shut. She withdrew the key and began to follow Mica out of the Cave Of Abandonment, but here was something in her way.

A dragon.

Nothing Good Idea had read, heard or imagined about dragons prepared her for what she felt upon coming across one face-to-face. She was shocked by the sheer size of the thing. His large, scaled head could barely fit into the entrance of the Cave Of Abandonment. A single puff of smoke filled the cave, setting them all to coughing, and the thin-slit eyes glittered angrily.

"Who," a low and cold voice said, "dares to delve into my chambers?"

Mica cleared his throat and stepped forward. "Now, Scale Face, we've talked about this before. This is actually part of the realm of Queen MerriDon, and —"

"Do not quibble with me, fool," the voice continued. "If this was MerriDon's realm, she would have banished me centuries ago. We both know to whom these tunnels and caves belong." Another puff of smoke. "Someone here has taken something. Someone here is planning to leave these tunnels with something that belongs to *me*."

Good Idea stepped forward. "Actually, we were taking this." She held up the notebook. "This belonged to my mother. We are not taking anything of yours. Really. We are just reclaiming a lost item."

Scale Face tilted his head to better look at Good Idea, opening one eye wider. "Are you kidding me? She gave that to me years ago. Left it right there, in that niche, as an offering."

"No," Good Idea argued. "She just left it here for safekeeping." She felt someone behind her and heard Weathervane's voice in her ear.

"It is not wise," the witch whispered, "to argue with a dragon."

Good Idea turned and glared. "What options do we have? With one 'poof' we're all roasted. We're standing in a large bread oven, just waiting for the heat."

Scale Face made a noise that could have been a chuckle. "Just return the notebook to where you found it, and, as a courtesy to Queen MerriDon, I'll let you all live."

Mica, who had been busy scraping mud off the bottom of his boot, looked up. "Sounds fair."

"But we need the notebook," Good Idea argued. "It's the reason we came." She looked around at the blank faces around her. "Ideas? Anyone?"

"Fighting our way out from this is a losing proposition," Left Ear said. "Even if he didn't crisp us in one breath, he could barricade the entrance there and we'd starve to death. Or he could drag us, one at a time, and throw us to the troll. Or he could—"

"Enough," Good Idea snapped. She looked at Weathervane. "Nothing?"

The witch shook her head. "The amount of magic needed to do anything with a dragon this size would drain me of everything, including my life force, and would probably only slow him down for a few seconds."

Scale Face smiled.

Good Idea stared down at the notebook in her hands. "Could we offer you a trade?" she asked. "Replace one treasure with another?"

"And what," the dragon asked, "could you possibly offer me that I don't already have? My lair is filled with gold and jewels, the finest swords and spears, countless shields and armor. I have grown quite fond of hob and feel no need for exotic food or drink. I despise the human race. Most races, in fact, so I have no desire for company. I have everything I want and need already."

"Surely," Good Idea said, desperately, "there must be one thing that you still desire?" Her heart was beating so hard she could barely breathe, especially since she knew the company had really nothing of value to exchange.

"The only thing I miss," the dragon said sadly, "is the night sky. When I was much younger, I would fly from my lair and soar through the clouds. I would play among the stars and dance with the moon. Now, I am too old to fly, and my wings are too frail to lift me." The glinting eyes narrowed. "Can you give that back to me?" he asked. "Can you give me the night sky?"

Good Idea heaved a sigh, then felt a tug in her pocket. She slid her hand down, and Fleet placed something at her fingertips. She drew it out and held it aloft.

It was the tiny star-shaped pebble that Fleet had found. It caught the dim light in the Cave Of Abandonment and twinkled.

Scale Face drew in a breath of astonishment. "You have a star?"

Good Idea drew herself upright. "Yes, I do. And I might be willing to trade this rare object for my mother's notebook. What do you say?"

The dragon pulled his head back. Good Idea ventured out into the much larger passageway, and saw, for the first time, the entirety of the dragon. His body filled the tunnel, thick and black-scaled. His head was down, and one large talon came forward. Good Idea held out the pebble, and the claw gently took it from her. Scale Face bowed his head and backed away with surprising speed, turned a corner, and was gone.

"Well done," Mica cried, coming up behind Good Idea. "That was one fancy bit of trading, if I say so myself. Now, let's get back to the throne room. I know the Queen will want to hear all about this."

They followed Mica, Weathervane fanning herself with her hand in obvious relief.

"That was very handy," She said. "I've not known many folks who bargained with a dragon and lived to tell the tale."

"That was a GillyWind Dragon," Left Ear said. "You can tell by the yellow streak in the eye."

"But letting us go for a shiny pebble?" Bruise said. "Bit of a pushover, that one."

Good Idea, slipping the Notebook Of Whim deep into her pocket, just breathed a sigh of relief.

THEY RETURNED to the throne room without encountering the promised troll, for which Good Idea was extremely grateful. She asked Weathervane to ease her aches again, but that had not done anything for the grumbling in her belly. They waited, standing quietly, for what seemed to be a long time before the Queen once again entered and was lifted onto her throne.

The wizened dwarf looked them over with a satisfactory smile. "Not dead? How nice. Good job, Mica. You are dismissed. And go directly to the laundry: your robe is a disgrace."

Mica bowed and hurried off.

The Queen shifted her gaze to Good Idea. "You do not look well, Inspirational Wink."

"I am extremely tired and hungry, your Highness. I feel as though we've been walking forever," Good Idea said. "As eager as I am to return home, I could do with a bit of a rest." She cleared her throat and tried to keep the pleading out of her voice. "And perhaps something to eat."

The Queen sniffed. "In recognition of your bravery, or possibly just your extreme luck, I will allow you all to spend the night here with us. I can see spatters of hobs blood on you all, so I imagine a good hot bath and a long night's sleep is needed. And I'll have some food brought. We recently traded for a very plump goose that has been roasting all day. I would be glad to share with you." She snapped her fingers again, and another dwarf stepped forward.

"This is Clatter. She will escort you to your rooms and arrange for your meal. I must consult with Mica. I'm eager to hear of your encounters."

The dwarf bowed to the Queen, then motioned for them to follow.

The tunnel she led them through was quite different from that what lead past the forges and furnaces: softly lit hallways, quite low-ceilinged, and carpeted in brilliant green. She finally stopped in a comfortable-looking common room, with fire burning cheerily in the grate, and motioned to the series of doors around the walls.

"You may each choose a room," Clatter said. "Someone will be here shortly with hot water, and if you'd like, we will provide robes so that your clothing may be cleaned. We have an excellent laundry."

"I want a robe," Good Idea called as she headed for the nearest door and heard similar requests from Weathervane and Bruise.

Left Ear shifted into a woman, naked of course, and said, "I'll have a robe as well."

Clatter ducked her head and hurried off.

The room, obviously designed for a dwarf, had everything low to the floor, but the bed looked soft, there was an inviting chair in the corner with a small table and lighted lamp, and a deep, copper tub by the lit fireplace. Good Idea thought it was the most inviting place she'd ever seen, especially since another dwarf arrived carrying buckets of steaming water as soon as she eased her boots off, followed by another dwarf carrying a quilted robe.

She slipped off her clothes, pushing the notebook and the contents of her pockets deep inside her pack, and stepped into the tub, sinking into the water and feeling the days of grit and ache soak away. She unbraided her long hair and washed it with scented soap and dried herself with a plush towel, slipping on the robe just as the door opened again and a dwarf poked its head in.

"Your meal is in the common room, unless you'd like it brought here?"

Good Idea, trying to untangle her hair, shook her head. "No, I'll be out shortly. Thank you." The robe was rather too short for her but a perfect fit, she reasoned, for a dwarf. It was soft and warm and covered all the necessary bits just fine. She beckoned to Fleet, who climbed into the side pocket, then slipped into the common room to find her companions already sitting around a small table, silently eating what looked to Good Idea a feast.

Bruise motioned to the food on his plate. "Best meal yet," he said.

Left Ear nodded in agreement. "These dwarves know a thing or two about cooking." She grinned. "Much more than I."

Weathervane shook her head. "Dwarves know nothing at all about cooking. I would guess this meal is the work of hobs. Before they were tiny terrors, they were quite useful for domestic things. The dwarves probably have a few on staff that they pay enough to forget old grudges."

Good Idea wouldn't have cared if Scale Face himself had made the meal. It was delicious. When they were all comfortably full, Bruise began cracking Wiffer Nuts that had been sitting in a stone bowl in the middle of the table.

"Congratulations," Weathervane said, popping one of the pale orange nuts into her mouth. "You have found the Notebook Of Whim."

"Yes, I have," Good Idea said. "Can you answer a question for me?"

"If I can," Weathervane answered.

"How did my mother come to have the Notebook Of Whim?"

Weathervane tilted her head. "Did she never tell you how the notebook came into her hands?"

Good Idea shook her head. "No. Although she said it should *not* have come to her."

Weathervane smiled wistfully. "She worked for me in my shop, beginning when she was just a little girl. Very talented, she was. And one afternoon, while I was out gathering herbs in the outlying fields, a man came in. He was poor and wanted to sell a notebook that he obviously didn't know a thing about. Belladona bought it. Because the exchange was with consent, the notebook then became *hers*. But once she realized what it was, she tried to give it to me. I refused."

"Refused?" Good Idea looked at Weathervane in astonishment. "Why?"

"We both knew the notebook was rare and important. She was very young and didn't want the responsibility of caring for such an object. I didn't either. I was already ambitious about building my reputation and knew that having such an object of power might very well lead to terrible things. I wanted no part of it. When she couldn't get it to her mentor, Jones, I was worried she might misuse it. But she didn't. She did the next best thing. She hid it. She was careful and prudent to the end." She sniffed. "Maybe too careful. Have you had a chance to examine the notebook?" she asked.

Good Idea went back into her room and pulled out the notebook where she had put it in her pack. She went back into the common room and sat back down. Fleet ran up her arm and sat on the table, whistlers twitching. Good Idea pushed away her plate and laid the notebook on the table, then looked toward Weathervane. "Would you like to look at it?"

Weathervane shook her head. "Only the firstborn child can retrieve the notebook. I imagine if anyone else tried to open it, something dreadful might happen to them."

"Oh, my," Good Idea said. She opened to the center of the

book, and it lay there, the pages glowing faintly. "What would happen if I tried to *use* it? Would my hands burn up?"

Weathervane frowned. "I don't know. I'm sure the wizard Mionarach could answer that question, but I can only guess. I don't think anything would happen to you, because Belladona has tied the enchantment to you. But I don't imagine whatever you wrote on the page would come to be. Magical possession is a very strict affair. This belongs to Belladona and Belladona only, unless she dies or gives it away willingly. Only she can work its magic."

Good Idea put a finger in the center of an open page and felt a tingle.

"What would you wish for?" Bruise asked.

"That we all return to Whisper safely," Good Idea replied.

Weathervane cocked her head. "What a simple and logical thing to wish," she said.

Bruise chuckled. "That's Good Idea all over. Simple and logical."

Good Idea blushed. "Speaking of which, we have to get back to the real world. My ewes are probably already dropping lambs all over Wink's Wold."

Weathervane smiled. "Yes. We can probably go directly through to the dwarves' above-ground entrance. It's a mine, just outside of Mirror City. We'll get back to my shop and slip back through the crack in the Veil. Then you can retrieve your companions and begin your trip back to Belladona."

Good Idea closed the notebook and put it deep into the pocket of her robe and spoke carefully. "You know, Bunny may still have no memory, and will probably be of little or no help to us on the road home."

Weathervane shrugged. "You're probably right, but that paladin looks very capable."

"Yes, she is," Good Idea went on. "But Bunny seemed to think that we would need his assistance, which makes *me* think he was expecting some sort of magical interference. And without him to counteract that interference, well, we could be in trouble."

Weathervane glared at her. "I agreed to take you through the Veil and help you find the notebook. I had made a Witches Vow to aid in finding the notebook. It has been found and my obligation has been fulfilled, and I believe I have done so admirably. But I am not leaving Mirror City. My responsibility ends back at my shop. I have customers, I have made some very careful plans for the next few weeks and have things to attend to. As I said, I have a reputation to protect. I cannot go off into the wilds of the Realm. My place is here. I will not take you back to whatever that place you came from is called."

"Whisper," Good Idea said. "We have to get back to Whisper."

"Well," Weathervane said, "I'm sorry, but I can't help you."

Bruise said, "She has gold."

Good Idea's face burned. "Yes," she said faintly.

Weathervane pushed away from the table and stood, staring down at Good Idea with narrowed eyes. "I am not going with you," she said. "I don't care about your gold." She turned and went into one of the open doors along the back of the wall, slamming it shut.

"That went well," Bruise grumbled. Fleet appeared on the table, holding a stub of candle out for Good Idea's approval.

"Thank you, Fleet," she said, taking the bit of wax between her fingers.

"I'm sure that will help us," Left Ear snickered.

"So far, Fleet has gotten us out of four very sticky situations," Good Idea said coolly.

"I suppose," Left Ear said. "And I must admit, in speaking to him, he seems very knowledgeable." She cracked a smile. "For a mouse, I mean."

"For a *familiar*," Good Idea corrected her gently. "And I think I need to get some sleep. I hope breakfast in the morning is as excellent as this dinner was. I have a feeling we won't be eating so well on the journey back to Whisper."

She left the table, went into her room, stepped out of the robe and crawled under the soft blankets, naked, and was soon asleep.

CHAPTER 12

*S*he awoke to the smell of roasted apples. Her clothes were neatly folded at the foot of her bed, and they were not only clean, but all the rips and holes had been carefully mended. She dressed quickly, looked around for Fleet, and called to him. He climbed into her pocket, but not before motioning to the small table that stood beside the chair. He had been very busy during the night. On the table was a coil of copper wire, a tiny silver thimble, an arrowhead made of a shiny, black stone, and what looked to be a fang from a very large snake.

"Thank you, Fleet," she said, then went out to meet her companions.

They were half-way through a most excellent breakfast when the Queen arrived without her entourage and carrying a pouch of purple velvet.

She stood in the doorway until they noticed her, and all hastily stood. She waved them back into their seats.

"Mica has told me of your remarkable adventure down in my tunnels. Brilliant in every way. I am sure, Inspirational Wink, that you are going to be successful in returning the Notebook Of Whim to your mother. However, you are right in thinking that someone in your party should be adept at magic."

Weathervane scowled. "You were listening to our conversation?"

The Queen rolled her eyes. "Of course not. I have minions for that."

She sat in a chair, arranging her robes around her. "I have indeed heard of you, Weathervane, Wynd. You are quite respected as a healer. Your potions are famed throughout the Realm. I am aware of your shop, it's place in the community, and understand your reluctance to go with these adventurers to Whisper. But I had someone check up on this Bunny person you mentioned. Buadhachan Jones? Apparently, he still has gaps in his memory, so I doubt he will be of much use to you."

She fixed her eyes on Weathervane. "You have had a bit of difficulty trading with the elves in the south for certain ingredients you need for your potion-making."

Weathervane nodded. "Yes. They insist on payment in Cordril, which, as you know, is extremely difficult to mine and is therefore very expensive. Even if I could afford it, it's so rare as to be non-existent."

The Queen held out the pouch. "I have here seven quips of Cordril. From my personal collection. I feel it is of utmost importance that the notebook be returned to Belladona. I don't know what her plans for it are, but since she took such care to hide it, I'm sure she will take equal care once she gets it back." She shook the pouch, and Good Idea heard a faint clink. "This is yours if you agree to go with them."

Weathervane narrowed her eyes, looked down at the pouch, then at the Queen. "You have made a very generous offer."

The Queen nodded. "Yes. I know. As soon as you return to Mirror City, I will have these delivered to you."

Weathervane took a deep breath. "Seven quips of Cordril would last me several years."

The Queen smiled. "And you could manufacture potions that no one else can. Imagine what *that* would do for your reputation."

Weathervane stiffened. So did Good Idea, holding her breath.

Finally, Weathervane nodded. "Fine. I will go with them."

Good Idea let out the air in her lungs in a loud breath, and she heard Bruise chuckle. The Queen looked at Good Idea and inclined her head. "I wish you speed and luck on your journey home," she said, standing and shaking out her robes. "Mica is coming. He will take you to the entrance to our mine. It is above-ground, and within a short walk to Mirror City." She nodded her head and swept out of the chamber.

Weathervane squared her shoulders. "Well, let's get going then. The sooner we set out, the sooner I can get back."

"Thank you," Good Idea said.

Weathervane gave her a cold look. "Seven quips of Cordril means a great deal to me. It's worth putting a few of my plans on hold."

And so, they left the common room with their packs and went down a long hallway, where they met Mica. He led them to a small antechamber, then upstairs for what seemed, to Good Idea, an entire day. At the top of the stairs was a landing with no doors or windows.

Mica placed his palm on the wall, and it slid open smoothly, showing a rough tunnel that ended with a point of bright sunlight.

"Follow the road to the fork, and head toward the City," Mica said. "You should be there in less than an hour."

Good Idea squinted ahead. She was learning that rarely was something as easy as it seemed, and nothing turned out as expected. "Left Ear, can you take a look out there?"

Left Ear shifted into a crow and sailed out, returning almost immediately. "There is a band of demons camped right outside the mine," she said. "They are wearing the livery of the Prince of Mirror City, which is rather odd for demons."

Weathervane spoke up. "The Prince has demons at his command, and since his regular troops would be ineffective through the Veil, it makes sense he would send them to intercept you."

Mica sighed. "Well, that's not good."

"Surely, there are other ways out?" Good Idea asked.

"Yes," said Mica. "There's another tunnel entrance that will let you out where the River Brown meets the sea."

"It will take us days to get there," Weathervane said. "And days again to get back to Mirror City."

"And we don't have days," Good Idea said. "This adventure has already taken much longer than I thought. I want to get back home. Are there any other ways to get to the surface from the tunnels?"

Mica nodded. "Of course. But we would never take you. They are sacred ways."

"Ah," Good Idea said. "Then can we get out the same way we came in?"

"No one ever has," Mica told her.

"That may be. But no one ever bargained with a dragon before, either."

Mica chuckled. "True. I will take you back to the spire lift."

They turned. Climbing down the stairs was easier than climbing up, but by the time they were back down and passing the familiar common room, Good Idea was once again hungry and starting to get tired.

"Can we spend another night, do you think?" she asked, turning into the common room they had just occupied.

Mica pursed his lips. "I doubt it, but I'll give it a try."

She sank into one of the chairs by the fire and looked at Weathervane. "How hard is it to find other cracks in the Veil for us to go through?"

Weathervane stretched out her leg and waggled her foot. "Ask Fleet."

Left Ear shifted, Fleet emerged from Good Idea's pocket, and another animated conversation took place. Left Ear shook her little mouse head. "Fleet only knows the one, because Belladona showed him. There may be others, but he can only know if he is close enough to sense them."

She shifted back and Good Idea leaned her head against the cushion behind her.

"Maybe the dwarves know of one," she mused. "Although going back would not be a hardship. We've already made peace with the Pidge Folk, and we know the way from the rooftops in Weir Town."

"But how do we get the spire lift to go up?" Bruise asked.

"The same way we got it to go down, I imagine," Good Idea said, now starting to feel very sleepy as well as hungry.

Mica stuck his head in the room. "No, you can't stay. The Queen is in a rather foul mood, after hearing of the Prince's demons literally on our doorstep. I imagine she will send a strongly worded letter. Follow me."

They did, down more corridors and through the narrow doors and back out to where the furnaces blazed, and the iron was shaped with pounding hammers. They followed until they recognized the long curving tunnel that led to the lift.

Mica bowed at the waist. "Again, best of luck to you."

They were back in the familiar spire room. Good Idea fished the green stone out of her pocket and Left Ear took it up to his perch while Fleet climbed the smooth wall. Once again, Left Ear flew over, dropped the stone, and once again, Fleet caught it. Left Ear went back to her perch and, sure enough, the room began to rise, much slower than it had dropped, but it eventually jolted to a stop and the door to the rooftops opened.

· · ·

THE ROOFTOPS LOOKED the same but were eerily quiet. They began their way back slowly, as it was growing dark. Good Idea was not exactly sure where she was going, and once again followed Weathervane, her head down to watch her feet on the different surfaces of the many roofs they crossed. Suddenly, Weathervane stopped.

"What?" Good Idea asked, looking up.

Bruise cursed softly under his breath. They were standing adjacent to the flat roof next to the Pints And Bread Tavern. It was littered with the bodies of the Pidge Folk. In the pale moonlight, Good Idea saw the twisted necks and broken feathers ruffling in the wind. And where the window to the tavern's attic should have been, there was a gaping hole and wisps of smoke.

"Oh, no," whispered Good Idea. "Who could have done this?"

"Someone looking for you," Weathervane said shortly. "Someone who followed us here and wanted to make sure we couldn't make it back through the Veil, which means my shop is probably burned to the ground as well." Her voice was cold, without regret, but brimming with anger.

Bruise looked down into the darkness that had once been the Pints And Bread Tavern. "I can probably climb down and look for a ladder or something," he offered.

Good Idea looked around, trying to keep her eyes off the bodies of the Pidge Folk. "Maybe there's another window we can climb into? And get out that way?"

Left Ear ruffled her feathers. "Don't you think every single Weir around here has been warned off you? No one is going to open any window or door. And if they did, it would be after they notified whoever is responsible. Or maybe there's someone posted right outside their doorway, waiting to grab us as soon as we walk out. Or —"

"Enough," Bruise grumbled.

Good Idea looked around. "Some rooftops back there were

lower than this. If we find one that's only, say, one story, we may get down without breaking anything."

"I can't make us fly, but I can cast a Pillow Spell," Weathervane said. "To soften the fall. That might help."

In the darkness they turned and worked their way back until they found a steeply sloping roof that seemed to be significantly lower than the others. Peering down to the street below, there was only a smokey blackness.

"How far down, I wonder?" Good Idea asked.

Left Ear flew down, then returned. "The house is only one-story and seems to be empty. We can slide down to the edge, hold on, then drop down without too much damage."

Weathervane pointed her staff into the darkness, and a faint glow lit up the cobbled street below. Bruise went first, sliding down, then hanging on by thick fingertips until he dropped. He landed on his feet, looked around, then up at the rest of them.

"Not bad at all, and there's nobody around," he called to them softly.

Good Idea went next, and as she hit the ground, there was a softness beneath her feet as she landed. Weathervane jumped last, landing like a dancer on one elegant foot. She looked around, then started down the narrow street. They followed.

If Weir Town had looked grim when they came through before, it looked even worse in the faint moonlight. No lights shone from any window. There were piles of smoking rubble as they made their way back toward Willow Way, and the only sign of life was a rat that slithered into an alleyway in front of them.

Weathervane put a hand up. Left Ear shifted into her hulking wolf-shape.

Bruise reached for Axe and snarled at Good Idea. "Jump up on my back and hold tight."

The rats that came out of the alley were at least as large as sheep, with very sharp teeth and three eyes on each side of their heads. Good Idea did as she was told and jumped up and clung to Bruise's back, her fingers clenching the straps of his pack, her long legs wrapped around his waist. Bruise swung Axe, and the rats scattered. Left Ear snarled and ran down the alley where they were still emerging, a stream of gray against the dark cobblestones.

Weathervane began sending small bolts of fire, just large enough to set the short, bristly fur of the rats on fire, and sending them twisting and turning, emitting high shrieks that pierced the silent night. The flaming bodies raced away from them, glowing until they disappeared in a puff of smoke.

Good Idea lifted her forehead from against the back of Bruise's bald head and looked at the bodies of the bleeding and dead rats all around her. More death. What had happened to the Pidge Folk had shaken her, and now more creatures were dying in her path. The cost of the Notebook of Whim came higher than she had imagined, and her heart was sick.

Left Ear loped back to them from the alleyway. "They're done," she said with some satisfaction.

"Here too," Bruise said.

Good Idea loosened her grip and let her legs drop to the ground. She knew it was a mistake, but curiosity overcame her. "What *were* they?"

"Zomp Rats," Left Ear answered. "Rarely find them roaming the streets, though. Like the sewers, Zomp Rats." She grinned a wolfish grin. "So, they don't make for very good eating."

Good Idea choked. "No, I don't suppose they do. Shouldn't they be underground then?"

They were walking again, skirting the charred bodies that Weathervane had set afire. "There are some from the Piney Ridge Mountains that live above ground. Never seen them this far south, though. And I never heard of them doing the bidding of another," Bruise said, worry in his voice. "I can't imagine what kind of power someone has to have to bend the will of creatures like that."

"Maybe a hedge witch?" Left Ear offered. She looked at Weathervane. "Any ideas?"

She was walking quickly, looking from side to side, her lit staff held high. After that commotion, secrecy was lost, and she was moving as fast as she could. "If I was to name one, I'd say Contentious Greenway. She often claimed she could control all manner of beasts."

"And she would be interested in the NoteBook Of Whim?" Good Idea asked.

Weathervane turned and Good Idea recognized Willow Way. At the end of the street, she could see the faint outline of ships docked along the River Brown. They hurried to the end and were back on the well-lit street that ran along the river.

Weathervane stopped and looked around. The eerie stillness of Weir Town was not apparent here. Lights shone from a few homes, and the taverns seemed noisy and crowded. There were even folks on the street, talking and laughing.

Weathervane sighed and looked at Good Idea. "*Everyone* is interested in the Notebook Of Whim," she said, and led them away from Willow Way.

WEATHERVANE'S SHOP WAS NOT, as she feared, burned to the ground. But Pink was no longer tied outside, and there was no shadow of Regret.

"How long have we been away?" Good Idea asked.

"Three weeks," Weathervane said.

Three weeks? She had reckoned on being away from home for less than two weeks. But three weeks? And they hadn't even begun their journey back to Whisper? Her heart sank. "I thought I would be home by now," she moaned. "This is terrible. My ewes!"

"Time is very different through the Veil," Weathervane explained. "And you have more serious things than ewes to worry about."

They made their way through the shop and through various passages and stairways until Fleet once again slipped through a sliver in the wall. Immediately, Good Idea felt different, and knew she was in a very different place. The air was damp and close, the air chill, and all the aches that Weathervane had been keeping at bay returned with a vengeance.

The dead creatures they had left behind had vanished. When questioned, Weathervane shrugged. "There are all kinds of things living in these tunnels, and many of them will eat anything they can find."

Good Idea winced as she began to climb the stairs and was so grateful to reach the door to the shop, she almost wept.

Weathervane looked at her. "Can you stand another flight of stairs? You can rest here tonight, rather than try to find your way in the dark."

Good Idea nodded. After all, at this point, what was one more night away from home? She went up another flight, and was surprised to find herself in a long, narrow room, just over the shop, which was warm and cozy, with a fire in the hearth, soft rugs underfoot, and a white cat curled up on one of the very comfortable-looking chairs.

"Sit," Weathervane said. "I'll get us some supper." She looked directly at Good Idea. "I know it's been a while since our last."

"Didn't expect this," Bruise muttered. He reached back into his pack and drew out a bundle of clothes. "Here," he said to Left Ear, who quickly shifted and even more quickly dressed.

Weathervane appeared with a tray laden with a teapot and several mugs, a stack of bowls, and a pot filled to the rim with something hot and smelling delicious. They sat around the small table by the fire and ate and drank, not talking about what they had seen or where they had been.

"This was wonderful," Good Idea said at last. "Almost as though you were expecting us to arrive this very night."

Weathervane looked pleased with herself. "My kitchen is always expecting company," she said. "As is my fireplace and the rooms to the back. Go off to sleep now, and in the morning, we'll try to find Pink and your paladin friend. I imagine they are together, along with this Bunny person of yours." Then she picked up her tray and bid them good night.

Good Idea fell asleep in a bed rather too short for her but nonetheless quite soft and did not think once about where her companions might be. But when she awoke in the morning, she felt a sudden dread.

"What if they left?" she asked Weathervane as they walked into the bright sunlight by the River Brown. "What if they thought we all perished and went home?"

"They were possibly kidnapped by the Prince, who seems to have taken quite an interest in our quest,," Left Ear said. "Or perhaps Contentious Greenway has them held in some dreadful dungeon. Or there's always a chance —"

"Enough," said Good Idea, Weathervane and Bruise, at the same time.

"The damage at Weir Town didn't seem new, and those poor Pidge Folk, well, obviously that happened to them days ago," Good Idea mused. "So, in the real world, the attack may have happened two weeks ago, right?"

Weathervane shrugged. "Possibly."

"Could Regret somehow have been taken?" Good Idea asked, "and given information to the Prince?"

Bruise made a noise. "That would explain why the Prince sent demons to grab us as we left the Dwarf Caves. But what about whoever sent the Zomp Rats? This hedge witch? How would she have known anything?"

Weathervane nodded. "We don't know who else is looking

for us. We can't trust anyone, and we certainly can't go anywhere they'd suspect. Where did you stash Bunny?"

"The Rider Man Inn," Good Idea told her.

"Then we can't go there," Weathervane said. "Come with me." She led them out of the shop and down Seller's Street, along the River Brown.

"How do we get him back?" Good Idea asked. "He needs to come with us. Perhaps in these few weeks he's gotten some of his memory back, but he must return with us to Whisper."

"Why?" asked Weathervane. "You have to give the notebook to Mionarach, right? Does it matter if Bunny comes with you or not?"

"I would think," Good Idea said, "that Mionarach would be rather upset if we left his nephew in the hands of an enemy. And I wouldn't want a wizard angry with me, no matter how old and frail he might be."

Bruise nodded. "Good point."

Left Ear grunted. "I'll scope out the situation. Where will you all be?"

Weathervane turned down a narrow alley and stopped in front of what appeared to be a former cheese shop, now shuttered closed. "Here," she said.

Left Ear shifted, shrinking down to a black rat, and scurried off. Weathervane passed her hand over the latch on the door, and the door creaked open. She pushed, and they went inside.

The interior of the shop was very dusty and smelled fairly terrible. Cheese, left on its own for too long, either ripens beautifully or rots away. Behind the filthy glass display cases was a lot of rotten cheese.

"This won't do," the witch said, waving a hand. The room was suddenly filled with a light floral scent. "That's better," she said. "This belonged to one of my husbands. No one really notices it. I made sure of it. I doubt anyone will look for us here.

There are a few rooms in the back where we can hunker down until we decide what to do next."

Good Idea waved a particularly persistent dust mote from her face. "We know where we left Bunny, but I have no idea how to look for Regret and Pink."

Bruise looked up from gazing at the rotten cheese. "If Regret had a lick of sense, which I believe she does, Pink is no longer pink and they're in the smallest, dirtiest inn around."

"Good," Weathervane said. "As soon as Left Ear returns, I'll be happy to take you to the smallest and dirtiest inn I know. And if they're not there, I know at least three more inns that run a close second."

She went behind the counter through an open doorway, beckoning Good Idea and Bruise to follow. The room was large, but with no windows. Weathervane lit her staff, and they all sat down around a small table on sturdy but very dusty chairs.

Weathervane adjusted her skirts, once again plain black. And they sat in silence. Bruise sat back. Closed his eyes, and after a few moments, began to snore.

Good Idea took a long breath and thought back over the past few days. The Pidge Folk and the dwarves, the hobs and the dragon. She hadn't had much of an opportunity to enjoy her adventure very much. She'd been too anxious and afraid. And she felt, very strongly, that she was not going to have all that much fun on the return to Whisper either, making her think that adventure was not at all something she would care to try again. All she wanted to do was get back home and start worrying about more familiar things, like sheep and corn, cows in the pasture and sweet rolls in the afternoon.

There was a noise in the front room, and Bruise woke and reached for Axe, but a black rat ran into the room and hopped on the table.

"That was quick," Good Idea said, impressed.

Left Ear grinned slyly. "You'd be surprised how fast people

get out of your way when you're a rat. Bunny is still where we left him, and the Rider Man Inn is surrounded by men in the Prince's livery, at least a dozen other men in black, and I sensed at least five other shapeshifters," Left Ear said. "There's barely an empty chair in the place. I found Plaid and scared the yaksun out of him. He said they all arrived about two weeks ago and are showing no signs of leaving. Bunny remembers his name, his mother's name, and about a half-dozen spells for turning objects into fruit."

"Oh, my," Good Idea sighed. "Then I think we should try to find Regret and Pink. If we are going to get Bunny out of there, we're going to need all the help we can get." A thought struck her. "What about Tuesday?"

"What's Tuesday?" Weathervane asked.

"Not what. Who," Good Idea explained. "One of our party, an elf, who was injured and in a Care Home."

Left Ear shook her head. "He wasn't with Bunny. Could be he found himself alone and went back to Whisper. Or maybe he was picked up by the Prince's guard for vagrancy and thrown in prison. Or —"

"Or Regret went and got him," Bruise finished.

Good Idea nodded. "Let's keep that thought. Everyone ready? I'm starving. I hope at least one of the smallest and dirtiest inns in Mirror City has good bread and soup." She stood, dusted the dirt off the back of her pants, and went out.

Bruise looked at Weathervane, then Left Ear. "Bit of an optimist, that one," he said.

Weathervane rolled her eyes and followed Good Idea out the door.

CHAPTER 13

The first of the smallest and dirtiest inns was called the Inn Of Little Comfort. It was farther down the dock, right on the River Brown. Left Ear, still a rat, went to see if Pink was stabled in the sagging barn behind the main building. Weathervane led the way and as they entered, the low rumble of conversation stopped. The man behind the bar narrowed his eyes and slowly bought a large axe from beneath the bar and set it on his shoulder. '

"Hey you," he snarled. "We don't serve the likes of you."

Weathervane drew herself up. "Are you referring to our companion, because he is an orc, myself and friend here because we are women, or do you mean *all* of us, because we are clean?"

The barman threw his head back and laughed loudly, and the once-surly customers joined in. The barman put the axe on top of the bar and leaned on it, pointing one finger at Weathervane.

"Weathervane Wynd now, isn't it?"

Weathervane dimpled prettily. "You've heard of me then?"

"Course I have. Everyone here knows the most beautiful witch on the riverfront."

Weathervane shot Good Idea a look that said, See?

"I love me a woman with a bit o'sass," the barman continued. "And to come in here and say somethin' like that, well, that takes *balls*."

The laughter grew and Weathervane joined in. "Is it possible there's soup and bread?" she asked.

The barman shook his head. "No, sorry. We send folk who want grub 'cross the street to the Small Pleasures Inn."

Good Idea sighed and almost heard her stomach grumble above the fading laughter. A small sparrow flew onto Good Idea's shoulder.

"Pink's not there," was all she heard before the bird flew out again.

"Then we'll try there," Good Idea said. "Thank you for the information."

As they crossed the street, Left Ear again flew to the stable at the back of the yard, and they entered another dark, slightly cleaner establishment where no one challenged them as they crossed the threshold.

Good Idea made for an empty table and sat. Weathervane followed her, frowning.

"What if they're not here?" she hissed, taking a chair across from Good Idea.

"I don't care. I need to eat something," Good Idea told her, then waved a hand at a stout woman weaving among the tables, holding a tray of empty mugs.

"Whatcha need?" the stout woman asked.

"Soup and bread," Good Idea said. "And ale." She circled her finger to indicate Weathervane and Bruise. "For all of us, please."

Left Ear flew in and perched on Good Idea's shoulder. "Pink is here, but she's not pink anymore. She's been dyed a dull black and I can tell you, she's not happy." She cackled. "She gave me an earful. I'd translate, but I don't think you want to hear."

Good Idea sat up and looked around at the people crowding

the tables. "Then they're probably here. We can just wait for them to come down from their rooms, or in from the street," she said.

"That could take hours," Bruise grumbled.

"Why, do you have someplace else to be?" asked Weathervane archly.

Bruise glared but said nothing.

The food arrived and Good Idea was relieved to find it hot and filling, if not exactly tasty. She drank her ale, then ordered another and sat back to watch the people coming in and out of the front door, many obvious regulars, as they all treated the barkeep with a loud "Hey there, Barty." Barty obviously knew his customers well, as did the stout woman, Magpie.

Left Ear and Bruise were discussing werewolves, which Good Idea had never really believed existed, with Weathervane adding a bit of magical insight. After Good Idea's third ale, when she was feeling rather sleepy and a bit stupid, she saw a couple come through the inn doors, a tall man with cropped white hair and a woman, covered neck to foot in a dull green cape, straw-like black hair falling across her face. The man lifted and hand and called to Barty, who called back.

"You and the misses staying for a pint?" Barty asked.

"Why, that would be lovely," the man answered in a rather high-pitched voice that Good Idea thought was somehow familiar. The man started off to one corner of the room, but his wife grabbed him by the arm and dragged him toward Good Idea's table.

"Cousin," the woman said in a raspy voice. "We've been waiting for you."

Good Idea stared, blinked, and stared again.

It was Regret, her red hair dyed, her clear skin roughened with soot, and at least three teeth blacked out.

"Ah, yes," Good Idea managed, completely shocked by the paladin's appearance. "Cousin…"

Regret dragged a chair from an empty nearby table over and pushed the man into it. The man pushed back the white hair falling across his face and grinned.

"It's me," Tuesday hissed. "In disguise."

"No kidding," croaked Left Ear, and Good Idea felt a giggle in the back of her throat.

Regret found another chair, sat next to the elf, elbowing him roughly. "And how was your journey from Midden?" the paladin asked loudly.

Weathervane leaned over to whisper in Good Idea's ear. "Do you *know* these people?"

Good Idea tamped down her smile and nodded. "The journey was longer than expected," she said to Regret. "I'm glad you waited for us." She turned to Weathervane and dropped her voice. "This is Regret, the paladin who was with me. And this is the final member of our party, Tuesday Fix. Er, he's an elf."

Weathervane raised an eyebrow. "I would never guess," she murmured. She leaned toward Tuesday. "You look hideous."

Tuesday blinked. "Really? I'm in disguise, to be sure, but hideous?" He pulled out a short knife and angled it, trying to see his reflection in the blade.

Magpie set down two more mugs of ale and turned away. Regret looked quickly over her shoulder and dropped her voice. "Do you have a safe place to stay? There are at least six different factions looking for you. Things are very dangerous at present."

"Can you lead them to Weathervane's cheese shop?" Good Idea asked Left Ear softly. "Do you remember how to get there?"

Left Ear ruffled her feathers. "Of course."

"Then wait a few minutes after we leave," Good Idea instructed. "We have much to discuss."

Bruise managed a huge yawn and stretched his arms wide. "Well, dearest," he practically yelled, "now that your cousin has found us, let's retire. We can meet them again in the morning."

Weathervane rolled her eyes, and Left Ear cackled.

Regret stood, smiling down at Good Idea. "Excellent idea. We'll see you in the morning, Cousin." She stood and looked down expectantly at Tuesday, who was still trying to see his reflection.

"Come, husband," she said loudly.

Tuesday looked up, and Good Idea noticed tears in his eyes. "Hideous?" he whispered.

Regret grabbed him by the scruff of the neck and pulled him to his feet, pushing him up the stairs, Left Ear perched on her shoulder.

Good Idea and Bruise followed Weathervane back out to the docks and hurried along the dark and now deserted street.

"At least with the streets so empty we can see if we're being followed," Good Idea muttered.

Bruise snorted. "You think you've got the only shapeshifter in Mirror City?"

"Oh. Right," Good Idea said, sighing.

Weathervane took them through the twisted narrow streets, doubled back several times and when the cheese shop was finally in sight, Good Idea had no idea how they had gotten there. Weathervane passed a hand across the door and it creaked open. She took a step in and paused, sniffing. Then motioned them inside. They made their way to the back room where Good Idea sank into a chair, drained.

"I'm too old to be skulking around this late at night," she groused. Her vision was blurred and her back hurt. She motioned to Weathervane. "Can you do that thing where I don't feel old anymore?"

"Not now," the witch answered. "I don't want too much magic in the air. We can't know if whoever is after you knows I'm with you. We can't risk it."

Good Idea pulled off her boot and rubbed the blister that had formed on her smallest toe. Fleet slipped out of her pocket and vanished into a dark corner. Bruise shut his eyes, put his head back, and almost immediately began to snore. Weather-vane sat, drawing circles with the toe of her boot in the thick dust on the floor.

Good Idea sighed. They were almost to the end, she thought. All they had to do was leave Mirror City and find their way home. Just four more days. Of course, the upcoming four days had been predicted to be the most perilous. She considered what she'd gone through already. This was not, she thought (again) what she had expected of her adventure. But at least she'd have plenty to tell her mother.

REGRET HAD BEEN VERY busy while Good Idea was off recov-ering the Notebook Of Whim. Tuesday Fix, looking and sounding rather subdued, had also been very busy — apparently by default — by following Regret all over Mirror City.

"I was quite alarmed when night was closing in and you had not returned to the shop," Regret said. She pushed off the hood of her cloak and Good Idea could see where the bright red of the paladin's natural hair was trying to peek through the dull black dye. "Then I remembered that I had once heard that time moved differently in the Veil, so I sought a place to stay for the night. That's when I noticed I was being followed." She shook her head. "I should have been more careful. Anyway, I tethered the horses and slipped down an alley. I was followed, of course, by not one but two men, one in all black, the other in the Prince's livery. Since I knew who had sent the liveried man, there was no reason to question him. So, I rendered him uncon-scious and took to questioning the man in black."

Good Idea widened her eyes. "You did this alone?"

Regret smiled grimly. "I am quite used to doing things alone."

"When she told me," Tuesday said, "I was astounded. Taking on those thugs single-handedly. Wasn't that just marvelous?"

Regret rolled her eyes. "There were just two of them."

"*Just* two?" The elf's eyes widened. "You don't say *just* a troll. Or *just* a Chomp Snake."

Regret cleared her throat. "Anyway, the man in black was hired by someone called Three Fingers."

Weathervane drew in a sharp breath. "Three Fingers is a very dangerous man. He is responsible for most of the smuggling and petty crime in Mirror City."

"I *knew* it!" Tuesday exclaimed. "With a name like Three Fingers, I had him figured as a true villain."

"Or maybe," Regret said gently, looking at Tuesday with a smile, "a careless pickpocket."

Tuesday rolled his eyes and shrugged.

Regret went on. "His thug wasn't very helpful, but he said that there were several other interested parties with an eye out for us. We were marked when we went through the city gates. So, I knocked him out as well."

Tuesday sighed. "She knocked him out. Can you imagine?"

"She's a paladin," Left Ear said. "I can imagine her slicing him up into little pieces with one arm behind her back."

"I spent the night on the docks," Regret went on, "stealing a few things that I needed, and in the morning, my appearance was quite different. I also managed to hide the fact that I was traveling with a pink horse."

"*So* resourceful," Tuesday said.

Regret glanced at him, shook her head, then continued. "The Prince's men are everywhere. Bunny was already under watch. Luckily, no one came looking for Tuesday here, so I could smuggle him out of the Care Home and into the Small Pleasures Inn, where we have been staying under the guise of man and wife." Regret's tone was carefully neutral, but Good Idea sensed something under the words that she didn't quite understand: a warmth, and a hint of humor.

"I was terribly weak," Tuesday said, "and of not much use. I spent a few more days in bed, trying to get my strength back, under the care of this most diligent angel."

Bruise snorted softly. "Bit of a stretch there, no?"

Tuesday shook his head. "No. For such a fierce fighter, she has the most delicate touch."

Regret exhaled loudly and buried her face in one hand. "Honestly, Tuesday," she said, exasperated. She looked at the faces around her. "I changed his bandage once and gave him water."

His face turned dreamy. "Best water I'd ever had in my life. When my strength and vigor returned, I asked to accompany Regret on her forays out into Mirror City." He paused, gazing at the paladin. "And she allowed me to accompany her."

"And what else was I to do?" she asked. "Tie you to the bedpost?"

Tuesday leaned in. "Folks around here don't think much of women, and I acted like a total fool, so we could sit around all sorts of places where people — and things — were talking." He smiled. "I've been in places I never would have had the nerve to enter if I'd been on my own. We even had ale with one of the Prince's demons."

Regret glanced at Tuesday, and a faint smile played on her lips. "That *was* quite an evening."

Tuesday looked around. "We were at the At Your Risk Tavern. Very disreputable."

"I would hardly expect demons to hang out in a more family-friendly sort of place," Left Ear said.

"The ale," Tuesday said with a shudder, "was swill."

"And yet," Regret said, looking at him with something of a twinkle in her eye, "you managed to drink three of them under the table."

"I felt it was my duty," the elf said. "We needed the information."

"And we got it," Regret said. "The Prince is your number one problem here in Mirror City. His troop of demons was sent to ransack Weir Town. They burned a few places and are responsible for the killing of the Pidge Folk. He knew you'd headed for the Dwarf Caves, but didn't dare follow you in, so I believe he set a trap at the main Dwarf Cave entrance."

Weathervane nodded. "Yes, he did. We saw them. The Dwarves are very powerful, and the Prince is very careful not to move against them. The Dwarf Kingdom has several allies that could easily bring down the Prince and his entire army of thugs."

Regret sighed. "That makes sense. There is a very tenuous peace between the Prince and the other forces trying to get the notebook. There are, of course, a handful of humans, especially Three Finger, who might also try to take the notebook from you. The real threat, though, is the Prince. This is his territory, and that is respected."

She took a breath. "But once we leave Mirror City, all bets are off. There are at least three hedge witches, a demon named Mftine, another just called the Green Guy, and a troll syndicate from the Bellorite Caves. The watchers are all camped just outside the city, waiting for you to leave. One of the hedge witches created the storm we went through. The Green Guy sent the Bug Bears."

With a sinking heart, all of Good Idea's hopes for an uneventful trip back to Whisper drifted away. Hadn't gryphons and Bug Bears been enough? Not to mention Cave Cats, hobs, and a real dragon?

Left Ear, who had led Regret and Tuesday through the darkened street as a black cat and was happily getting scratched right behind the ears by Good Idea, stopped purring and said, "This is sounding pretty bleak. Trolls from Bellorite Caves are known for being stupid but terrific fighters. Hedge witches are vicious and shrewd, and don't even get me started on demons."

"Yes, please," muttered Weathervane. "Don't get her started."

Good Idea turned to Tuesday, carefully looking at him in the flickering candlelight. With his hair cut and dyed, and beautiful skin roughened with soot, he looked very different from the lighthearted elf that rode out of Whisper on a spirited black horse "I trust you have fully recovered from your injury?" she asked.

He nodded. "I can still feel a certain stiffness in my leg but have otherwise recovered. And thankfully, I proved to be of some use to our brilliant paladin here."

Regret rolled her eyes again but managed a wry smile. "To be honest, he was of some use."

Good Idea took a deep breath. "First, we must rescue Bunny."

Regret shook her head. "There is someone with him at all times. Two guards, actually. And there is an entire company camped in the main room of the Rider Man Inn, and more of the Prince's men in all the streets surrounding."

Good Idea frowned. "I'll think on it. There must be a way."

"Is he so important, then?" Regret asked.

Good Idea nodded. The paladin still did not know the entire story, and still had not asked, so Good Idea finally told her.

Regret listened without so much as a nod or grimace, lifted her shoulders, and sighed. "Thank you for telling me. I am glad I've earned your trust. But that all is nothing to me. All I'm concerned with is protecting you."

Good Idea was now too tired to even speak any more, to they went upstairs to a low-ceilinged space with plump mattresses on the floor.

"Sleep here," Weathervane said. "This place will be safe for us until the morning, at least."

Good Idea crawled thankfully under a thin, faded blanket just as Fleet scurried up, holding the wishbone of a very small bird.

"Thank you, Fleet," she mumbled, before closing her eyes to sleep.

THE NEXT MORNING, over hard bread and cheese, Good Idea related to Regret and Tuesday their adventures through the Veil. Tuesday's eyes grew wide in places, and Regret grew more and more thoughtful.

"I must admit," Regret said, "that I always assumed you were just a rather ordinary sort of person."

Good Idea's shoulders slumped. "I am."

Regret shook her head. "No. You're not. You killed a Cave Cat. You negotiated with the Pidge Folk. You figured out how to get down to the Dwarf Caves. You convinced the Queen of the Dwarves to help you. You defeated hobs. Outsmarted a dragon." She tilted her head. "I think you're not ordinary at all."

Good Idea sighed. "Well, I feel ordinary. And old. Too old to be sleeping on the floor of dusty places and not having hot tea with my breakfast. Too old to be worrying about the Prince of Mirror City on my trail, not to mention demons and hedge witches. I wish I had never left Whisper, and now I wish to get back there as quickly as possible and have this entire thing done with." She stood up and brushed breadcrumbs off her hands. "This enterprise was grossly misrepresented from the start. I thought I would be having a great adventure. I was expecting excitement to be sure, but not danger and exhaustion and hunger and total lack of rest. Most disappointing." She drew a breath. "But at last, we're almost at an end. The first thing we must do is get Bunny."

"Tuesday and I have spent a great deal of time at the Rider Man Inn," she said.

"Excellent lamb stew," Tuesday interjected. "Avoid the fish."

Regret shot him a look then continued. "We know every inch. I told you, there are two guards with him. Even if we overpower them and try to sneak the wizard out of a window or back door, he will be missed as soon as he doesn't appear in the common room at the usual time. Then the entire city will be looking for him."

Good Idea looked at Left Ear. "I've seen you shift into woman. Is that the only human form you can take?"

Left Ear, still a cat, stopped grooming her whiskers. "What other human form would I *want* to take?"

"A man. Bunny," Good Idea answered.

Left Ear stood and arched her back. "Of all the men whose shape I could take, I wouldn't have thought that *Bunny* would be the one you'd ask for." There was a teasing note in her voice, and Good Idea chuckled.

"I think you misunderstand what I want, exactly," Good Idea explained. "If you can shift into Bunny, then you can take his clothes and pretend to be him with the guards and everyone else. We can then sneak him out of the Rider Man Inn and to a safer place. Here, or maybe even outside of the city. Then you can shift back and meet us."

They all stared at her, jaws open.

Weathervane spoke first. "Well, that's brilliant."

Left Ear grinned a cat-grin. "I can do that."

"But the guards are always with him," Tuesday protested.

"Not in the privy I'll bet," Good Idea said.

Tuesday thought. "You're probably right."

Good Idea stood. "Okay then, let's head over to the Rider Man Inn and check out the situation." She brushed down the wrinkles in her trousers. "Left Ear, you need to see how everything looks outside of the City. Where our enemies might be hiding, where the traps may be. If getting back to Whisper is going to be more difficult, we must be extra careful."

Weathervane stood as well, then turned sharply toward the door. "Someone is here," she said softly.

Left Ear slunk off to hide behind an overturned barrel. Regret drew her hood back up over her head.

"Is there a back way out?" Regret whispered.

Weathervane nodded as a fist pounded on the door. "Weathervane Wynd," a hoarse voice shouted. "Are you there?"

Weathervane swore swiftly and hurried to the back of the shop, past decrepit furniture and shattered crates. She pointed to a narrow doorway. "Through there," she whispered.

Regret and Tuesday hurried off. Good Idea grabbed the witch's arm. "Are you coming?"

Weathervane shook her head. "No. They know someone is in here. I'll answer and try to throw them off your trail."

Good Idea went out, Bruise behind her.

They were in a narrow alley. Regret looked up. "Let's climb," she said. "They might know about the alley, but they probably won't be watching the rooftops."

There was a rusting ladder bolted to the brick building across from them, and she swung up and began climbing.

Tuesday paled. "I hate heights," he muttered, but followed.

Good Idea looked at Bruise. "I feel terrible leaving her," she said.

Bruise shook his head. "Don't worry about her. Worry about you."

Good Idea put her hands on the bottom rung of the ladder just as the narrow door behind her burst open. A man stood there, in bright purple livery, and put a long, glittering sword to Bruise's chest. Several men swarmed out after him, filling the alleyway. One of them, in the same bright uniform but wearing a larger, much more flamboyant hat with pink feathers, bowed before her.

"Inspirational Wink? I am Captain Beauregard Storm, in service to Toto, Prince of Mirror City. The Prince requests an audience. If you could just follow me?"

Good Idea glanced up. The rooftop was bare. Left Ear, her fur sleek and fading into the dark cobblestones, crept out.

"Where is Weathervane Wynd?" she asked the captain.

"She is in our company. She will not be harmed. Nor will you or your companion. We are here to escort you to Castle Splendid. The Prince would just like a word."

Good Idea drew herself up. "Is this how the Prince treats strangers in his city? Has them followed and hunted like beasts?"

The captain flashed a grin. "Not at all. We knew you were traveling with Weathervane Wynd and knew she owned an interest in this building. It was just natural for us to seek her — and you — here."

Good Idea sighed in relief. If they hadn't been followed, then maybe the Prince's men didn't know of Regret's and Tuesday's existence. Which meant the two of them were again free to travel the city in search of helpful information.

Like how to escape from the Prince's castle.

NEVER HAVING BEEN inside the castle of a Prince — or the castle of anyone else — Good Idea wasn't sure what to expect. So the large bright green snake, tightly coiled, its eyes covered by a black cloth and tethered by a golden chain to the throne, came as a real surprise.

"Croddack Basilisk," Bruise muttered as they approached. "Nasty little buggers. They have to cover the eyes. One look from a basilisk and you're dust."

"Do all princes have basilisks?" Good Idea wondered aloud.

Weathervane sighed. "No. Only ones who are so insecure they feel the need for window dressing."

The guard walking beside her, clothed in a brilliant green uniform with gold buttons and heavy braid, snorted. "Got that right," he said, just loud enough for them, but not the strutting captain, to hear.

For the rest, the throne room was wide with polished marble on every horizontal surface, large windows letting in bright light that reflected off the marble, and mirrors hung on all the available wall space, also reflecting the sunlight. The place was so bright, Good Idea had to squint.

The Prince only left them standing for about twenty minutes before hurrying in from a narrow side entrance, followed by six bearded men in long silver cloaks. The Prince patted the basilisk, who tightened its coil, then relaxed, and mounted the three steps and sat upon his throne. He arranged his elaborate golden robe, folded his hands on his lap, and looked at them expectantly.

One of the bearded men stepped forward. "His Royal Majesty, Toto, Prince of Mirror City, Protector Of The Western Realms and Master of Castle Splendid welcomes you. I believe one of you is Inspirational Wink?"

Good Idea stepped forward. "I am Inspirational Wink. What kind of welcome is it to be hunted down, chased through a deserted cheese store, and brought to the Prince at the point of a sword?"

Weathervane closed her eyes and Bruise grunted.

"Bit of a rough start, that," the orc mumbled.

The Prince leaned forward, eyeing Good Idea with curiosity. "How else was I to get you here?" he asked with genuine curiosity.

Good Idea shrugged. "A simple invitation? Maybe one of those pretty, engraved things that some folk use to announce a wedding? With a seal or something?"

The Prince tilted his head. "And had I issued such an invitation, would you have come to me?"

Good Idea shrugged again. "We'll never know now, will we?"

The six bearded men huddled together, whispering furiously, as the Prince slowly rose, walked back down the three steps, and stood in front of Good Idea.

His face was quite handsome, she thought, but his eyes were cold and flat. "You have something that I need," he said in a quiet voice.

"And what is that?" Good Idea asked.

"The Notebook Of Whim."

"I don't have it," Good Idea said stoutly.

The Prince was a tall man, but not quite as tall as Good Idea and had to glare up at her. "Where is it?"

Good Idea pointed to Bruise. "He has it."

The Prince turned his gaze to the orc. "Is this true?" he asked.

Good Idea held her breath.

"Yes," Bruise said.

Good Idea blew out in relief.

Weathervane jumped in. "Look at her. She's just an ordinary old woman who doesn't even know how to show respect to those who deserve it." She paused. "I am Weathervane Wynd. Perhaps you've heard of me?"

The Prince nodded briefly. "Indeed, I have."

Weathervane could not quite hide the smile of satisfaction as she continued. "Being someone quite experienced with magical objects, having surrounded myself with them most of my life, I took the notebook from her. I felt that, since she was so unaware of its importance, she might lose it somewhere from sheer thoughtlessness. But I was also afraid that someone might take it from *me*, so I entrusted its care to the orc."

"I would not," Good Idea said loudly, "have lost it."

The Prince moved in front of the witch. "What would you do with the notebook?" he asked.

"I don't know, but I certainly wouldn't give it to a bumbling old wizard who can no longer travel to retrieve it himself,"

Weathervane said. "Which is what *she* was planning to do with it."

He then moved to Bruise. "May I have it? Please?"

Bruise let out a long, grumbling sort of sigh, rummaged for a moment in his pack, and drew out a small book, bound in rich tan leather, with intricate gold embossing on the cover.

The Prince narrowed his eyes as he reached for the book. "No one may use it until the witch who first found it is dead," he said.

Weathervane nodded. "That is true. And I have no idea what would happen to a person who would *try* to use it. Magical objects are very odd, you know." She cleared her throat as the Prince's fingers touched the book. "I'd be afraid of opening it myself. Maybe nothing will happen. Or, if someone tries to open it, they could be turned into a pillar of fire." She shrugged. "I don't know what the enchantment is, but I've known of curses that condemn a person and their entire family to lifelong pain and suffering. Or one hundred years of bad luck and impotence. Why, I know of one magical book being opened and everyone in the room turned to stone."

The Prince paled and withdrew his hand. "Oh. I can see there might be danger here." He motioned to one of the bearded men. "Binder, come and take this. Put it somewhere safe."

The bearded man, whose face had gone white, approached Bruise slowly and took the book from his hand with two fingers. Then he backed away and ran from the throne room, holding the book in front of him as though it was on fire.

Good Idea, keeping straight face, turned on Weathervane. "You have betrayed us," she wailed. She turned to Bruise. "All of our trials have been in vain. Now the notebook will never be returned to my mother."

Bruise grunted sympathetically and tried to pat her on the back.

Weathervane sighed and folded her arms across her chest. "I

suppose you can just let her go now. She has failed. She may as well go home."

The Prince smiled at last. "No, I think not. Her...mother, is it? That woman in, what is the name of that place...Whisper? She must be killed. As soon as possible." He turned to one of the now five bearded men. "How long to get men to Whisper?'

They conferred in hushed tones until one said, "About four days."

The Prince clapped his hands. "Excellent." He turned and started toward the same door he'd come in through, speaking over his shoulder. "You all can rest in the dungeon until we know what's-her-name is dead." He stopped, turned, and bowed briefly to Good Idea. "I will be very sorry for your loss," he said, then left the room.

Part Four

In which Inspirational Wink and her valiant
companions make a daring escape,
engage in a rescue,
and finally return to Whisper.

Wink's Wold

CHAPTER 14

*G*ood Idea had never been in a dungeon, either.

"Well, this is certainly a day for firsts, isn't it?" Bruise said as he inspected the heavy iron bars before him.

Good Idea sighed.

"At least the notebook is safe," Weathervane said. "Quick thinking by the way."

Good Idea sighed again. "On all our parts," she said. "We are beginning to work together very well." She looked around the cell. There was plenty of straw on the floor, a pile of blankets in the corner, and it appeared to be quite dry. The same bars that had closed behind them were pounded into the rock of the walls.

"It's not terrible here," she said.

Weathervane glanced around and nodded in agreement. "No, it's not. Clean, dry, and apparently no mice."

Fleet, from the depths of Good Idea's pocket, chirped.

"Except for you, Fleet," Weathervane said.

Bruise slumped into one of the corners. The guards had not

taken anything from them, not weapons or packs, which indicated to Good Idea that whoever was in charge of the dungeon was so confident in its ability to keep them inside that their having any weapons would be a moot point.

"We need a plan," Bruise said, fluffing up the straw behind him. "In four days, they will kill Belladona. Four days after that, they will return to the Prince. He will then open the book and instead of ruling the world, he'll learn fifteen ways to kill a Whitmeer Goblin."

"Is *that* what the book was?" Weathervane asked.

Bruise grunted. "Very good book if you're interested in that sort of thing. But we need to be out of here by then."

"We need to be out of here now," Good Idea said. "This is a very busy time at the farm, and I have already been away too long. Besides, I do not want those men to kill my mother. Or even try. There are lots of people in Whisper sworn to protect her, and I wouldn't want any of them hurt."

"There is good news in all this, I suppose," Weathervane said slowly. "The Prince will undoubtedly announce that he has the NoteBook Of Whim. The man announces *everything* he does, no matter how insignificant. If we get out of here, no one will impede our journey back to Whisper."

"That is good news," Good Idea said. "So, all we have to do is find a way out."

"I would guess," Bruise said, settling back and stretching out his thick, tree-trunk like legs, "that no one has *ever* found a way out. They left me Axe. Obviously, they figured I'll never have a chance to use it. After all, twenty guards marched us down here, and all twenty of them are still lining the corridor. See them bars? Altrunic Iron. Can't cut it, burn it, or magic your way through it. And see the iron in the walls? Same thing. We're surrounded." He heaved a sigh. "We're stuck here," he said, then closed his eyes and began to snore.

There was the sound of heavy footfalls in the corridor, and six guards in green, all heavily armed and led by a short man in brilliant purple robes, appeared. The one wearing purple held out a tray laden with a large tureen, a stack of bowls, and a loaf of bread. It smelled delicious.

One guard slid open a wide but quite short opening at the bottom of the barred door, and the tray was slid into them. The opening was then drawn shut.

"Welcome to the Dungeon Of All Hope Lost," the guard in purple said. "I am Key Hold, the Head guard. You will be fed twice a day and given all the fresh water you ask for. Your chamber pots will be emptied morning and night. You cannot escape. There are one hundred guards here in the Dungeon, and only two ways out, through the East gate, or up through the palace. The East Gate is also where the Prince's troop of demons camp. And Castle Splendid above us has Grimby."

"Grimby?" Good Idea asked.

"Yes. The basilisk," Key Hold explained. "At midnight, when the castle guards go off duty, and everyone in the castle is safely locked away in their rooms, he is let off his chain to wander freely. Also, to feed on anything that may come up from the dungeon entrance. He is still blindfolded, but he has a keen sense of smell, and manages quite well. So, make yourselves comfortable. You'll be here until the Prince tells us to let you out." He nodded. "Good evening and sleep well."

He turned to go.

"Excuse me," Good Idea called. "May I ask a question?"

Key Hold turned and smiled politely. "Of course."

"Do you hold the keys to all the cells here?"

He shook his head, fished in his pocket, and drew out a single brass key on a long, thin chain. "Only one key. This unlocks all the doors. But stealing it will do no good. There are two hundred guards living down here, and half of them are always on the alert. No one has ever escaped from the Dungeon Of All Hope Lost." His smile broadened. "No one. Ever." He snapped his heels together, bowed, and walked off, his guards marching behind him.

"Well, that was discouraging," Weathervane said.

"Yes," said Bruise. "Bit of a soul-crusher, that one."

Good Idea lifted the lid of the tureen. "Chicken stew with dumplings," she said happily. "How lovely."

Bruise ladled stew into one of the bowls. "Well, I guess we'll get eight days' worth of good meals."

Good Idea was also scooping out her portion of stew. "Only one day of good food, so enjoy while you can. We need to get out of here tomorrow."

"And how are we going to do that?" Weathervane asked. "While I have been quite impressed with your ingenuity until now, I feel like we are at an impasse."

Good Idea blew on her stew to cool it. "I have to talk to Left Ear first."

"And you are sure she will find us?" Weathervane asked.

Good Idea nodded. "She will always find us," she said.

THE NEXT MORNING, Good Idea found Left Ear curled up in the straw next to her as a cat, purring loudly. She woke and scratched behind her ears.

"I like you very much as a cat," Good Idea said, although, in truth, she found she liked Left Ear as pretty much anything. "Where are Regret and Tuesday?" she asked.

"Back in the Small Pleasures Inn. They weren't followed. They're waiting for instructions," the cat said.

Weathervane pushed herself up and stretched. "Tell them that, when they claim my body, I want to be returned to Middling, the Home Place of my order."

Left Ear cocked her head. "That bad?"

"We have been told," Good Idea said, "that there is no escape from here." She told her what Key Hold had said. "Can you confirm all that?"

Left Ear grinned a cat-grin and slipped out between the bars. Fleet ran up to Good Idea's shoulder, carrying the dried shell of a dead beetle.

"Thank you, Fleet," Good Idea said, slipping it into her pocket.

Fleet's ears twitched, and he looked around.

Good Idea frowned. "Is there something I need to know?"

His ears twitched again.

"Left Ear will be back soon," she assured him, and the mouse disappeared into her pocket.

Bruise woke, rolled over and stood, stretched, and rubbed their stomach. "When's breakfast, do you think?" he asked.

Weathervane shot him a look. "How can you be hungry? We have seven days left to live."

Bruise made a face. "Maybe not. I trust Good Idea here. She's come through in tight spots before."

Good Idea smiled bravely but was not heartened by his words. This situation seemed rather dire.

They got a breakfast: toasted bread, soft butter, cold bacon and hot tea. Bruise ate with relish, Weathervane barely ate all. Good Idea munched the bacon and waited for Left Ear.

It took half of the day for the shifter to return, once again as a cat. She settled herself comfortably on Good Idea's lap.

"Well, there are, in fact, only two ways in or out of this dungeon, and the gate to the outside opens onto the edge of a large campground of what look to be the Prince's demons."

Bruise grunted. "How many?"

Left Ear rolled over on her back and let Good Idea scratch her belly. "At least a hundred, and from what I overheard, they're itching for a fight." She purred at Good Idea. "They say the Prince has the notebook."

Good Idea shook her head. "The Prince has *a* notebook, which is why we have to get out of here as soon as possible. He has sent men to kill my mother, and once that is done, he will open the notebook and be very disappointed. Then, he will probably search us, take the real notebook, and kill us all."

Left Ear brought up a paw to scratch her ear. "Well, the demons think that someone or something will try to steal the notebook from the Prince, and they will be called into duty. They are looking forward to that very much."

"If we managed to escape our cells," Good Idea asked, "could we get past them?"

Left Ear shook her head. "No. Absolutely not. Even if you could get past the dozens of guards filling the hallways down here, once you pass through the door to the outside, you would immediately get caught."

Good Idea sighed and felt Fleet running up her arm. "Left Ear, would you mind?" she asked. "I think Fleet has something to say."

Left Ear shifted quickly to a mouse and Fleet ran down to the stone floor to meet her. Their conversation was short.

"Fleet says he can sense another crack in the Veil," Left Ear told her.

Weathervane straightened. "That's promising."

Good Idea nodded. "Go with him. Find out where the crack is."

The two mice scurried off.

"We still have to figure out how to get out of this cage, through the corridor, and past all the guards," Bruise said.

Good Idea nodded. "Yes. I'm working on that."

When the two mice returned, Left Ear rubbed her two paws together in excitement. "The crack in the Veil is in the passageway between the guard's room and the outside door. We could slip through there. We would have to make our way up and back through the palace though, because the demons outside of the door would still be there through the Veil. But once outside the palace, we can get back to Weathervane's shop and re-enter our world as before."

Good Idea looked at Weathervane. "If we could get to the crack, would there be an advantage of going through the Veil?"

The witch thought. "Well, any human guards in the palace would not see us, so we could quickly get out and through the gates," she said. "But any magical creatures, such as the basilisk we were told roams freely, would find us all the same."

"Ah, yes. Grimby." Good Idea looked at Bruise. "Can you defeat the basilisk?" she asked.

Bruise scratched his chin. "Craddock basilisks are nasty little buggers," he said at last. "Never fought one single handedly before. What do you say, Left Ear?"

Good Idea closed her eyes, waiting to hear the litany of terrible things the Craddock basilisk could do to them, how long it would take them to be eaten, if they'd be pulled apart or burned alive. But...

Left Ear rubbed her paws together. "The easiest way is, of course, to get it to look at itself in the mirror. Then it would turn itself to dust."

Good Idea opened her eyes. She glanced at Weathervane, who had tilted her head and was looking at Left Ear with interest.

Bruise grunted. "We'd have to find a mirror first."

"The throne room had mirrors hung on every wall," Good Idea said.

"That's probably why he's kept blindfolded," Weathervane mused. "to keep him from seeing his reflection."

"So, all we have to do is get him to the throne room and take the blindfold off." Good Idea said. "Easy."

They stared at her.

"Do you know how fast a basilisk moves?" Bruise asked. "Even blind, old Grimby up there could strike us down before we even had a chance to run."

"Can you freeze it, like you did the Cave Cat?" Good Idea asked, looking at Weathervane.

The witch sighed. "I am only a healer. I don't have the kind of power needed to stop a basilisk. I could only freeze the head of the Cave Cat for a few moments, remember?" She lifted her staff. "I can cure the blind, heal the lame, and take away the pains of childbirth. That's what healers do. The other skills I've learned along the way through luck and a generous teacher, but I don't have the skill to take down a creature like the basilisk."

"How about the SloMo spell," Bruise asked. "Like with the hobs?"

She shook her head. "They were very small creatures. This basilisk is too big. I'm afraid magic is out."

Good Idea looked at Bruise again. "And you don't think you could fight him?"

"Well, sure. I could fight him," Bruise huffed. "I just don't think I could kill him before he kills me. Like I said, they move too fast. We'd need something to keep him distracted. And then someone to help me to fight him. Maybe two or three some-ones, and at least one of them would need a sharp sword and fast feet."

"We know someone with a sharp sword and fast feet," Good Idea mused. "Regret. And Tuesday could be useful."

Left Ear chirped. "Well, he would make a very good distraction."

"Tuesday is an elf, so he's not a problem. But Regret can't get through the Veil," Weathervane said.

Good Idea thought. "Can we get another talisman?"

Weathervane nodded. "Such things are expensive and rare. I

know where she could purchase such things, but she would need gold."

"That is not a problem," Good Idea said. "When she gets her talisman, the two of them must come immediately to Castle Splendid."

"Regret hates magic." Bruise said. "Do you think she will be willing to put on a talisman and step through the Veil?"

"She has sworn to protect me. And against a basilisk, I will need all the protection I can get," Good Idea said.

"And if Tuesday comes, she will surely follow," Weathervane said dryly.

Good Idea frowned. "Really? My impression is that she doesn't think all that much of him."

Weathervane stared at Good Idea for a moment, then shook her head. "I think staying in Whisper for all of your life was not as good a thing as you've always thought."

Good Idea shifted in the straw. "Whatever. The point is that people can enter the castle freely, so they should be able to slip in with the crowd. The trick will be to find their way down to the dungeon entrance and then hide there."

"And then what? They'll just waltz down here and wait for what? How are you going to get us all past the guards?" Weathervane asked, annoyed.

"There won't be any guards. The fey said they would help us, so I'm going to ask them for help." Good Idea said, feeling with one hand into her pocket.

She withdrew the small pouch that had been given to her with the small, gold-flecked linnets inside.

"We need to burn it in a silver chalice," Bruise reminded her.

"I know," Good Idea said, rummaging in her pockets again.

"And if you are going to summon the fey," Weathervane warned, "it will not work here. We're surrounded by Altrunic Iron."

Good Idea paused. "I hadn't thought of that. Thank you. Left

Ear, can you tell me if there are any guards in the corridor? I don't hear any, and they rarely walk past."

The mouse hurried out, returning a few seconds later. "All clear."

"Good," Good Idea said.

She stuck both of her arms out of the cell. In one hand was the dented thimble, with a tiny seed inside of it. With the other hand, she struck one of Fleet's matches. It flared briefly, and she dropped it in to the thimble. There was a puff of purple smoke, and Thistle appeared.

"You are in need of our aid?" the fairy asked.

"Yes. Tonight, just at midnight, I would like you and all of your brethren to come back into this dungeon and drive everyone out," she said. "But just down here. We will have friends waiting at the top of stairs at the entrance to the dungeon waiting to assist us. Can you do that?"

"Of course, but is that all?" the fairy asked. "That seems such a simple request."

"It is simple," Good Idea conceded, "but it would mean very much to us."

Thistle said. "We could do this right now, if you like."

Good Idea shook her head. "No. We need to inform our friends of our plan, and we need to obtain the key to our lock. That will take time."

The fairy bowed. "As you wish. Midnight then." And he disappeared in a puff.

Good Idea drew in her hands, slipped the charred thimble back into her pocket, and brushed the dirt from her palms.

"I will not even ask how the fey came to owe you a favor," Weathervane said, "although I imagine it's because they fear the notebook will fall into the wrong hands."

Good Idea nodded. "Yes." She looked at Left Ear. "Once again, so much will depend on you. You must get back to Regret and Tuesday and inform them of our plan. They will have to buy the talisman, get to the castle, and wait until they see all the guards flee. They can then come down and come with us through the Veil. Stress to Regret how important her role in in this."

"If that fails," Weathervane interjected, "tell her Tuesday will surely perish if he comes alone."

Good Idea continued. "We will defeat the basilisk, leave the castle, and find our way to Weathervane's shop. From there, we can cross through the Veil again. If Weathervane is correct, and it is believed that the Prince now has the notebook, then we should be able to move through the streets without bother."

"Once the Prince knows we're gone," Bruise asked, "won't he send men after us?"

"That would mean the Prince would have to admit we escaped," Weathervane said, "and he would never do that."

"So that's the plan," Good Idea said brightly.

Bruise made a noise. "That all?"

Weathervane cleared her throat. "You are placing a great deal of faith on a great many things going exactly the way we need them to go."

Good Idea shook her head. "I am placing a great deal of faith on the known behavior of others, and a logical chain of events."

Left Ear sat straighter. "This faith of yours goes against my way of thinking, but I trust your judgment, even when things look bleak. There is nothing you can ask of me I would not do, so what else do you need from me?"

"Thank you, Left Ear." There was a small glow in Good Idea's chest that she did not recognize, but thought that maybe it had to do with Left Ears words. "When the fey arrive, I assume all the guards will begin to leave the dungeons. You must find Key Hold and take the key from him. I'm hoping that in his haste to get away, he won't notice or care if someone slips into his pocket."

"Not a problem," Left Ear said. "But who is Key Hold?"

"Oh, my," said Good Idea. "That's right. You haven't met him." She looked around. "Any ideas?"

"Well," Bruise suggested, "we can always just holler for him and see if he shows up."

Weathervane rolled her eyes. "Like that would work," she muttered.

Good Idea walked to the bars of her cell, pressed her face against them, and began yelling. Bruise moved up beside her and began yelling as well.

In moments, Key Hold appeared, frowning. "What's this? What's going on?"

Good Idea stepped back in surprise. "I, I didn't think you'd show up so fast. I mean, I thought a guard would have to go and get you."

Key Hold frowned. "Why would someone need to get me? I'm sitting right around the corner there, and since you're the only prisoners we have right now, it's not like I have excessive duties to attend to."

Bruise looked surprised. "We're the only prisoners?"

Key Hold smiled meanly. "No one in Mirror City wants to end up down here, because it's a known fact that, unless you get a pardon, you only way you leave is in a burlap bag. Folks are very law-abiding. You're the first prisoners we've seen in months."

"And yet," Good Idea asked, "you have a hundred guards here? For just us?"

"Oh, no," Key Hold said. "That's not why they're here. They're here to keep the good citizens of Mirror City from even thinking about breaking the law." He showed his uneven teeth in a grin. "And it works very well, wouldn't you say? Now, what do you want from me?"

"Would it be possible," Good Idea said, thinking fast, "to send a letter?"

"Absolutely not," Key Hold said. "Anything else?"

Good Idea shook her head. "No but thank you."

Key Hold stomped off, and Good Idea looked down at the mice.

"Good enough?" she asked Left Ear.

"Yes," she said. "And where do we find this talisman seller?"

Weathervane gave her an address.

Good Idea dug into her pocket, drew out a gold coin and held it out to Left Ear.

She shifted into a crow so that she could carry the gold piece in her talons and flew out of sight.

SHORTLY BEFORE MIDNIGHT, Left Ear, as a sleek black rat, scurried into their cell.

"All set," she said. "Regret and Tuesday are waiting for you at the top of the entrance to the dungeon. They are disguised as guards, and no one has given them a second look."

"That's perfect," Good Idea said, shaking the straw out of her hair. "I knew they could do it."

They suddenly saw a pale purple light outside the bars, and a dozen fairies, their long fingers aglow, trotted down the corridor.

"They're here," Good Idea whispered. Then she frowned. "Why don't I feel anything?"

Bruise grunted. "Altrunic Iron. It won't let magic out. Or in."

In moments, they could hear the shuffling of feet. The passage was suddenly filled with guards, all muttering and grumbling, their feet moving quickly down the hallway. Key Hold was easy to spot, his bright purple uniform flickering among the dark gray. Left Ear shot out of the cell and returned in seconds, a large key dangling from her jaws.

"That," she said, breathing heavily, "was by far the hardest thing I have ever done. That fairy dust is potent."

Good Idea bent down and scooped up the rat in her hands

and placed a kiss on the top of her sleek head. "I can always count on you," she said. Left Ear curled her tail and twitched her whiskers.

They waited, and it seemed that it took no time for the corridor to be empty and silent. There was a glow again of purple, and Thistle trotted up to their cell.

"It will take another few minutes for the effect to wear off," the fairy said. "But they are all gone to the upper floors. I hope you have a plan for getting past them once you get out of your cell."

"We will pass through the Veil," Good Idea explained. "They won't be able to see us."

Thistle nodded, then stroked his chin with a long finger. "You know about the basilisk?"

Good Idea nodded. "Grimby? Yes, but we have a plan."

"Would you like us to help you with that plan? Our magic will not work on a basilisk, but we can be annoying in other ways if we choose," Thistle offered.

"That's very kind of you," Good Idea said. "I think we'll need all the help we can get. But won't you, won't we —"

"We can make ourselves quite tolerable to humans when we wish," Thistle explained. "We will find you when you need us." And he was gone in a puff.

Bruise used the key and opened the cell door. Good Idea stepped out and felt an immediate unease in the corridor. She stopped and felt the hairs on her arms send on end.

"It's the fairy dust," Weathervane explained. "There are still traces in the air. It doesn't bother me as much. Let me find Regret and Tuesday and bring them here."

Weathervane went down the corridor in one direction, and Bruise and Left Ear went off in the other. Good Idea stepped back through the now-open cell door and her discomfort eased. Moments later, Bruise was back.

"They're all gone," he said.

Left Ear trotted toward them in the shape of a large, shaggy wolf. She sat back on his haunches, panting slightly.

They waited in silence until Weathervane turned the corner, Regret and Tuesday behind her, dressed in the green uniform of the guards.

"Grand uniform," Tuesday said, spinning around, arms wide.

"Yes," Regret said dryly. "You look marvelous."

Tuesday blushed. "Why, thank you," he mumbled.

Good Idea stepped from the cell. She still felt slightly ill at ease, but that could have been because of the thought of their next challenge.

"So, I'm unsure of the plan here," Tuesday said. "We just slip through the Veil, back up to the castle proper, then out the front door? Sounds simple enough. Which makes me think that there must be something more.'"

"There *is* a bit more," Good Idea said. "There's a basilisk running around the castle we have to get past."

Tuesday paled. "You mean the one that was in the throne room?"

"That's Grimby," Bruise said. "He's let out at night to patrol the castle. He's a Craddock basilisk, so I'm sure you know all about killing it."

Tuesday cleared his throat. "I certainly know how it can kill us," he said.

"But he's nothing we can't handle," Regret said. "Right Tuesday?"

Tuesday looked at her and straightened his shoulders. "Right."

Good Idea followed as Fleet then watched as the mouse moved through a sliver of light in the damp, dark stone of the passage. She stepped through and moved away as the others followed.

Weathervane came last, her dull gown now a splendid red,

her staff aloft. She looked around. "I can make one of you faster than the rest," she said. "For a short time."

Good Idea nodded. "Good to know," she said, and they all turned and walked swiftly back to the dungeon entrance, up the steep flight of stairs, and into the castle.

CHAPTER 15

They opened the door of the dungeon slowly. Regret stuck her head out, took a step, then another, then motioned for the rest to follow.

"Where did all those guards go?" Good Idea wondered softly.

"There's a basilisk roaming around these halls," Bruise said. "If they were smart, they found the nearest empty rooms and locked themselves in."

The hallways were brightly lit, and Good Idea saw none of the shadows that meant a non-magical person was about. Fleet, sitting on her shoulder, trembled slightly and clung to a tendril of hair that had escaped her braid.

"Do you know how to get us out of here?" Bruise asked.

Regret threw him a look over her shoulder and rolled her eyes.

"Just asking," Bruise grumbled.

They climbed another stairway, and the hallway was wider, the floor of inlaid marble. They moved quickly, turning right, then left, and then Regret held up a hand.

"The throne room is ahead," she whispered.

"Where's Grimby?" Good Idea whispered back.

In answer, she heard a faint noise, as though a harness of scales was being dragged across the floor.

She looked behind her, and her breath caught in her throat.

When she had seen the basilisk the day before, it had been in a tight coil, its head resting on the marble floor. She had no idea how big it might have been. But now, looking at it as it slithered slowly up the wide marble corridor, she could see that it was at least thirty feet long, and its body was so thick she could not have encircled it with both arms. Its bright green body reflected the light from the torch-lined walls, and a split tongue moved in and out of its mouth, testing the air. The black cloth covered its eyes, and the head moved restlessly.

Good Idea stopped and heard Regret and Tuesday draw their swords, and Bruise unleashed Axe. Left Ear seemed to grow in size, and they all backed away from the monster in the direction of the throne room. Fleet, who had been tightly holding into Good Idea's hair, ran down her arm and into her pocket, and she could feel the small creature tremble.

The body of the snake undulated, and its tail rose in the air, quivering. The massive head turned one way, then another, before it burst forward, the massive body shooting across the slick marble floor, fangs bared.

"You're with me," Regret said to Tuesday.

"Always," he answered, and they ran toward the basilisk. So did Bruise and Left Ear, and as Grimby moved forward, Regret and Tuesday moved to the left, Bruise and Left Ear moved right. The snake — smelling, hearing, sensing, for Good Idea could not tell — stopped, head up, tail moving back and forth.

Regret struck first, a quick, darting blow several feet behind the massive head. As Grimby turned its head , looking for her, Bruise struck from the other side.

The head moved, but then it was Tuesday's turn, then Left Ears...

Good Idea immediately saw that they were very successful at

keeping the basilisk occupied, and the blows they struck were drawing a pale green blood that oozed from the between the scales, but she also saw that they could spend a great deal of time stuck in the hallway, when they needed him in the throne room.

"Drive him forward," she called, but then realized that to do that, they would have to move closer to the head, making it easier for the snake to strike one of them with its fangs.

"Never mind," she called. Then turned to Weathervane. "You see the problem?"

Weathervane nodded. "Does anyone know if there is anything it's afraid of?" She called.

Tuesday, ducking as Grimby whirled and snapped at him, swung his sword and grunted. "Left Ear, can you weasel?"

Left Ear had jumped upon the creature's body and was hanging on by the power of her massive jaws and teeth, which she'd sunk into the scaly back. She twitched her tail in answer.

"Get ready to run," Tuesday shouted. "Old Grimby here is going to shoot forward like an arrow."

Weathervane grabbed Good Idea's hand as they moved farther down the hallway to the throne room. The two began to run. Good Idea glanced over her shoulder. Left Ear had jumped off Grimby and was now a small, sleek creature who raced down the body of the snake to the tail and then…squatted? Was she actually trying to pee on Grimby?

The basilisk roared and shot forward, away from Left Ear, and Weathervane muttered a few words. Good Idea felt her legs tingle, and she was suddenly running faster than she could ever imagine. She and Weathervane burst into the throne room just seconds before Grimby shot past them, wailing and thrashing.

Good Idea stared at the beast, then looked back again. Regret and Tuesday were running full out, as was Bruise. Left Ear was a crow, black wings flashing. How long would it take for them to get there? And what were she and Weathervane to do in the meantime?

Weathervane grabbed Good Idea by the arm and pulled her back against the wall. Grimby was in the center of the throne room, coiling and uncoiling, hissing furiously, tongue out. The massive head turned in their direction and the snake began to move toward them.

There was a poof of green smoke, and at least twenty fairies, wings fluttering, swarmed the head. The snake snapped its massive jaws, but the fairies were too quick, darting back and forth, poking Grimby with their pointy fingers. This enraged the basilisk which, Good Idea could see, was not the best idea, but it kept the massive snake in the center of the room, head moving, tail waving angrily.

Bruise, Tuesday, and Regret came running from the hallway and immediately attacked the rear of the basilisk. This caused even louder roars and more frantic movement. Bruise was hit by a brutal lash of tail and went flying across the marble floor. He lay there, stunned, trying to rise, then falling back onto the polished floor. There was a high-pitched cry as three fairies were caught by the slashing tongue and fell with a series of soft thuds. Regret jumped into the air and brought her sword down in the center of the tail and pulled herself until she was straddling the rear of the beast and riding it like a bucking horse, holding on to her sword.

Tuesday ran forward, his sword bouncing off the rough scales on the basilisk, but it was enough to slow the thrashing head and turn Grimby's attention from the fairies. It turned its covered eyes to Tuesday and opened its massive jaws.

"Left Ear," Good Idea screamed. "His eyes!"

The crow soared upward, turned, then began a breakneck descent. Just as the jaws of the Basilisk opened to grab Tuesday, the crow snatched at the scarf with her talons, tearing it off.

Weathervane stamped her staff on the marble floor. The

room was flooded with bright light, and the basilisk, frozen for a second by sudden sight, turned and stared directly into one of the now brilliantly lit mirrors.

The basilisk's eyes glowed red. The reflected eyes did the same. The fairies shot away as the massive beast threw back its head in an anguished cry, sank to the floor and turned to dust.

The silence was so sudden and shocking that Good Idea could hear the pounding of her heart and the thrumming of blood in her veins. Nothing moved for what seemed a very long moment.

Regret rose out of the dust that was left of the basilisk and leaned on her sword. Tuesday turned and went to Bruise, holding out a hand. The orc took it and hauled himself up.

The fairies, in a cluster around their fallen comrades, wailed shrilly. Thistle flew to Good Idea.

"We must attend to the injured. We must return home. I'm sorry we can be of no further help to you right now."

Good Idea clasped her hands to her chest. "Oh, Thistle, you saved us. Please, do what you need to do. I hope they'll be okay."

Thistle's wings fluttered. "They will be fine. We will all be fine. Just make sure the notebook is made secure. If it falls into the wrong hands, we will be the first to be destroyed. We are not loved by many."

Good Idea nodded. "You are loved by me. And you have my word."

Thistle flew back to the cluster of fairies, and then they were all gone in a cloud of green smoke.

Good Idea crossed to Bruise, who was rubbing his head and grimacing. "Are you okay?" she asked.

The orc grunted. "Should have been more careful."

Good Idea threw her arms around his thick neck. "You were brilliant," she gushed. She stepped back and looked at Regret and Tuesday, then at Left Ear, who settled onto Bruise's shoulder. "You all were." Then she looked at Left Ear. "Why did you try to pee on him?"

Tuesday answered. "I'd heard there was an old wives' tale that weasel urine can kill a basilisk. I don't know if it's true, but I've read that most basilisks don't want to wait to find out if it is."

"I heard the same thing," Left Ear said, "I'm a great fan of old wives' tales."

Good Idea smiled. "Thank goodness for that."

Weathervane lifted her head, listening. "We've attracted some attention. People are coming. We need to move."

They walked to the end of the throne room, and as Good Idea looked back, she saw shadows streaming from the hallway they had come through minutes before, and the shadows crowded around the ashes of the fallen Grimby.

"That will give them something to talk about for years," Weathervane said with a dry chuckle. "Now, let's get back to my shop and out of the Veil. We still have things to do."

In Whisper, the hours after midnight had always been dead quiet and pitch dark. But, in Mirror City, through the Veil, the streets were anything *but* quiet. Nor was it dark. The streets were lit with a pale, greenish glow that illuminated everyone and everything around them.

"Who are all these...whatever they are?" she asked Weathervane in a hushed whisper.

The witch, head high and heels loud on the cobblestones, looked around her. "The usual folk. Merchants and shoppers, going about their business." She glanced at Good Idea. "The Veil is less crowded with regular people and things after midnight." They passed a small group of Weir Folk huddled around a small cart full of loudly squealing creatures that looked to have six legs.

Their troop passed through the small crowds for what seemed to Good Idea for quite a while before they came to the waterfront. After crossing a few of the small bridges, Weathervane drew up quickly, turned around abruptly, and motioned them all to go back the way they had just come.

"What?" Good Idea whispered.

"Seller's Street is blocked," Weathervane said under her breath.

"By what?" Regret asked.

Good Idea looked over her shoulder. She could see four or five men lounging along the entrance of Seller's Street. "They're just men," she said.

"No, they aren't. They're shifters, looking like men. Which means they've been hired," Left Ear said.

"By whom?" Tuesday asked.

Weathervane shrugged and turned down a small alley, walking briskly until she ducked into a small alcove. The witch sighed. "Probably Three Finger. He has connections on both sides of the Veil. We need to find a way to get into my shop."

"We can always fight our way through," Bruise said. "After all, there are only five of them."

"That would alert the entire riverfront," Weathervane said. "We don't want the attention."

"Can Fleet find another crack?" Regret asked.

"Only if he's close enough to sense one," Good Idea said. "We could wander the streets for days, and we don't have that kind of time."

"Where does Seller's Street End? We can find a back way through." Tuesday suggested.

"Don't you think that would be watched as well?" Bruise said.

"Can we go up the river?" Good Idea asked. "Then up the canal?"

Weathervane frowned, thinking, then nodded. "Let me find

us a boat. Left Ear, let's go." She abruptly turned and went back down the alley, Left Ear flying above her.

The wall behind Good Idea was cool and rough as she leaned against it. She had been so ready for this long night to end. "I'm exhausted, but I don't think I could sleep a wink."

Regret folded her arms across her chest and shifted her weight from one foot to the other. "Tuesday and I have been going without sleep for days now. Listening is a twenty-four-hour a day job."

Bruise looked at the paladin. "You don't seem very impressed with the Veil. Most folks find it, well, interesting at least."

Regret shrugged. "I've never been through the Veil before, but that doesn't mean I haven't encountered all sorts of magical types. And I imagine every low-life and paid informant on both sides of the Veil has been through the Rider Man Inn."

Tuesday nodded in agreement. "All sorts there, three deep at the counter and hanging out by the door most days. Like kids hanging around the stage on Market days, waiting for a show to start."

Good Idea looked at him. "You almost make it sound like you enjoyed it."

A faint blush appeared under the soot and grime on his face. "Some of it was rather fun." He glanced at Regret, who stood, arms folded, staring ahead.

It didn't take long for Left Ear to come flying back to them. "She's found someone," she croaked, and they followed her out of the alley, turned away from Seller's Street, and threaded through a warren of shabby buildings as the River Brown twisted through the city. She finally fluttered down by a weathered dock where Weathervane sat in a small scow, sitting low in the water, a single lantern burning at the bow.

Regret stared. "Will this keep above water with all of us?" she asked.

It was a fair question, Good Idea conceded, as the boat was

so low in the river that to reach it required a descent on a narrow ladder over eight quellegs long.

Weathervane motioned them down and into the boat. "Don't complain," she hissed. "Murk is doing this as a favor to me. We must be silent. Not only because of the men at Seller's Street, but because there are things in the River Brown we do not want to attract."

Murk, huddled by the lantern, was not much bigger than one of Good Idea's sheep, and similarly shaped; broad and four-legged, with tufts of stiff hair sticking out from beneath its hood.

They sat still in the bottom of the scow and Murk moved through the still water, using a long pole to stay in the darkness at the middle of the river. The shoreline was crowded with wooden piers and all sizes of vessels. Good Idea saw the looming shadows of the commercial ships she'd first seen the River Brown. But now there were fantastical boats of a very different sort, with colorful sails and fanciful names inscribed on their bows, all part of the world that existed through the Veil.

She had dozens of questions she wanted to ask, but heeded Weathervane's request for silence, as she could easily see shapes moving in the water as well, long, slithering kinds of shapes with large heads that occasionally turned to show gleaming teeth.

Good Idea glanced back at Bruise and Left Ear, now a sleek water rat, who were having a complete conversation with just expressions and gestures about, she was sure, the names of these water creatures, as well as their dangers and various ways to kill them. She tried to hide a smile but caught Weathervane's eye. The witch, as though reading her thoughts, grinned and rolled her eyes.

The small scow suddenly rocked, one side dipping into the River Brown, water spilling into the bottom of the boat. Murk turned and, with the long pole he'd been using to steer the boat, swiped at a dark figure hugging the side of the boat.

Murk made a noise, a guttural kind of noise, and Weathervane paled. Regret, who had been scanning the water on the other side of the boat, turned quickly. The paladin, drawing her sword, looked at Weathervane and raised her eyebrows.

Weathervane bit her lip, then nodded.

Regret slid to the other side of the boat and, with one swift stroke, hit the thing in the water, and it sank without a sound.

Tuesday also drew his sword and, without so much as a boastful grin or knowing look, slashed at something on his side of the boat as well.

There was a strangled sound, and a gurgling sound, and suddenly there were tentacles on either side of the boat, pulling it down into the River Brown.

Bruise stood, causing the scow to rock violently, and the orc hewed at several tentacles with Axe. Regret and Tuesday also slashed wildly, as Good Idea and Weathervane clung to each other in the center of the boat. Left Ear dove into the river, and in seconds there was a roiling in the water that became more desperate as the tentacles began to drop away. Regret, breathing heavily, leaned over the side to jab several times at what was left in the water.

There was a call from the docks to the right. The noise had attracted the attention of a few of the figures working the bright-colored vessels along the shore.

"What's goin' on?" one voice called.

"Sounds like a SixLegg Seripant got hold of something," another voice said.

"Sounds like several SixLegg Seripants," said another with a laugh. "Hey, anyone need help down there"

Odd shapes rose to the surface of the water, and Good Idea saw the water stained with something dark and viscous.

Murk, who had been moving his scow through the water

with quiet determination, turned back to give Weathervane a quick nod. Good Idea heard her sigh of relief.

Regret and Tuesday sat back down, settling the boat, but Bruise still stood, his eyes searching the river. Left Ear, Good Idea suddenly realized, had not come back to the surface.

Good Idea grabbed Weathervanes hand and tugged, gesturing with her finger to all on board. Weathervane frowned in the darkness, then her face changed. She reached over and put the tip of her staff in the water, and Good Idea saw a shimmer of purple light leaving a faint trail in the water.

Of course, Good Idea thought. Down in the dark water of an unfamiliar river, Left Ear probably lost her bearings, and could be swimming in any direction. The alternative was that she'd been badly injured, or even killed by the SixLegg Seripant, and Good Idea found her chest tightening at the very thought.

The voices on the shore faded, and they were once again gliding in complete silence. Good Idea had moved to the edge of the boat, her eyes straining in the darkness for a flicker of movement. Nothing. She reached down to put her hand in the water, but Weathervane tugged at her arm, shaking her head violently. The witch's staff was still in the river, leaving a pale glimmer of a trail.

Finally, Murk turned the boat into a canal. They glided past the men who were watching the street and not paying attention to what was happening in the water. Good Idea felt the scow bump and bounce against the boats that appeared as shadows until it stopped before a narrow ladder.

We can't leave her, Good Idea thought as she climbed up to the dock. "I won't leave her," she said in a strangled voice

Bruise obviously felt the same, as he remained on the scow, bent low, looking into the water.

Murk made a noise and Weathervane gestured impatiently for him to shush. The pale light she had made was beginning to fade, and they all stood, staring down, with a growing sense of dread.

"We should go back," Tuesday whispered.

Regret shook her head. "Not all of us. You and I will go. Weathervane, can you —"

At that moment, there was a splash, and something leaped up into Bruises' arms. The orc chuckled, and the sleek shape of a water rat slid across the bottom of the scow and up the ladder.

Good Idea scooped the bundle of wet fur up in her arms, hugging tightly. "We were so worried," she said, her voice breaking. "We thought we'd lost you."

Left Ear wriggled in her arms. "You almost did. Black as mines of Clerridach down there, and when I finally broke the surface, I was downriver. Thank you, Weathervane, for your light. If I hadn't seen it, I'd be halfway to Berrin by now." She looked over Good Idea's shoulder to the street. "Are we safe? Can't see anyone about."

"Relatively," Weathervane said. "And we're not too far from my shop. Thank you, Murk. Your debt is paid."

The huddled figure on the boat waved and pushed away. Left Ear jumped from Good idea's arms and climbed up onto Bruise's shoulder.

"Ever come across a thing like that before?" Left Ear asked.

The orc shook his head. "Someone on shore called it a SixLegg Seripant. Now, I've heard of seripants, but I don't spend much time near rivers."

"Me neither," Left Ear said. "But believe me, they had more than six legs."

Good Idea smiled and sighed and followed Weathervane through the pale light of Seller's Street.

THEY WERE BACK in Weathervane's shop just before dawn, but Good Idea was too nervous to even think of sleep.

"We must rescue Bunny, then get back to Whisper as soon as possible," she said. "We need horses."

"We can buy horses where Pink and Vigilant are stabled," Regret said. "We would need to purchase one for Tuesday, Bunny, Weathervane, Bruise—"

"I can run as fast as any horse," Bruise said.

"And I can become a horse," Left Ear said, perched as a crow on Bruise's shoulder.

"Good," said Good Idea. "Then two horses. That will save my gold. And Weathervane, is there something you can do to help us along?"

Weathervane nodded. "Yes. I can create a potion that will give the horses extra strength and speed."

Good Idea nodded. "Very good." She dug out two more gold coins and handed them to Regret. "The best and fastest you can buy. How much time will you need to prepare your potion?" she asked Weathervane.

The witch thought. "Less than an hour."

Good Idea turned to Bruise, Tuesday, and Left Ear. "We will go to the Rider Man Inn. It is still so early that Bunny could still be asleep. We will have to find out where we can sneak the real Bunny out while Left Ear takes his place."

Tuesday spoke up. "Regret and I scouted the inn for several days. There's a small window over the kitchen that we can use. From there, we can drop down to the alley and no one will notice."

"Very good. We'll need clothes for Bunny." Good Idea frowned, thinking. "Preferably some sort of disguise."

Weathervane sighed. "Well, I have a nun's robe."

Good Idea looked up in surprise. "You do not strike me as someone who would have use or need of a nun's robe."

Weathervane sniffed. "Well, you would be wrong. Do you want it or not?"

Good Idea nodded. "Yes, thank you. That would be perfect."

She looked around at her companions. "We will meet in front of the Rider Man Inn, and we will begin our journey back to Whisper."

They all nodded and went out the door onto Seller's Street. Regret turned one way toward the stable. Weathervane came out of the back room holding a dust-colored bundle, which she handed to Good Idea, then watched as the party disappeared down the street.

Rider Man Inn looked closed, the shutters still barred, the door closed, but when they pushed against the door, it opened with a long creak.

There were men asleep at the tables, some wearing the livery of the Prince, others in different colored livery, some in plain black robes. Left Ear shifted to a mouse and darted up the steps.

Bruise made his way to one of the few empty seats and sat. Good Idea and Tuesday withdrew and went around the Inn to a narrow alley that ran behind.

Tuesday pointed to a small window above a wooden door. "That's where he can get out," Tuesday said.

Good Idea glanced around. The alley was deserted. "Good. I'll go in and find Bunny." She had the nun's robe in her pack. "Do you know where the window is on the inside?"

Tuesday nodded. "On the second floor, at the end of the west-side hallway. It's in a closet."

Good Idea nodded. "You and Regret did a good job scouting out this place," she said.

"We spent a lot of time here," Tuesday said. Then he dropped his voice. "I think she's starting to like me," he said.

Good Idea did not know how, exactly to respond. "Well," she said at last, "she did say you were a help."

"I know," Tuesday gushed. "Can you believe it?"

Actually, she couldn't. But she smiled, patted his shoulder, and went back into the Rider Man Inn.

She glanced at Bruise, who had apparently attracted the

attention of someone because there was a mug of something in front of him. She felt suddenly very hungry. How had she forgotten about breakfast?

She went up the stairs, turned, and found the closet. The window, thankfully, was larger than it had looked from the outside. Buddy could easily crawl through. She turned back into the hallway and realized she had no idea what room Buddy occupied.

She slumped against the wall. How could she have been so shortsighted? The inn was four stories tall, with dozens of rooms. Unlike Left Ear, she could not creep under the doors of those rooms, looking for Bunny. Then she straightened. Left Ear would find Bunny, and she was confident she would let her know where and when the switch would take place.

Sure enough, after a few minutes, she saw a mouse scurry down the staircase.

"Left Ear?" she hissed.

The mouse turned and ran to her.

"Bunny Jones is still completely useless," Left Ear grumbled. "He doesn't remember me, or you, and tried to kill me with a fireplace poker when I spoke to him. You're going to have to meet him in the privy and convince him I'm not the spawn of a demon, then convince him he should come with us, then get him to change clothes and escape his guards, who have apparently become his best friends in the past few weeks."

"Oh, my," Good Idea said. Once again, a difficulty where she had been expecting none. It was becoming exhausting. She squared her shoulders. "Where is he?"

She followed Left Ear up the stairs.

There were two large men wearing the Prince's livery seated on wooden chairs outside one of the doors. Keeping her head down, she followed Left Ear as she crept along the hall, passed the guard, turned, then stopped in front of a smallish door marked "Privy."

Inside was rather spacious, considering its function, and didn't smell nearly as bad as it could have. Good Idea leaned against the wall.

"Left Ear," she whispered, "you'll have to tell me if someone other than Bunny is heading this way."

The ears twitched, and the mouse squeezed under the closed door.

It wasn't a long wait. The door opened and Bunny stepped in, Left Ear sliding in behind him. The young wizard turned, saw Good Idea and opened his mouth, but she put a finger to his lips.

"Shh," she whispered. "I have a very important message from, ah," she thought. What had he remembered again? "Your mother."

Bunny's shocked expression became one of concern. "Mummy?"

"Yes. We want to take you to her, but unfortunately, the guards won't let you come with us," Good Idea said earnestly.

Bunny made a face. "Yes. They are rather insistent they never leave my side."

"But if you give me your clothes," Good Idea went on, "Left Ear can pretend to be you, and we can escape, and then we can go to your mothers."

Bunny frowned. "Well, that *sounds* okay, but…" He narrowed his eyes. "Who's Left Ear?"

Left Ear shifted into a human form, naked, of course.

Bunny blinked. "Where did she come from? Why is she naked? And how do I know you're really from Mummy?"

Good Idea exhaled, thinking again which question was easier to answer, then brightened. "If we didn't know your mother, how would we know about your Uncle Mionarach?"

Bunny continued to frown. "I have an Uncle Mionarach?"

Good Idea nodded. "Yes. He's a great wizard. Old, but still

sharp." She circled her head with one finger. "Lots of white hair? One leg?"

Bunny's face lit up. "Yes. Uncle Mionarach."

Good Idea nodded. "Now, if you could just change into this," she pulled the robe from her pack. "And give Left Ear your clothes..." She handed him the robe and turned her back. She could hear the rustle of clothing. The privy had become very crowded.

She turned and saw Bunny in a shabby brown robe with a hood and simple rope belt, and Left Ear, looking exactly like Bunny, in the wizards' robes, now slightly dingy with constant wear, but still rather splendid with the golden stars and crescent moons.

Left Ear adjusted the robe. "You might want to go back into his room and retrieve his staff," she murmured. "It might be magical and useful at some point." Left Ear brushed the front of her robes and left the privy.

Good Idea pressed her ear to the door but couldn't hear much. Bunny tried several times to speak, but each time she shushed him. She finally opened the door and crept down the hallway, looking around the corner.

The guards were gone.

"Where did they go?" asked Bunny in a whisper.

"They followed Left Ear. After all, they thought she was you,"

"That's quite a trick," Bunny said as they crept down the hallway.

"Yes," Good Idea greed.

"Is that something anyone can do?" Bunny asked.

Good Idea shook her head as they hurried into his room. There, he hastily stuffed items into his pack and grabbed the beautifully carved staff. He looked at her.

"Did she say magical? Can this do what what's-her-name just did?"

Good Idea nodded. "Possibly. I don't know much about it,

but you never can tell. If not, you can always use it to hit things with."

Bunny twirled the stick in one hand. "I can't wait to try this out!" The stick fell from his fingers, hit him above the right eye and clattered to the floor.

"Maybe not today," Good Idea muttered as she pushed him out into the hall.

The stairwell was empty, as was the second-floor hallway, but sounds of activity came up from the main floor. They found the closet and Bunny climbed out the window, hampered by his robes, then dropped to the ground below with a thud. Good Idea threw his pack, her pack and the staff out the window, then she climbed out, hung for a minute by her fingertips, then dropped to the ground.

Tuesday went first down the alley to the street, then motioned for Good Idea and Bunny to follow.

Regret was on Vigilant, with Weathervane astride a massive gray stallion. There was another horse standing with them, a sleek sorrel. And there was Pink. The mare was dyed a hideous color that should have been brown but, against the pink of her coat, looked purple. Good Idea ran to Pink, who whinnied softly and proceeded to kiss Good Idea's cheek with her long tongue. Good Idea threw her arms around the slender neck and whispered, "We're going home."

Regret looked down at Good Idea. "Are we waiting for Bruise and Left Ear?" she asked.

Good Idea shook her head. "No. Tuesday and I will, but you all start ahead now. Travel as quickly as you can, we'll catch up."

Bunny made to mount Pink, but Good Idea pulled at his sleeve. "You will ride the other horse. I must leave Mirror City as I arrived, on Pink."

Bunny looked embarrassed but climbed onto the sorrel.

Regret nodded briefly. "Good Luck," she muttered, then sat

forward and Vigilant took off at a quick trot, the other horses behind them.

Good Idea looked at Tuesday. "Well, my friend, just one more trick and we're on the way home."

Tuesday ran his hand over his cropped, ugly hair. "Let's go."

THE MAIN ROOM was louder and bustling with activity, and Good Idea immediately saw that it was because of the appearance of Bunny Jones. He—she—was seated at a table in the center of the room, two guards standing over her, and every other person in the room was awake, alert, and watching.

Bruise, still in the same chair, was now eating a substantial breakfast. Good Idea and Tuesday hurried over to him. Good Idea grabbed the only empty chair left and pulled it next to the orc. Bruise eyed her.

"Hungry, I expect," he grumbled.

She nodded, and he pushed the half-empty plate of eggs, fried apples and bread in front of her.

"That our girl? She looks just like him." Bruise asked in a low voice.

Good Idea nodded, piling the eggs on a torn chunk of bread. Her stomach was in knots thinking about the men riding toward Whisper, but it was also empty, and since they had to wait for LeftEar to make her move... She glanced up at Tuesday. "Want any? Or you could buy your own."

Tuesday shrugged. "No money. Luckily, Regret had coin to pay for our stay at the inn."

Good Idea felt in her pocket. She still had plenty of change from the innkeeper at the Stop Here Inn. She placed a handful of coin on the table, and Tuesday snatched it up and shouldered his way to bar.

The noise was a low and steady rumble, and Good Idea watched Left Ear. She looked exactly like Bunny and even had the slump of his shoulders and hesitant manner. She mimicked a sore throat, which, Good Idea thought, was an excellent way of getting out of any conversation with the guards, who probably knew Bunny fairly well by now.

Tuesday returned with a plate heaped with eggs and cheese in one hand, and two steaming mugs of tea in the other.

"I know you like your tea," he said, putting one mug down in front of Good Idea.

She smiled gratefully. "Yes, I do. Thank you." She looked at Bruise. "I'm sorry I ate your breakfast. You can have some of mine. I don't *think* I can finish it all."

The orc waved a hand. "I'm good. Besides, I doubt there will be much left." He looked around. "I trust the real Bunny is on his way?"

She nodded and watched the faces of the others in the Rider Man Inn. Some of these faces were obviously not human.

Bruise followed her look. "That's a Mud Ruck goblin," Bruise informed her in a low voice. "Probably for hire. Maybe from that Bellorite syndicate? Then there's that." He pointed with a discreet finger. "That's what I'm pretty sure is a Flea Fig."

Good Idea squinted at a smaller figure, cloaked in dull blue, with what appeared to be a tree branch protruding from the bottom of its cloak, where a leg should have been.

"A what?" she asked. Without Left Ear's commentary, she found herself wondering what a Flea Fig could be.

"Flea Fig," Tuesday said. "Woodland creature. I read about them, actually. Quite rare to be seen out of its native habitat. North Jundre Woods, up close to the Wild Side Border."

"Maybe working for Contentious Greenway?" Good Idea asked softly.

Bruise nodded and stretched. "Possibly. All sorts here. All waiting."

"But don't they know that the Prince has the notebook?" Good Idea asked.

"This place isn't nearly as crowded as it was when Regret and I were here three days ago," Tuesday said. "They were stacked three deep on the floor."

"What are they waiting for?" asked Good Idea.

"Dunno," Bruise said. Then he leaned away from Good Idea toward the table next to theirs. "Hey, you. Whatcha waiting here for?"

The person he spoke to, hunched over a cup of tea and hooded, like most of the others not in livery, shrugged. "Well, the Prince has whatever my boss was looking for. Don't know what, exactly. I'm not important enough to know that. But I'm supposed to watch that guy over there." He motioned to Bunny. "Report if anyone talks to him or if something odd happens around him."

Bruise turned back to Good Idea and sniffed. "Get that?"

She nodded, finished her tea, and tried to get Bunny's, er, Left Ear's eye. They had to get out of there sooner rather than later. But as she craned her neck and tried to get her attention, Left Ear's mug slipped off the table, sending ale over one of the guards. The guard stood up and began to shake out his clothes. Bunny bent down to retrieve the mug, and...

"Hey!" The guard sprang back, yelling. "Hey, where'd he go?"

Sure enough, there was nothing left but a purple robe puddled on the floor.

Bruise stretched and stood. "Ready?" he asked Good Idea loudly.

A rumble of voices grew in the Rider Man Inn. The chairs scraped against the hardwood floors as everyone stood. Good Idea noticed a few other disappearances as cloaks fell to the floor. More shapeshifters, she thought.

They made their way outside just as things inside got raucous. They walked quickly to the entrance of the alley where Pink stood. Her head turned as she looked at the horse standing beside her, a large white horse with a flowing mane and tail.

"Now, *that's* a horse," Tuesday breathed, and he leaped easily onto Left Ears' bare back. "Where did this grand fellow come from? Why, look, one of his ears is larger than the other."

Left Ear snorted and muttered, "Twit."

Bruise sighed. "Still a bit of an ignoramus, that one."

Good Idea smiled and patted Pink. "As soon as I can, I'll get you back to your own beautiful color," she whispered. Then she mounted, and they trotted down the cobblestone street, leaving something of an uproar behind them.

And so, Good Idea left Mirror City just as she arrived — on a pink horse. As she passed out of the city limits, she felt a tingle in her pocket where the Notebook Of Whim seemed to sigh with relief.

hey passed several groups camped right outside the
city, huddled around small fires or in front of tents,
all heavily cloaked. There seemed to be a variety of shapes and
sizes among them, three so large that Good Idea thought they
must be giants.

Left Ear confirmed. "Look like Drunner Giants. Stupid, but
very fast."

Bruise, trotting effortlessly beside Pink, nodded. "Don't like
weapons, Drunner Giants. Like to kill things with their hands."

Good Idea waited for an additional comment from Left Ear,
but none came.

It was close to midday when they came to a faded signpost in
the road where the rest of their party waited.

Regret hailed them. "If we are to catch up to the Prince's
men, we should take the Marsh Road."

Good Idea pulled Pink to a halt. "The Marsh Road is dangerous," she said.

Regret nodded. "Yes. It is. But we must take it."

"Quicksand," Good Idea said, remembering the litany of
danger Left Ear had recited on their way to Mirror City.

"Swamp Rats and harpies. And those snakes." She looked at the white horse beside her. "What else Left Ear?"

The horse shook her head. "Staying on the road is half the battle," she said. "We can deal with harpies, and Swamp Rats are terrified of fire. If Weathervane here can cast a SloMo spell, any Choke Snake can be dispatched by Regret here with one stroke of her sword. Even Tuesday could do the job."

Tuesday grinned. "Yes, I probably could."

Good Idea looked at Left Ear. "Your attitude has changed, Left Ear," she said slowly. "You used to enjoy telling us all the worst that could happen."

The horse snickered. "Not everything is gloom and doom," she said.

Good Idea looked at each member of the party. "It is up to all of you. I would do anything to get to my mother before the Prince's men Following me has put you all in danger before. But this is different. You know the risks, and I will not demand you take them. I will not take any of you down the Marsh Road against your will."

Bruise shrugged. "The only thing I'm worried about is the quicksand. Once you're in, you can never get out. The rest I can deal with."

Weathervane sighed. "I'll go."

Tuesday looked at Regret, and when she nodded, he said, "I'll go as well. Speed is of the essence."

Left Ear snickered. "I know to stay on the path. I'll be fine."

Bunny stood up in his stirrups and looked down the Marsh Road. "Why, it looks perfectly fine to me." He smiled brightly. "Besides, aren't I a wizard? If we get into trouble, can't I do wizard-y things?"

Good Idea patted Pink's neck. "It's important to stay on the road," she said. "Do you understand?"

Pink nodded, then turned and trotted down the Marsh Road, although Good Idea thought that calling it a road was quite a stretch. The narrow path twisted through a bleak landscape of dead trees, shrouded in a pale mist of dull red.

They couldn't go faster than a trot, and even then, Good Idea was nervous. She sometimes couldn't even see where the road was, but Pink went first, picking her way surely among the occasional cobbles and stretches of packed sand. Once, they saw a flock of large birds—if they were birds—off to the west.

Regret pointed out the divide of Rocky Tops, way off in the distance and barely visible beyond the tops of the skeletal trees. "We're already halfway to Edge Of The Marsh Inn," she said. "We're making good time. We've cut half a day off our journey,"

In the late afternoon, they stopped for water and food. The road seemed broader, enough for the horses to stand side-by-side. Good Idea slid from Pink's back and stretched gratefully. The little horse had a gentle trot for all of its speed, but Good Idea felt her bones ache from the ride. She stood with Pink, leaning against the horse's side, when there was a sudden yell.

She looked up and saw the sorrel horse turn suddenly, and it bumped into Bruise. The orc put a foot back to keep from falling, and the foot disappeared into the sand. Bruise teetered, arms flailing in an attempt to balance himself, or at least fall forward rather than back, but Good Idea saw the sand surge up the stout yellow leg, pulling it in, and Bruise tumbled back into the quicksand.

Eyes on her feet, and staying as close to the line of horses as she could, Good Idea hurried down to where Bruise had fallen in. Left Ear's head turned, the bright eyes wide with fear.

Regret, sliding from Vigilant, stood looking helpless.

"How do we save him?" Good Idea asked.

Regret shook her head. "We don't. If we try to pull him out, he'll get sucked down faster."

"What if we use the horses?" Good Idea asked, watching Bruise's face as he sank slowly.

"It doesn't matter what we use," Regret said softly. "If we pull one way, the sand will pull the other." She laid a hand on Good Idea's shoulder. "I'm sorry."

Good Idea looked at Weathervane. "Can you use magic?"

"To do what?" Weathervane asked.

"The only force that can get me out," Bruise said, looking up at them as his knees disappeared, "would have to come from within. And I don't have any kind of power within me that would be of use."

Good Idea fought down a feeling of panic. "I'm getting you out," she told him.

Bruise shook his head. "No, Good Idea, I don't think so. I can't see a way out of this."

Good Idea set her jaw. "Terms, remember? I will not leave you behind."

Bruise grinned ruefully. "I'm not injured. I was just careless. Notify my family."

Good Idea turned to Weathervane. "Okay then, is there a spell that can give him a power? Like the ability to jump? Or fly?"

She nodded. "I know of such a spell. You cast it on the thing you want the ability to come from, like a bird or a frog. Then, if you eat that thing, you absorb the ability. It's called a Transference Spell, but I don't know how to cast it."

Bunny, who had been leaning down in his saddle to hear their conversation, waved furiously at them to get their attention. "I know that spell," he said.

They all turned and looked at him.

"You do?" Good Idea asked.

"Well, I know the words. I don't know what else I need," Bunny said, then his face lit up. "But I have a book!"

Good Idea edged to the wizard's side. "What book?"

Bunny reached back into his pack and drew out a large, rather shabby book, its edges frayed, and the spine cracked.

Good Idea saw the title on the cover in faded gold letters, The Big Book Of Important Spells And Potions.

He opened the book and turned a few pages. "Here it is! Why, this is easy. I need teeth and bone and skin. Burn with witch fire. Then, what did you say? A bird or a frog? Roll in the ash, say the words, and it's enchanted!" His smile was broad. "I can make the witch fire, and can speak the words, but the rest is on you."

Tuesday groaned. "We can scrape skin and pull teeth, but where can we find a bone?"

Weathervane frowned. "And there's not a bird or frog to be seen anywhere."

Good Idea rummaged through her pockets and pulled out the snake fang, the wishbone, and the beetle shell. She laid them on the ground.

"Will these do?" she asked Bunny.

"I have no idea, but I don't see why not," he answered. The wizard narrowed his eyes and the items burst into flame on the packed earth of the road.

Good Idea looked at Bruise, who was now waist deep. "Does it have to be a living thing?" she asked the wizard.

Bunny shook his head. "No clue. But I would think it has to be something that he can use to pop up out of the quicksand."

There was Fleet on her shoulder, holding the wine cork. She took it, rolled it in the ash, and held it before Bunny.

Bunny pushed back the sleeves of his tunic, stretched out his hands, and closed his eyes. His face became still, and there was a vibration in the air. "Take the power from this seed," he intoned, "and let it bloom in those in need."

Good Idea felt the cork tremble in her hand.

Bunny opened his eyes. "That's it! Did I do it right?"

"Get off," Left Ear said to Tuesday. The elf slid down and the horse became a familiar crow who fluttered to Good Idea's hand and gently plucked the cork from her palm. She flew to Bruise, now neck deep.

"Open wide," the crow called.

Bruises' mouth opened, and the cork dropped straight down his throat. Bruise coughed, coughed again, and chewed a few times before swallowing.

Left Ear flew down to land beside Good Idea, where she quickly became a woman. She reached out and grabbed Good Idea's hand and held it tightly as they watched Bruise's mouth disappear.

Good Idea felt a sob in her throat. She stepped closer to Left Ear, who put an arm across her shoulder and squeezed.

Bruise's eyes blinked shut and sank beneath the sand.

"Oh, no," Regret said softly.

Bunny looked around. "It didn't work? I'm so sorry. I really thought I got it right."

Good Idea turned to the wizard, her eyes streaming tears. "It's not your fault. I know you tried."

Tuesday sniffed. "I'm going to miss him," he said softly.

Weathervane held her hand to her mouth, her eyes full.

Left Ear made a strangled sound, and Good Idea turned to her and put her arms around her. Left Ear sobbed, and Good Idea's heart ached, knowing how close Left Ear and Bruise had become. She felt her own grief as well for the loss of such a valiant companion. Good Idea held the smaller woman until the sobbing stopped and her own tears were gone.

They stood in silence until Regret cleared her throat. "We must move on. We can't be on the Marsh Road at night."

Good Idea nodded, and Left Ear stepped back, glanced up at Good Idea with a look of gratitude, and shifted back to a horse. Good Idea walked up the line to Pink, who stood with her head up, ears perked.

Good Idea swung on top of the mare and picked up the reins, clucking softly.

The horse did not move.

"Come on, Pink," Good Idea coaxed. "We must be off. There's nothing we can do for him now."

Pink shook her head and shifted on her hooves.

Good Idea frowned. "We have to go," she said, loudly. She dug her heels into the mare's side. Pink turned her head all the way around to glare at Good Idea.

"What?" Good Idea asked in frustration.

There was a very loud, wet sounding pop. Good Idea turned around and saw Bruise shoot up from the quicksand, limbs flying.

"Weathervane!" Good Idea cried.

The witch lifted her staff and the orc, who had begun to fall back to the same spot he'd popped out of, suddenly stopped his descent and hovered in the air, barely a foot above the quicksand.

"I can't hold him long," Weathervane cried out.

Bunny slid off his horse and, with his staff, hooked Bruise's belt and pulled him forward. Tuesday reached out a hand and Bruise grabbed it and tumbled against Left Ear. Left Ear planted her hooves, and the orc grabbed on to Left Ear's neck and put his feet on solid ground.

Bunny looked at his staff. "What a handy thing to have," he cried out in delight. "I wonder what else it can do?"

THERE WERE lights shining in the Edge Of The Marsh Inn, and they entered the courtyard wearily. The sun was just setting, and from the shadows a stout figure emerged.

"Welcome," it cried. It was a woman, tall and broad, dressed in a rough dress and apron. "You all look done in. Are you stopping for a meal, or would you be staying the night? We have rooms."

"We are staying the night," Good Idea said as she slid from

Pink's back. Left Ear, who had shifted into a woman and donned a simple shift, caught her as she stumbled. She leaned against her. "I could sleep for a week," she mumbled. "And we had no lunch."

Left Ear chuckled. "And no lunch makes for a very long day."

The woman, whose name was Bright, called for a young boy who took their horses, and she led them into the inn.

The main room was much different from when they had passed through weeks before. The fire burned cheerfully, and the tables were full of laughing, chattering men and women.

"A hot meal for all?" Bright asked. "And ale?"

Good Idea nodded and sank into a wooden chair, leaning her elbows on the tabletop and looking around.

"Food smells good," said Bruise.

"A bit of a change from the last time we were here," Regret said.

"I would love a clean bed," Tuesday said. "And a bath."

Good Idea slipped her hand into her pocket. "I have three gold pieces left," she announced. "One is for Bruise," she said. "The other will pay for the Stop Here Inn, so tonight I will splurge for everyone to have a bath."

Bunny leaned toward her. "Were we here before?" he asked.

"Not you," Good Idea said.

"Where was I?" he asked.

"In Mirror City."

"Ah. Why?"

"You were to meet us there. Your uncle, Mionarach, sent you ahead," Good Idea explained.

Bunny frowned. "I don't think I enjoyed my time there very much," Bunny said

"You had been cursed and your memory erased," Bruise said.

"Why, that was rather harsh," Bunny said, as mugs of ale were set down before them. "Don't imagine I enjoyed that at all. Did I ever get my memory back?"

Good Idea patted his hand. "Bits of it, yes."

Bunny leaned closer and lowered his voice. "Why is that lady there sitting with us?" he asked, motioning toward Left Ear. "I don't think we were introduced."

Good Idea smiled. "That is Left Ear," she said. "She has been with us from the beginning. She just changes form every once in a while."

Bunny's face brightened. "She popped in for a moment on the Marsh Road," he said. "She was naked, I believe."

She nodded and looked at Left Ear, leaning back in her chair, talking to Bruise. "I used to think my favorite shape was of a crow," Good Idea said. "But I'm beginning to think I like her very much as a woman, naked or not."

"Weathervane," Tuesday asked, "is there something you can give us to erase this dreadful dye?" He ran his hand over his stiff, white hair.

Weathervane nodded. "Yes. I packed just the thing." She looked at Good Idea. "You can also use it for Pink."

Good Idea smiled gratefully. "Thank you."

Food arrived, steaming bowls of boiled mutton and roasted potatoes, simmered squash and chopped greens. They all ate, then drank some more, and then Good Idea informed Bright that they all needed baths and a bed, and one by one the table emptied until just Good Idea, Tuesday and Left Ear remained.

"What do you think?" she asked them. "We are a day-and-a-half behind the Prince's men. We will never get to Whisper before them, no matter how hard and fast the horses run tomorrow. What will they do?"

Left Ear and Tuesday exchanged a look.

"Well, first they have to cross Three Creek Bridge," Left Ear said slowly. "My clan will do whatever it takes to keep them out of Whisper altogether."

"But if they should fail," Tuesday continued, "they will have to fight my father, mother and brother Friday. Now, granted, my brother has no real-world experience, just as I did not. And he will probably be just as useless in a fight."

Good Idea started to speak, but Tuesday held up a hand. "I have seen what a real warrior is," he said. "I have seen true courage. But Mother and Father are soldiers. They were trained by the Guardians of Yellen."

Left Ear let out a low whistle. "I didn't know that."

Tuesday nodded. "Yes. And then there's Mr. Gold, who probably has more experience in weaponry than all the Prince's guard has together. I don't know what use the gnomes are." He looked at Left Ear. "Do gnomes fight?"

Left Ear nodded. "They can. And there's a bit of magic about them as well." She grinned. "Although I'd say their thoroughly disagreeable appearance is their best weapon."

Good Idea snorted a laugh.

Tuesday went on. "Then there are the Barnstable Sisters. I think they have a great deal of power between them. And the wizard, Mionarach. Surely, if he knows we're on the way back, he would be in Whisper as well?"

Good Idea took a deep breath. "I would hope so." She looked at them. "Whisper has been my whole life."

Left Ear nodded. "Yes. We know."

"All I want is to get back home and work in the garden and tend my chickens," Good Idea said.

Tuesday tilted his head. "You have been to Mirror City and back. You've been through the Veil. You've spoken with Queens and Princes and dragons. Hasn't all that made you want more? Hasn't it shown you something else?"

She looked down at her hands as a feeling she'd been keeping at bay rose to the surface. "This was something beyond what I could have imagined. I saw magic working in a way I never had before. I saw bravery and determination unlike anything in Whisper. And I saw friendship and loyalty. All of those things made the danger and exhaustion seem not as important."

She lifted her eyes as her heart swelled with emotion. "I never wanted this. You both know that. But now, as things are finally over, I don't think I would have missed it for the world." She smiled. "Still, Whisper is still the only place I want to be. Once I return, I will never leave it again."

Left Ear reached across the table and covered Good Idea's hand with her own. "I understand. My clan is from the Widdering Mountains. The air is so clear you can stand upon Two Step Ridge and see all the way to the ocean. The trees stay green, and there's always the scent of morning. I've traveled farther than you and seen much more, but when the clan is done here, I can't wait to get back."

Good Idea looked at Left Ear and a thought suddenly struck her. "You will be leaving Whisper?"

Left Ear nodded. "Yes. I have been here long enough, and it was agreed that once I returned from this journey, I would return home."

"But I thought —" Good Idea stopped. What she had thought was that Left Ear was becoming her friend. The kind of friend she'd never had before. The kind of friend she never thought she'd needed before.

True, she considered Tuesday her friend. After all, she'd known him most of her life, and they would sometimes meet on Market days and wander the stalls together. They always ate together during the Harrowmount Feast, and sometimes danced with each other on Jennwarren Eve. But Left Ear had come to mean something quite different, something she could not quite understand in herself. She would miss the shifter's company very much.

"I was just looking forward to meeting you at the river and fishing off Three Creek Bridge," Good Idea said.

Left Ear laughed. "Usually, I fish *in* the river."

Good Idea laughed with her and recognized that she had

laughed a great deal with Left Ear, something else she didn't know she'd needed before. True, the shifter's constant talk of the worst that could possibly happen had tired her at first, but lately...

Lately, there had been much less of that.

"So, you don't like Whisper?" she asked.

Left Ear shook her head. "That's not it. I like Whisper just fine. But it's nothing like the Widdering Mountains." The shifter's hand still lay atop Good Idea's, soft and warm, and she gave it a squeeze. "Some places stay in your heart."

Bright shuffled up to the table. "There's a new bath being drawn. Who wants it?"

Good Idea stood wearily. "I do."

Bright nodded. "Come away then. I'll show you first to your room."

Good Idea followed the woman upstairs. She was shown into the same room she had used when they had been there before, when the inn and stable yard had been deserted, and half-empty plates sat on silent tables. "You run a good inn," she said.

Bright nodded as she turned down the covers and helped Good Idea with her pack. "We do a good business here most of the time. But the strangest thing happened to us just a few weeks back. This way here to the bath. We were all just getting ready for dinner, you see, and suddenly, this terrible feeling came over everyone. Not terrible, exactly, but so strange. Why, I tell you...here's the tub, and that water is hot...I tell you we just stopped what we were doing and left. Walked as far out into the swamp as we dared. It was the oddest thing."

Good Idea smiled as she shut the door, stripped off her clothes and sank into the steaming tub. Fleet, perched on the nearby chair, squeaked.

Good Idea flicked a drop of water his way. "Come on in

then," she said, and the mouse jumped into the tub, dove beneath her legs, and broke the surface of the water with a grin.

GOOD IDEA GAVE Bright a whole gold piece the next morning and refused the change offered. "You did us a great service once," Good Idea explained, "even if you didn't know it."

Then, she spent a few precious minutes washing Pink, adding drops to the bucket of water from a small vial that Weathervane had given her. Since Regret's glorious red hair was back, and Tuesday's short and rather sad looking curls were at again their original color, she was confident in her mission. And sure enough, as Good Idea splashed water on the mare, the black dye dripped to the ground and the coat returned to its original pink.

Next, Weathervane poured a thick, dark green liquid into the palm of her hand and let each horse lick a few drops. Left Ear, again a white horse, looked doubtful.

"It won't hurt you, I promise," Weathervane said, so the shifter stuck out a long tongue and took her portion.

It did not take long for Weathervane's elixir to take effect. The horses moved from a steady lope to a full gallop, hooves pounding the worn road. Good Idea flattened herself against Pink's neck and clung to her mane. She worried about Bruise, but the orc increased his speed as well, the stout legs practically flying.

They pulled up and stopped by the waterfall and slid off their horses for a quick meal of bread and cold bacon. Good Idea recognized the spot where they had camped the night that Regret had joined them.

Regret nodded. "Yes. We'll be at the Stop Here Inn by nightfall. We'll only be half a day behind when we reach Whisper."

"What do you think can happen in half a day?" Good Idea asked.

"They'll be turned back, of course," Tuesday said. "What can a dozen of the Prince's men do against the defenses in Whisper? I bet we'll meet them running back to Mirror City on the road tomorrow."

Good Idea still felt uneasy. "Maybe we can ride through the night?"

Weathervane shook her head. "No. The potion gives the horses speed and stamina, but they must also rest and eat. If we ride them through the night, they might not make it to Whisper at all."

It was barely dark when the Stop Here Inn came into sight. They led their horses into the stable, Left Ear shifting to a woman.

"Bruise and I will mind the horses," Tuesday said. "Get us food and rooms."

The women entered the inn, and the innkeeper recognized Good Idea at once.

"You're back, then? That's good news." He led them to a table. "When I saw the Prince's men had returned, I feared the worse."

Good Idea stared. "The Prince's men stayed here?"

Full nodded his head. "Not all of them. Why, there must have been near a hundred camped out along the road last night. But the captains and the wizard spent the night here."

Weathervane sat carefully in her chair and arranged her skirts. "Wizard?"

Full put his hands on his hips and leaned toward them, obviously eager to tell his tale. "Yes and dressed in the most splendid robes of crimson and gold. And there were three captains as well in that purple livery. They asked how far it was to Whisper, then ate and sat right here at this table and talked until I put out the fire. Went up to their rooms and were gone before the sun was up. But I heard them. On a special mission, and one captain mentioned his troop, a hundred strong, he said." Full bobbed his head. "Nothing like that's ever happened here, I told the regulars. The closest was when you came through, Miss, and that man in gray came a looking." He clapped his hands together. "Now, what can I get you?"

Regret glanced at Good Idea, saw the white, pinched face, and spoke. "We'll be joined shortly by two others. Ale and food for all. And we'll need rooms."

Full nodded and moved off, and Good Idea shook her head. "No. We mustn't stay. We must get to Whisper tonight."

"I told you," Weathervane said slowly, "we can't. The horses must rest. If you push them so hard again, they will fall down dead in their tracks. How long do you think it will take to *walk* to Whisper?"

"One hundred men," Good Idea said, her voice hushed. She tried to picture a hundred of the Prince's guard crossing Three Creek Bridge. How many otters were there?

She tried to remember. There had been Left Ear and Tooth. Then, how many more? Four? That meant only five otters left protecting the bridge. Of course, Good Idea reasoned, there could also be five dragons, and that made her feel better. "And a wizard?"

Weathervane sighed. "Of course, the Prince has a wizard. He has a few, but the most important is Cascade Goodbody. He's the worse kind of wizard: pompous and vain, thinks he's the last word in all things magic. I've actually heard him speak a few times. Nothing good to say, of course. He thinks witches can never be as powerful as wizards, which is *not* necessarily true. He comes and goes as he pleases. But he is in service to the Prince. It was probably he who cast the Short-Term Memory Curse on Bunny and the rest."

Tuesday came through the door first and saw Good Idea's face. He pulled up a chair and quickly sat beside her. "What?"

"The Prince's men," Good Idea said, her breathing coming

short. "There are one hundred of them. And three captains. And a wizard."

No one spoke. They pulled chairs around the table and waited in silence as Full set out mugs of ale and cutlery before them.

"How may rooms then?" he asked.

Good Idea pulled out a gold piece from her pocket, trying to think clearly. "I would say just three this time. We'll be sharing all around."

Full went off and Good Idea stared at the coin on the table.

"This doesn't mean anything," Tuesday said at last. "The defense will hold. No one will hurt Belladonna. You'll see."

Good Idea stared back at him and felt a rush of despair and sudden rage. "They will kill everyone," she choked. "My mother, the witches, the gnomes..." She turned to Left Ear. "Your clan. Can they all become dragons?"

Left Ear nodded.

"But what about against a wizard? Can a wizard stop them? There are only five of them. I mean, five is a lot, when you're talking about dragons, but...can they keep a wizard and one hundred men from crossing Three Creek Bridge?"

"A wizard," Left Ear said slowly, "a powerful wizard, can stop us from shifting."

Good Idea felt a chill run through her entire body. "So, it may very well be otters against an army of one hundred." She closed her eyes and saw the face of her mother and brothers, as well as the folk of Whisper: the shopkeepers in town, the sheepmen farther down the valley, the workers in the mill. What would happen to them all? Even if they all didn't fight against the Prince's men, what would become of them? "When we get there, we'll be met with ash and blood," she said, her voice breaking. "When the Prince learns he doesn't have the Notebook Of Whim, he will send the same troops back to kill us as well. And with Mionarach dead, what will become of the real notebook? This has been a fool's journey."

Weathervane put her hand on Good Idea's shoulder. "If all that should come to pass, *you* will have the notebook. And you will do with it whatever you wish."

Good Idea returned the witch's gaze. "Will I be able to bring back the dead?" she asked.

Weathervane shrugged. "It is said to grant any wish."

Good Idea breathed. It was, at least, something to hold onto. "Let's hope that is true."

CHAPTER 17

*T*hey crossed Three Creek Bridge in the late morning. There were no soldiers awaiting them. There were no otters either. Left Ear, still in the simple dress from the night before, searched beneath the bridge and returned to them with a very puzzled expression.

"I don't know what happened," she said. "They aren't here, but there's no blood or sign of battle."

Weathervane was sitting still on her horse. "There is magic all around here," she said. "But there is also magic confined. I can smell Altrunic Iron."

"That makes sense," said Regret. "The Prince's wizard would have access to Altrunic Iron."

"But why," Weathervane asked, "would he bring it here?"

"To keep all the magic that might defend my mother in check," Good Idea said.

"But they have only been here since last night," Bruise said. "And there is no sign of battle. Even if they sneaked up on the shifters —"

"No," Left Ear said.

"But what other explanation is there?" Bruise argued. "And

look. There is no smoke from fires. No sound of fighting. Almost as though they slid in unseen."

"Could that be the work of the wizard?" Good Idea asked.

"It would have to be," Weathervane said.

Good Idea took a deep breath. "There is only one way to find out," she said, and urged Pink across Three Creek Bridge.

They found the Princes' army of men easily enough. They were camped out across Wink's Wold. The horses and men filled the cornfield and gardens and stretched out down the road to the town of Whisper. Good Idea felt her throat tighten and tried to pull Pink to a stop, but the little mare went down the drive and into the yard, stopping only when she reached the front porch.

"Mother?" Good Idea called as she slipped from Pink's back.

"In here," came a faint reply.

Good Idea mounted the steps on trembling legs. The army of the Prince's men were still and silent, watching her. Left Ear walked on her one side, Weathervane on the other, and Good Idea cautiously pushed open the front door.

"Mother?"

"She's right here," A loud, vigorous voice called. "We've been waiting for you.

Bringing up the rear, Bunny lifted his head. "Uncle Arch?" he said excitedly. "Uncle Arch? Is that you?"

It was. Sitting in the front parlor, the room Belladona saved for only the most important occasions, sat Mionarach. Belladona, in her wheelchair, was next to him, her gray eyes red-rimmed and teary.

"I'm so sorry," she whispered as Good Idea stepped in.

Good Idea felt her eyes widen as she stared at Mionarach. He was no longer stooped over and frail. He looked quite robust; his skin had a healthy glow, the halo of white hair was thick and glossy, and both of his legs were intact. He was wearing lavish red and gold robes, with a tall, pointed hat on his head.

Weathervane, standing behind Good Idea, let out a gasp. "Cascade Goodbody?"

Good Idea felt her jaw drop. "Who?"

Mionarach let out a laugh. "I've gone by many names in the past few centuries," he said. "And served many masters."

Belladona turned in her chair. "But you always served yourself first," she said coldly.

"That's true," the wizard said. He motioned with both hands. "Come in, everyone. Have a seat. This little adventure is finally at an end, and you all should be very proud of yourselves for getting the notebook here, as I asked."

Good Idea lifted her chin. "The Prince took the notebook."

Mionarach laughed. "You may have fooled him, but not me. I knew it was a fake the moment I laid eyes on it." He folded his hands in his lap. "And now, you will give the notebook to Belladona so that she may give it to me."

The parlor was crowded. In all of Good Idea's sixty years, the only time she had seen the room so full of people was after her father's funeral. She looked at the faces of her companions, those who had fought and stayed with her to help her do what she had told them was the right thing. And now she knew it was exactly the wrong thing.

"Where is everyone?" she asked. "The otters. Mr. Gold? The others?"

"Well, no one is dead. Yet. All of those defenses you thought were going to protect your mother are gathered in your barn, surrounded by Altrunic Iron, and quite incapable of giving you any aid."

"Uncle?" Bunny said at last. The young wizard had sat on Belladona's red velvet settle and perched on the edge of the seat. "Why aren't you happy to see us?"

"But I am," boomed Mionarach. "You don't know how much.

I have waited over sixty years to lay my hands on the Notebook Of Whim, and now, finally, my wait is over."

"What will you do when you have it?" Good Idea asked.

Mionarach narrowed his eyes. "Rule the world," he said coldly. "As it should be ruled. Not by a petty, arrogant prince, nor a simpering benevolent witch, like your mother. I'm sure if Belladona had the notebook, every morning would bring rainbows and sweetly singing birds to all in the land."

"And what is wrong with that?" Belladona challenged. "This world could use a few more singing birds."

Mionarach waved a hand, then suddenly turned and Bruise, who had inched forward, Axe in hand, went flying across the small room and slammed into the wall where he remained, arms splayed, frozen.

"Don't think," Mionarach said easily, "that any of you can do anything to stop me. I completely took over this whole town, and this farm, by myself, in one afternoon."

"Then why do you have one hundred men outside?" Tuesday asked.

"Because I couldn't tell the Prince what I'd already done." He leaned back. "As soon as the Prince had the notebook, and he decided to send his troops, I told him I would be needed to quell the magical forces. I told the captains I would meet them on the road, and I hurried back here." He smiled, his teeth bared and white. "I can get here in less than a day, you know. And since everyone knew me and knew that I was the one who was going to make everything right again, no one questioned a thing that I did. I was trusted, you see. That's how I managed to imprison a magical force that, if they had known better, would have put up quite a fight. Then, I joined the army at the Stop Here Inn and entered Whisper without a single sword being drawn." He took a deep breath. "Good Idea, give your mother the notebook."

Good Idea stood across the room from Belladona, her back

against the wall because she was afraid her knees would buckle. She shook her head. "No."

"I can take it from you," Mionarach said irritably.

"No, you can't," Belladona said. "It cannot be taken by force. If it is not given willingly, then it will return to the place it was hidden." She had a look of smug satisfaction on her face. "You wizards always boast how much stronger you are than witches, how you have so much power and we don't. You always forget that what we have lacked in strength, we've made up for in cleverness."

Good Idea saw a flicker of anger in the wizard's eyes. She also felt a tremor on her shoulder. Fleet was there, his whiskers quivering.

"Well then, how shall I convince you?" Mionarach said. "I know." He picked up his staff that had been lying on the floor beside his chair and pointed it at Tuesday. "Give it to her or I'll kill him."

Tuesday looked at her. "Don't. He's a monster. Don't give in."

"Then he will probably kill all of you and everyone else in this room," Good Idea said. "And once I hand it to my mother, if she won't give it to him, he will kill all of my family, and probably the whole town. This is what I believe is called an impossible situation, and I must think for a moment." She closed her eyes and whispered. Fleet, his ears twitching, listened.

She opened her eyes. "My mother would have wished for rainbows and singing birds. I will give her the notebook, but you must allow her one wish before she hands it to you. Will you grant her that?"

Mionarach tilted his head, then nodded slowly. "And why not? But Belladona, you cannot wish for anything against me. Nor can you wish that the notebook to not obey me. Is that understood?"

Fleet ran down Good Idea's leg and edged around the room. All eyes were on Belladona, and no one noticed the mouse creep up and find its way to Belladona's ear. Fleet rubbed his front paws together, and Belladona nodded. She met Good Idea's eye and smiled.

Belladona said. "Of course."

Mionarach placed his hand on Belladona's. "Witches' Vow?" he asked.

Weathervane inhaled sharply.

"Witches' Vow," Belladona answered.

"I know what that is," Good Idea said. "My mother is no longer a witch."

"I will always be a witch," Belladona said. "I may have lost all my powers, but that has not changed who I am."

"Then you must make a Witches' Vow too, Mionarach," Good Idea said.

He puffed impatiently. "What are you talking about?"

"I assume you won't tell the Prince you have the notebook."

Mionarach nodded. "Of course, I won't"

"So, when the Prince finds out his notebook isn't real, he'll come looking for it. And he'll come here. He'll probably destroy all of Whisper."

Mionarach narrowed his eyes. "Yes. That's true."

"And others will come looking. Whisper will be overrun. You must make a Witches' Vow to return to the Prince and tell him that the notebook has been lost again, and that you, and only you, can find it. And you must protect us from the others." Good Idea stared at the wizard, her heart in her throat. "All of us in this room. And our kin. Will you make that vow?"

Mionarach smiled. "Why not? After all, I owe you a debt. You found the notebook for me. Yes. I will tell the Prince the notebook has been lost again, and that only I can find it. In addition, I will ensure that all of you here, your clans and kin, and all of Whisper, will not be harmed in any way by anyone connected to the notebook. Witches' Vow. Are you happy now?"

Good Idea slid her hand in her pocket and withdrew the

small book. She felt it hum in her hands as she took the few paces to where her mother sat in her wheelchair, hand outstretched.

Mionarach leaned forward, his glittering eyes on the notebook. Belladona took it, stroked the smooth leather with her hand, and opened it.

The room vibrated. The open page glowed. Belladona smiled.

"I don't have anything to write with," she said softly.

Mionarach opened his hand and there, on his palm, lay a gold pen. "And what will you wish for?" he asked, his voice cruel and mocking. "An eternity of sunny days? Ever-blooming flowers? Chickens that lay eggs forever?"

Belladona took the pen and put the nib on the pearly page, open for all to see. Then, she wrote two words.

Get. Lost.

The notebook vanished.

THERE WAS silence in the tiny parlor until Bruise began to laugh.

Belladona handed the pen back to Mionarach.

The wizard stared at the empty place where the notebook had been, his jaw agape, all the color draining from his face.

Weathervane chuckled and crossed the room to put her arms around Good Idea. "Brilliant again," she whispered. Then she turned to Belladona. "It is good to see you again, my friend. I'd know you anywhere."

The room erupted into noise. Left Ear let out a whoop, and Tuesday applauded. Bruise, freed from the wizard's spell, dropped to the floor. Regret looked at Good Idea admirably.

"Well played," the paladin said. "I'm beginning to think that you were never really in need of my protection at all."

Good Idea shook her head. "You made this happen as much

as I did. We all did." Her eyes never left Mionarach's face. "And now it is done."

The wizard finally turned his amazed gaze to Good Idea. "You tricked me," he whispered harshly.

"As you tricked me," Good Idea said. "As you tricked all the folk here in Whisper who believed you would do the right thing. As you tricked those you swore loyalty to." She leaned forward, smiling. "And now, I believe you need to go outside and tell all these soldiers you are going back to Mirror City."

Mionarach rose, and the emotion on his face was so strong that Good Idea questioned just how binding a Witches Vow was, but he did not raise a hand to her, nor did he take his rage out on anyone else. He just seemed too astonished by the turn of events to do anything but gaze around in wonder.

"I say, Uncle," Bunny said. "If you were in service of the Prince, were you the one who cursed me? And stole my memory?"

Mionarach looked startled. "Yes, of course. I didn't mean for you to be targeted, actually. I didn't want you hurt. After all, you are my sister's only son. I recruited a few local wizards to do the actual work, and you just got caught up in it." For the first time, emotion caused his face to change. "I'm sorry. But not to worry, in another day or two, you should be fine."

"But why?" Bunny asked.

Mionarach took a moment before answering. "I didn't want any wizard who was not loyal to me to try to come after the Notebook Of Whim. I wasn't sure how things would play out and wanted no interference."

Bunny looked long and hard at his uncle. "I will return with you to Mirror City," he said. "I will work to make amends for your actions. You have disgraced my name and my Order. I will make sure you never do that kind of harm again."

Bunny went up to Good Idea and kissed her gently on the cheek. "You could have left me in Mirror City. Who knows what would have happened to me there. Bringing me here has shown me the truth. Thank you." He swept out the door and Mionarach followed.

Good Idea ran after Mionarach and stopped him on the porch. "You killed the Pidge Folk?" she asked him.

He stared at the sea of soldiers spread down the drive and across the road. "The Prince ordered it," he said.

"But it was your idea." It was not a question. "And the burning of the Pints And Bread Tavern?"

Mionarach nodded, then turned to her. "I did what I had to do," he said coldly. Bunny, on the steps, made a noise of disgust.

"Why?" Good Idea asked in a whisper.

"To make sure you returned to Whisper as soon as possible. I did not want you growing comfortable in Mirror City. I wanted you to think you were being hunted."

"We *were* being hunted. And we were caught. By the Prince."

Mionarach shook his head. "Yes. That was a mistake on my part. The Prince got the idea of chasing you into his own silly head and sent that captain after you. I should have been paying more attention. I don't know what I would have done if you'd given him the real notebook." He looked at her almost admirably. "That was quick thinking on your part. And you figured out how to escape. I would have had a tough time getting you out of that dungeon and back on the road."

"All those lives," Good Idea said softly. "All of them lost for nothing."

Mionarach shrugged. "I regret none of my actions."

Good Idea shook her head. "You are lucky that I will never have a chance to write in the Notebook Of Whim. I would wish for all those you have killed to haunt you for the rest of your life."

She turned and went back into the house, into the parlor, and went straight to her mother's arms.

"Oh, my darling girl," Belladona whispered. "Who would

271

have thought you'd be so smart and brave? This journey must have truly changed you."

Weathervane, sitting comfortably in the chair Mionarach had just vacated, snorted. "Possibly. One hopes all journeys change a person. But since the moment I met her, she's been clever and brave. She's been unafraid of making decisions. And she's cared about every one of us. She's quite unusual, your daughter."

Belladona tilted her head and smiled tenderly at Good Idea. "And here I thought you were always rather ordinary."

"I am," Good Idea said, straightening. "But ordinary people can do extraordinary things."

Belladona nodded, her eyes shining with tears. "Yes. That is very true. Just like Steadfast. How lucky I am that you took after him so much."

Tuesday looked out the front window. "Well, it looks like the soldiers are leaving. Maybe we should see about who's in the barn?"

Good Idea put her hand to her forehead. "Of course." She looked at Weathervane. "How do you un-enchant Altrunic Iron?"

"You don't," Weathervane said. "It's the very nature of the iron itself that renders magic powerless. But you can just tear it off the bars and let them free."

Good Idea hurried out of the house and made her way to the barn. The large double doors were firmly shut, and Good Idea saw that a thin band of metal had been fastened all the way around the walls of the barn and across the doors. As she got closer, she saw that the doors were held shut by the same large latch that had always been there, and that just the metal had been replaced. She lifted the latch and pulled the doors open.

The first thing she saw was Montgomery Gold, holding a pitchfork before him like a spear, surrounded by huge, snarling wolves. He blinked at her, squinted in the sunlight, then lowered his pitchfork.

"Oh, it's you. You're back then?" Mr. Gold said.

As the doors were pulled open, the barn was flooded with light. The Barnstable sisters were perched in the hayloft, in a position ideal for dropping down on anyone coming through the doorway, and Mr. Tip and Mr. Tap were hanging from the rafters, teeth bared. Button and Wrench Fix, and their son, Friday, brought up the rear, each holding a shovel.

Mr. Gold looked past her. "Where are they? The Prince's men?"

"Gone," Good Idea said. "And so is Mionarach Jones."

Mr. Gold leaned on his pitchfork. "He tricked us," he told her.

"As he tricked me," Good Idea said. "But he is gone now and will not be returning to Whisper. I don't know how long you've all been in here, but I imagine you're hungry. Would you like to stay for lunch?"

Tress Barnstable came forward. "What about the notebook?"

Good Idea sighed. "It's gone. Lost again, this time for good."

Tress nodded. "Well then, thank you for the lunch, but we go. Our work here is done, and it's time to return home."

"But this is your home," Good Idea said. She had grown quite used to the sisters and their odd little ways. And no one had a better way with livestock. "Didn't you tell me that you had lived a long and peaceful life here? Why would you want to leave it?"

The two witches exchanged glances. Cropped frowned. "You have a point," she said.

"Yes, things are going along just fine, just as they always have," Tress said.

"It would be foolish to ruin a good thing," said Cropped.

"But we've been in here all night, and the horses haven't been fed," said Tress.

"And that new cow is due to drop a calf, so thank you again

for the invitation, but we must be going." And the two sisters linked arms and went away down the drive.

Mr. Gold, Mr. Tip and Mr. Tap followed Good Idea out of the barn, as did the Fixes, who ran forward and embraced Tuesday as he came toward them from the house, his mother exclaiming over his shorn head. Regret had followed him out, and Good Idea saw the paladin shaking hands with the elves.

"Miss Wink?"

Good Idea turned. Mr. Tip was standing before her. "We would love to hear your story," he said. "An account of your undoubtedly exciting adventures in your search for the alto-gether extraordinary notebook. We could run it in three or four parts over the course of the month. It would guarantee a boost in circulation."

"Yes, it would," grunted Mr. Tap.

"Don't you two have somewhere to go back to?" Good Idea asked. She wasn't quite as fond of the gnomes as she was of the Barnstable sisters.

Mr. Tip made a face. "I've gotten quite used to sunshine," he said. "There's not a chance to get a lot of sunshine underground, you see."

"Nope," said Mr. Tap.

"And it's quite exciting to see things in the world around, even the not-so-good things," said Mr. Tip. "Where we come from, not much happens."

"Nothing happens," said Mr. Tap.

"So, what do you say, Miss Wink? Can we get an exclusive?" asked Mr. Tip.

Good Idea smiled. "Let me spend a few days with my mother first, but I will be happy to speak with you both."

Mr. Tip grinned, showing rather hideous teeth. "That is most excellent, Miss Wink. We eagerly await your first visit." Then the two gnomes bowed and hurried after the Barnstable sisters.

Good Idea saw that the wolf pack was rolling in the grass and tumbling over each other like pups. She saw the pile of clothes that had been Left Ears, and immediately found a wolf, dark gray and very beautiful, that had one ear larger than the other. She watched them gambol in the sunlight and felt a tightening around her heart.

Mr. Gold, still leaning in his pitchfork, cleared his throat gently. "I would love to have luncheon with you," he said gruffly.

Good Idea smiled at the dwarf. "Wonderful."

"Can you tell me of my aunt, the Dwarf Queen?" he asked as they walked toward the house.

Good Idea laughed. "Your aunt was quite helpful and generous," she said.

Mr. Gold made a sort of huffing noise. "That doesn't sound like her at all. Say, was that dragon still around?"

"Oh yes, Mr. Gold."

"And that knife I gave you? Did you use it?"

"Just once, Mr. Gold. But when I used it, it counted very much."

"So, I guess you had quite an adventure, then?"

Good Idea pushed open the door and saw the kitchen table, crowded with bread and cheese, cold ham and dried apples and a pitcher of sweet berry tea.

"Yes, Mr. Gold, I did indeed. It was not at all as I expected, and it is so good to be home at last."

CHAPTER 18

*B*efore and After, who had been locked up in their bedroom by Mionarach Jones, insisted on cleaning up after the impromptu feast. Mr. Gold lounged on the porch, a small pipe between his lips, puffing contentedly as Good Idea told her mother the story of her journey to Mirror City and back. Bruise and Weathervane spoke up when Good Idea seemed reluctant to take too much credit for something, and Regret and Tuesday filled in what happened to them when Good Idea had gone through the Veil.

Belladona listened with eyes wide and filled with fear, admiration and delight, finally telling them what had happened when Mionarach appeared in Whisper.

"He must have come in the night with that Altrunic Iron and wrapped the barn. He locked the boys upstairs and said if I warned anyone, he'd kill them. How could I warn anyone about anything? But still, I feared for their lives."

"First, he bewitched the Fixes, and led them into the barn like three sheep. Then the Barnstable sisters came by on their own accord, just checking in, and he lifted them off their feet and in through the open doors only to shut them behind. Mr.

Gold, well," she looked at him fondly. "I believe you put up quite a fight."

Mr. Gold smiled grimly. "We dwarves don't have much real magic, just what we can forge into our weapons. He woke me at dawn and marched me through town at the point of a sword."

"Finally," Belladona continued, "he went down to Three Creek Bridge and told the otters they needed to be smaller to help with his plan. They all shifted into mice, and he put them all to sleep, gathered them in a basket and put them in the barn as well. Then he left and came back early this morning with all those men." Belladona shuddered. "He told me you had the notebook, and that all I had to do was give it to him and we'd all be safe. I didn't believe him, of course. I don't know when he went from a kind and good wizard to one with such a thirst for power, but I was defenseless against him and so afraid." She reached out and grabbed Good Idea's hand. "How lucky I was to have such a daughter."

"How lucky we all were," said Bruise, sprawled across the steps. "Although I was looking forward to a good, final fight against one hundred soldiers." The orc grinned at Left Ear, who was dressed quite nicely in one of Belladona's dresses of pale green wool.

Left Ear grinned back. "And I spent all that morning trying to figure out how to defeat a wizard," she said.

"What?" Weathervane said. "Instead of finding twenty ways the wizard could kill us?"

Left Ear laughed sheepishly. "I told you. I've changed."

"Yes," Good Idea said, looking at her fondly. "You have. You were a valuable ally. You went places and did things that no one else could have. I'm so very grateful." She looked around the crowded porch. "I want to thank all of you. I could not have done this without you."

Regret smiled. "And it wouldn't have been done at all without you."

Bruise sniffed, and Good Idea sprang up, her face flushed.

"Bruise," she stammered, putting her hand into her pocket. "I owe you another gold piece. I should have paid you in the kitchen. That was the agreement, and I just forgot. I'm so sorry." She pulled out the last of her gold and held it out to him, her palm open, the gold piece shining.

The orc looked at Good Idea's hand for a very long time, then folded her fingers over the coin. "There are some things more important than gold," he said at last. "We did a good thing here. That's payment enough."

Tuesday Fix made a strangled kind of noise. "Zeppins, Bruise, you'd better not let anyone else hear you say that. Your reputation will be ruined forever."

Bruise chuckled. "She's a bit of a diamond in the rough, that one." He pulled himself to his feet and bowed, very formally, to Good Idea. "It has been an honor to walk in your company. If you ever need assistance again, Mr. Tip will know how to reach me. I wish you the best of luck here on Wink's Wold."

Good Idea hugged the orc, and the orc hugged back.

"Stay safe, Bruise," she said, then stepped back.

The orc nodded, then walked down the long drive, disappearing in the dusk.

Left Ear sniffed. "I'm going to miss him."

Good Idea sighed. "Yes. He was quite a character." She looked at Left Ear. "Are you going back to your clan?"

She nodded. "Yes. We're all going home."

"The Widdering Mountains?" Good Idea asked.

Left Ear smiled. "You remembered me telling you that?"

She felt herself blush. "I remember everything," she said softly. "Please stop by tomorrow before you leave."

Left Ear nodded to her, gave a quick salute, the also disappeared down the drive.

"You have managed to collect more than allies," Belladona said softly. "You have found friends."

Good Idea nodded. "Luckily, not all of them will be going back to their old lives. Tuesday, you'll stay in Whisper?"

The elf nodded. "Yes. Mother and Father are returning to Yellen, but Friday and I will stay here and run the shop. After all, things will still need fixing."

Good Idea smiled. "That is good to hear. And you, Regret? Will you go in search of another stranger in need?"

The paladin shook her head, her glorious hair shining in the lantern light. "No. I think I will make a home in Whisper as well. Sometimes," she looked at Tuesday with a gentle smile, "sometimes you find a *friend* in need."

Tuesday smiled back. "Yes. And I think we should go as well. But I will see you again, Good Idea." He stood, then leaned over and gave her a soft kiss on her forehead. "You are a most extraordinary woman," he said, and they were gone.

"Something else I did not expect," Good Idea said, watching as the two figures walked away together, hands clasped between them.

"One thing you didn't learn," Weathervane said, "was that the heart speaks louder in action than words."

Mr. Gold cleared his throat. "Well, I, for one, will be returning to Mirror City. The Dwarf Caves, more precisely. As much as I have almost enjoyed forging horseshoes and mending plows, I cannot wait to return to making swords and armor. What say you, Weathervane Wynd? Are you returning to Mirror City as well? We can travel together."

The witch nodded. "Yes. I have a business to attend to."

"And thanks to the Dwarf Queen," Good Idea said, "your business will be booming. Not to mention your reputation."

Weathervane frowned. "What do you mean?"

"Seven quips of Cordril from the Dwarf Queen. Remember?" Good Idea said.

Mr. Gold looked shocked. "My aunt? Offered seven quips of Cordril? Whatever for?"

Weathervane sighed. "To bribe me to accompany Good Idea back to Whisper. I had quite forgotten in all that has happened these past few days." Her face softened. "And I'd also quite forgotten about my reputation. How odd. But I wish to stay a while longer and visit with my friend, Belladona Wink. Is that a problem for you?"

The dwarf shook his head. "Not at all. I must find someone to take over my forge. And now I will bid you ladies good night."

And off he went.

The three women sat as darkness fell, the glow of the lantern illuminating their faces. Good Idea could hear Before and After climbing the stairs to bed. She stared out over the quiet fields and up at the twinkling stars. This was her favorite place in the world, and she was so grateful to be back.

"I'm glad," Good Idea finally said, "that you at least had one chance to use the Notebook Of Whim, Mother."

Belladona laughed softly. "Actually, I had used it once before."

Good Idea and Weathervane both turned to stare at her.

"What?" Weathervane asked.

"When?" Good Idea asked.

Belladona's eyes grew soft, and her voice became a whisper. "I wrote in the notebook just once. I asked to meet a man who would make me happy for all of my days." Tears glistened in her beautiful gray eyes. "And my wish came true."

Good Idea felt her heart swell with love and grief. She looked out into the darkness and watched the moon rise slowly in the north.

Belladona cleared her throat. "And what do you think of the world beyond Whisper, daughter?" she asked.

Good Idea thought. "I think it is a wonderful, frightening and totally surprising place. Everything that happened to me, the bad and the good, would never have happened here. I never bothered with magic, but it is a very good thing for people who know how to use it. And, like everything else, it can be very dangerous in the wrong hands. I am glad that I have none. But I am also glad that it is found in others that I love and trust."

She shifted in her seat. "There is evil out there, but there was evil here too, just beyond Three Creek Bridge. I just never saw it. And there was courage and danger and teamwork and love, things that have always been right here in Whisper. But out there," She stopped and looked down the dark drive of Wink's Wold. "Out there, it just meant so much more."

Belladona reached out to squeeze her daughters' hand. "Then it was well worth the journey?"

Good Idea nodded. "Oh, yes." Then she felt an overwhelming urge to crawl into her own bed. She kissed her mother good-night and made for her own small room, leaving the two witches talking quietly into the night.

WHEN GOOD IDEA awoke in the morning, she didn't know where she was for a moment. The bed was soft, the linen clean and smelled of lavender. There was the soft sound of clucking chickens coming through the open window, and the smell of frying bacon wafting in the air.

Then she sat up and took a long, deep breath.

She was home.

She dressed hastily in the simple cotton dress she had left hanging on a hook the day she left for Mirror City, and quickly combed out and braided her hair. She could hear the morning sounds in the yard: the clank of the milk pails, the bleating of hungry sheep, the snuffling snorts of pigs in the pen. She hurried downstairs and found her mother and Weathervane Wynd sitting at the table, drinking hot berry tea and whispering conspiratorially.

"I'm late," Good Idea said. "I'm so sorry."

Belladona waved a hand. "You were tired. You had quite a day yesterday. The bacon isn't quite cold, and the bread is still warm from the oven. Sit. We have things to discuss."

Good Idea filled her mug with tea and her plate with bacon, bread and apples, then sat across from her mother.

"Mr. Gold was here again this morning," Belladona began, "and it would appear that Before and After will be taking over the forge for him."

Good Idea was dumbstruck. "Before and After? But they know nothing of iron and forges."

Belladona shook her head. "Actually, they know a bit, enough to get started with, and they'll spend the next few days learning even more. They are both eager to step away from farming, and this would be a wonderful opportunity for them both."

"But…" Good Idea looked down at her plate. "What about the farm?"

"Oh, I'm sure one of your other brothers can find an extra son or two and send them this way," Belladona said. She folded her hands on the table. "The thing is, I'm leaving."

Good Idea lifted her eyes. "You're what?"

"I'm going back to Mirror City with Weathervane. As much as I've loved Whisper and living at Wink's Wold, I never stopped being a city girl."

"But, what about the protection spell? The one that will stop working as soon as you leave Whisper?" Good Idea asked.

Belladona and Weathervane exchanged glances. "It is possible that as soon as I cross the line and leave Whisper, I will drop dead in my tracks. If that happens, Weathervane has promised to bring me right back for a proper funeral. But there are plenty of old people in Mirror City, and I could live out my life there, helping Weathervane in her shop, finally surrounded by the sights and sounds I always loved."

Good Idea felt something crack inside of her. The farm

would mean something completely different without her mother. She had felt a shift, deep and profound, when she'd buried Steadfast. She didn't think she could bear another change. "I thought you loved the farm," she whispered.

"I loved your father and my children," Belladona said. "But now Steadfast is gone, my sons are off on lives of their own, and I finally see that you are your own woman. You don't need me or anyone else to make your life complete. Your strength has given me my strength back."

Good Idea's eyes filled with tears. "But…I shall be here alone," she said, her voice breaking.

Weathervane chuckled. "I don't think so, Good Idea. Remember what I said about the heart? And actions rather than words? I think that if you don't want to be alone, all you have to do is ask."

Good Idea blinked back tears, pushed herself away from the table, and ran out the door into the barn, past Before and After who obviously wanted to tell her their news. She pulled Pink out of the barn, mounted her quickly, and cantered down the drive, turning toward Three Creek Bridge.

There was no sign of anyone or anything when she got to the bridge. She slid off the mare, her heart in her throat, when she saw Left Ear walking up from the creek, dressed in the pale green dress. She stopped when she saw Good Idea.

"I was just coming to say goodbye," she said.

She clasped her hands together. "I-I-I was afraid you would forget," she stammered.

Left Ear tilted her head and smiled. "How could I forget? You have taught me so much, Good Idea. I am so different from when I left weeks ago. My mind is clearer, and for the first time, I see the light in the world first, instead of the dark. Thank you for that."

They stood a few feet apart, and Good Idea leaned forward and blurted, "I want you to stay."

Left Ear frowned. "Stay? Here in Whisper?"

She nodded. "Yes. My nephews are leaving to work Mr. Gold's forge, and Mother is going to Mirror City with Weather-vane Wynd, and even though I will probably get two more nephews to work the farm with me, I'd like *you* to do that with me." She spoke in a rush and ended feeling completely breathless.

Left Ear looked thoughtful. "I suppose I could do that. I know nothing of farming, of course, but I imagine I could be very useful. As an eagle, I could keep crows from the cornfield. As a wolf, I could protect the stock against other wolves. As a horse, I could pull a plow. Why, I could even produce milk or eggs." She nodded thoughtfully. "Yes, I could be very helpful."

Good Idea faltered. This was not going exactly as she had planned. Again. She took a breath. "I don't want you to work for me. I want you to work *with* me. As my, well, partner."

Left Ear tilted her head. "A partner? I have always worked in a pack before, but never with just one other person. I don't know if I'd be very good as a partner."

"Well," Good Idea said, "as an otter, you were quick. As a crow, you were observant. As a dragon, you were protective. As a horse, you were strong. As a mouse, you were quiet. As a rat, you were clever. As a crocodile, you were as an armor. And, as a cat, you curled against me, and gave me comfort. These things would make you a very good partner."

Left Ear smiled. "That is all very flattering. But I still know nothing about farming."

"I know enough for both of us," Good Idea said. "And I promise you, this winter, when the farm is sleepy and chores are few, I'll go with you to the Widdering Mountains. I want to see the ocean from the top of Two Step Ridge. I want to walk among trees that are evergreen, and smell like morning."

"You mean leave Wink's Wold?" she asked, her voice gently teasing. "I thought you were never going to leave it again."

"I have learned too much in the world beyond Whisper to think I will never travel out there again. This is my home, and I still think it's the best place for me to be, but if you wish, I will leave it for you," Good Idea said. "I wouldn't want you to never return to a place that holds your heart."

Left Ear stepped closer and took Good Idea's face in both of her hands, stood on tiptoes, and kissed her softly.

Good Idea closed her eyes. Her heartbeat quickened and her lips trembled. As she stepped back, she heard whispered words.

"I may have found a new place for my heart to be."

At last.

Pink shook her head and whinnied, then turned and began to walk. Good Idea and Left Ear, arm in arm, walked behind her, all the way back to Wink's Wold.

THE END